Also by Jennifer L. Schiff

A Shell of a Problem

Something Fishy

In the Market for Murder

Bye Bye Birdy

Shell Shocked

A Sanibel Island Mystery

Jennifer Lonoff Schiff

Shovel
&Pail
Press

This is a work of fiction. Names, characters, businesses, places, events, and incidents are either the products of the author's imagination or used in a fictitious manner. Any resemblance to actual persons, living or dead, or actual events is purely coincidental.

SHELL SHOCKED: A SANIBEL ISLAND MYSTERY
by Jennifer Lonoff Schiff

Book Five in the Sanibel Island Mystery series

http://www.SanibelIslandMysteries.com

© 2019 by Jennifer Lonoff Schiff

Cover design by Kristin Bryant

Formatting by Polgarus Studio

ISBN: 978-0-578-53086-4

Library of Congress Control Number: 2019907986

Every seashell is beautiful and unique, and each has a story to tell.

PROLOGUE

Susan Hastings, known to her thousands of shell-loving blog fans as Suzy Seashell, prided herself on being the first to break any big shelling—or shell-related—news. So when she heard that shell artist extraordinaire Samantha Hutchins had been commissioned to design a sculpture for the City of Sanibel, to be unveiled at the annual Sanibel Shell Festival in March, she knew she had to get the scoop. And it seemed like fate when Samantha emailed her about one of her rental listings.

Like many Sanibel residents, Susan wore many hats. In addition to running a popular blog devoted to beachcombing (and Sanibel gossip), she managed vacation rentals on the island. And she had been only too happy to help Samantha Hutchins find a place, away from prying eyes (well, except for her own), where she could work on her shell sculpture. Which she did. A charming two bedroom with a big garage and lanai on the West End of the island. But Susan had been miffed when Sam, as she had told Susan to call her, said she couldn't reveal anything about her commission. Even worse, Sam's project manager, Rita, had made Susan sign a non-disclosure agreement, which stated that Susan was not allowed to reveal Sam's whereabouts or any aspect of the project without prior permission.

Susan had tried to cajole Sam and Rita into letting her

blog about the project, revealing juicy tidbits as the sculpture took shape. But they had refused. The fewer people who knew they were on the island or what they were working on, the better, they told her. (Though Sam had quietly recruited a handful of volunteers to help with the project, all of whom had signed non-disclosure agreements.)

Susan had smiled and nodded her head, saying she understood, but inside she raged.

Weeks went by, and she would drive by Sam's house, wondering what was going on in there. She had heard that Sam and Rita had recruited volunteers to help them find local shells. And rumor had it that a couple of lucky islanders were actually working on the sculpture.

Well, when Susan heard that… something inside her snapped.

She had made it a point to drive by Sam's place first thing in the morning and late afternoon or evening, hoping to learn who might be helping them out. Then one evening, just past dark, as she was driving by, she saw two women leave. No doubt Sam and Rita.

This was her chance!

She parked her car down the street and made her way stealthily back to Sam's place. Then she went around to the side door and let herself in with the spare set of keys she had kept for emergencies.

She checked the garage first. There were bins filled with all different kinds of shells, but no sculpture. She then went into the house.

She paused in the kitchen and quickly looked around. She didn't hear or see anything, so she made her way quietly down the hall, to the spare bedroom. The door was closed, so she slowly opened it.

"You forget something, Sam?" called a female voice.

Susan froze.

Coming out of the bathroom, dressed in cutoff shorts and a t-shirt, was Rita, her long, brown hair pulled back in a cross between a ponytail and a bun.

"What are *you* doing here?" Rita asked.

Susan stood there, unable to speak for several seconds. Then she forced a smile on her face.

"I was just checking to see if you needed anything."

Rita looked skeptical.

"How did you get in here?" asked Rita.

"The door was open," Susan lied. "And I was concerned."

Rita looked even more skeptical.

"Well, we're fine," said Rita. "You can go."

She walked over to the door and held it open for Susan. Susan reluctantly walked through it, then made a sudden dash down the hall, to the master bedroom.

"Don't go in there!" Rita cried, charging after her.

But it was too late. Susan had gone in and locked the door behind her.

Rita pounded on the door.

"Come out of there right now!" she boomed.

But there was no reply.

"Fine. I'm calling the police," said Rita.

She went to get her phone.

Susan's husband Karl had thought she was joking when she called to tell him that she was at the Sanibel Police Department and needed him to bail her out. But she wasn't. She was mortified.

"What possessed you to break into that woman's house?" he had asked her, as he drove her home.

Sam and Rita had not pressed charges, but the police had given Susan a warning to not go near Sam's house again. And, of course, word had quickly spread that Suzy Seashell had been arrested. Though Susan threatened to sue anyone who printed that. Still, the damage had been done. She was now the chief topic of gossip on the island, a laughingstock—Suzy Seashell, whose blog was one of the main sources of shell-related gossip on the islands. The irony did not escape her.

Worst of all, she couldn't even write about what she had seen, not that there had been much to see. And, to top it off, she had just heard that her nemesis, Guinivere Jones, a reporter for the *Sanibel-Captiva Sun-Times*, had gotten the exclusive. Instead of Suzy Seashell breaking possibly the story of the season, it would be Guin, that little interloper from New England, who had probably never heard of a junonia or a Scotch bonnet until she had moved to Sanibel less than two years ago. It positively galled Susan.

No doubt Ginny was behind it. She and Ginny Prescott, the publisher and editor of the paper, had been rivals for years, since shortly after Susan had scooped her on a big story. But Susan was not giving up. Somehow, some way, she would get to see that sculpture again and deliver the scoop before the *San-Cap Sun-Times* did.

CHAPTER 1

The 81st Annual Sanibel Shell Festival was just over a week away and Guin was still jet-lagged from her recent trip to Australia to see Ris, her beau, who was spending his sabbatical in the South Pacific. She had had a wonderful time exploring Sydney and Noosa with him, and now, instead of not seeing him again for another two-and-a-half months, she would be seeing him in less than a week.

Ris, a professor of marine biology at Florida Gulf Coast University, known to his students and those who attended his lectures as Dr. Harrison Hartwick (and as "Dr. Heartthrob" to his legion of adoring female fans, who had voted him one of Southwest Florida's sexiest men), had been asked to interview for the chairmanship of the Department of Marine & Ecological Sciences at FGCU. The current chair, who was not only Ris's boss but a friend, had announced his retirement shortly after Ris had left for Asia, and he had recommended Ris for the position.

Of course, it would mean Ris would have to interrupt his trip abroad, as the committee was conducting interviews the first two weeks of March. But Ris had felt he could not say no, especially when it would mean he could help with the Shell Show—and see Guin. So he had booked a ticket back to Fort Myers and would now be there for two weeks. Then he would continue his sabbatical in Japan.

Guin took another sip of her coffee and absent-mindedly stroked Fauna, her black cat, who had fallen asleep in her lap.

"You suffering from jet lag, too?" she asked the feline.

Guin stared out past the lanai at the golf course and watched as some birds flew by. A few minutes later, after finishing her coffee, she gently removed Fauna from her lap and got up.

"Sorry, kitty cat. Gotta get dressed, then get to work."

She made her way to the bathroom, then threw on a pair of capris and a t-shirt. A few minutes later, she was at her desk, which was conveniently located in her bedroom.

Only around a half-dozen people actually worked out of the *Sanibel-Captiva Sun-Times*'s Periwinkle Way office: Ginny Prescott, the publisher/editor; Jasmine, the head designer; Mark, the copy editor; and the advertising folks. Everyone else worked remotely. Though Guin made it a habit to go to the office at least once a week, usually on Tuesdays, if for no other reason than to get the local gossip. (Ginny had eyes and ears everywhere and knew everything that happened on Sanibel, seemingly minutes after it had occurred.)

Guin pulled up her notes on Samantha Hutchins and reviewed them. She hadn't heard of Samantha Hutchins before the announcement that she would be creating a sculpture to honor the City of Sanibel. So she had been doing research online, trying to glean as much information as possible about Sam and her work before interviewing her in person. And she had been impressed. Samantha Hutchins was the real deal. Her work had been exhibited in galleries and museums around the world and was in several private collections.

"I wonder what she has planned for Sanibel?" Guin mused.

All sorts of images popped into her head: a dolphin made

of shells, or perhaps a manatee. Or maybe a life-size sculpture of "The Birth of Venus" by Botticelli, the famous painting of a naked Venus hovering over a giant clamshell. That would be quite a sight. Though it would probably be too scandalous for Sanibel.

She finished making some notes, printed out the set of questions she had typed up, then grabbed her microcassette recorder, her bag, her keys, and her camera and headed out.

Guin drove to the address in East Rocks Sam had given her, on a street called Chert Court, which Guin hadn't heard of before. To be fair, Guin hadn't been living on Sanibel for that long, and there were swaths of the island she knew nothing about.

She parked her purple Mini Cooper in front of the house, then made her way to the front door. The house was simple yet cheerful, white with teal shutters and an attached garage. She rang the doorbell. It was opened a minute later by a woman a good head taller than Guin (who stood around 5'4" barefoot), dressed in cutoff shorts and a t-shirt, her brown hair pulled back in a half ponytail, half bun.

"Hi, I'm Guinivere Jones," Guin said, smiling up at the woman. "I'm with the *Sanibel-Captiva Sun-Times*. I have an appointment to interview Ms. Hutchins."

"I'm Rita, Sam's project manager," said the woman. "Come in."

Guin glanced around as Rita led her out back, to the lanai.

"Sam, that reporter's here," Rita called as she opened the slider.

Outside, seated in the enclosed lanai, was a petite woman with short blue-black hair, surrounded by bins of shells.

"Hi!" said the woman, holding up a hand in greeting.

"Hi," Guin replied, glancing around.

The woman got up and made her way over to Guin.

"I'm Sam," she said, smiling at Guin.

"Guin Jones, with the *San-Cap Sun-Times*."

Guin glanced around.

"The sculpture's not out here," said Sam. "Too exposed. I'm just sorting through shells."

"I'd love to see it," said Guin.

"You want to warn CiCi and Marta?" Sam said to Rita.

"CiCi texted a few minutes ago," Rita replied. "She's running late and said she'd be here in a few," Rita informed her.

"Let me guess, she went out looking for shells again late last night and overslept."

"Probably," said Rita.

"CiCi, one of my assistants, is obsessed with finding me the perfect shells," Sam explained to Guin. "She knows our project is top secret, so she goes out looking for shells late at night or before dawn. Then she sleeps right through her alarm. I told her we had enough shells, but…"

She trailed off and shrugged.

Guin understood. For the serious conchologist (i.e., collector or student of mollusk shells), there was no such thing as too many shells.

"Speaking of top secret," said Guin, "I signed the NDA you sent me."

She reached into her bag and handed Sam a neatly folded piece of paper.

"Thanks," said Sam.

She placed it on a nearby table, then turned back to Guin.

"So, would you like to see the sculpture?"

"I'd love to," said Guin.

Guin followed Sam and Rita back into the house, to the master bedroom.

"Ta da!" said Sam, opening the door.

There was a woman with short, silvery blonde hair, who looked to be around 60, on her knees, placing shells on what looked to be a fountain, a very large fountain. In the center of the fountain was a dolphin, and along the outside were images of sea turtles, manatees, and seashells. In the background classical music was playing.

"Wow," said Guin, moving closer to the fountain, which took up a good chunk of the room.

Sam smiled.

"Whatcha think?"

"I think it's amazing," said Guin, walking around the sculpture. "It's a fountain, yes?"

"It is," said Sam. "The dolphin is going to shoot water into the air, and at night it will be all lit up."

"Wow," said Guin, continuing to walk around the fountain.

The woman who was working on the fountain ignored her.

"This is Marta," said Sam.

"Hi," said Guin, stopping and looking over at the woman, who, even kneeling, she could tell was quite tall.

Marta glanced over at Guin, barely acknowledging her, then resumed what she was doing.

Guin wasn't offended. She could tell the older woman was intent upon her work.

"Marta here's a woman of many talents," said Sam. "She teaches yoga, sings in the local choir, and is a member of the Shell Crafters. Her shell sculptures are amazing."

The Shell Crafters were a group of Sanibel artists who made one-of-a-kind creations using seashells. Every Monday morning they held a shell crafting class at the Sanibel Community House, something Guin had been meaning to try but hadn't yet gotten around to doing.

"Impressive," said Guin.

She turned back to Sam and Rita.

"You guys are doing a great job. I can't wait to see the sculpture when it's finished. Though it seems like it's nearly done."

Sam smiled.

"There's still a lot to do, but I would have never been able to get this far without Rita—and Marta and CiCi and all the people who brought me shells," she hastily added.

As if on cue, a young woman, probably in her early twenties, bounded into the room.

"Sorry I'm late!"

Guin guessed this was CiCi.

"You find anything good?" asked Rita.

"No, but there's supposed to be a big storm blowing through tomorrow, so there should be good shelling Thursday," said the young woman.

"You know you don't have to get me more shells, CiCi," Sam said. "We have more than enough."

"I know," said the young woman. "But I have my heart set on getting us one more Scotch bonnet."

"What we could really use is another set of hands," said Rita, looking over at CiCi.

"I'd be happy to help," Guin offered.

"Thanks, but the four of us can handle it," Rita replied.

"Okay, but if you need an extra set of hands…" said Guin. "I did sign an NDA."

Sam smiled at her.

"That's really nice of you, Guin. But like Rita said, we're good."

"So, what's left?" asked Guin, still looking at the fountain. She saw only a few bare spots.

"Well, CiCi here needs to finish up the manatee," said Rita.

"But it's so gray!" complained CiCi. "Can't I work on the sea turtle?"

"That's what you get for being late," said Rita.

"Rita's the real boss," Sam explained to Guin. "I'd be lost without her."

"You two know each other long?" Guin asked.

"Since college," Sam replied. "I was majoring in studio art and Rita was studying mechanical engineering."

"So how did you two meet?" Guin asked. Artists and mechanical engineers didn't typically run in the same crowd.

"At a concert near campus. Rita and I share a love of music," Sam replied.

"And Denny," said Rita.

Guin looked confused.

"Denny is Rita's brother," Sam explained, "and my significant other. He's a musician. He was playing guitar in this band that was playing at a bar near school my senior year. Rita happened to be standing next to me and asked if I'd like to meet them, after she saw how into them I was."

"And it was love at first sight," said Rita.

"More like lust," said Sam, grinning. "At least for me."

"Where's Denny now?" asked Guin. "Did he come to Sanibel with you?"

"He's supposedly flying down this weekend," said Rita. "Though with Denny you never know when he'll show. Musicians," she said, with a shrug.

"So he still plays?" asked Guin.

"Oh yeah," said Sam. "He's the guitar player for No Signal. They're about to go on tour. The only reason he agreed to come down is because it's freezing up north."

"Wait, you're going out with Denny Sumner?" said Guin, looking at Sam.

"Guilty," said Sam. "You a fan?"

"Back in the day," said Guin. "No Signal was huge."

"I don't know about huge," said Rita.

"So how did you go from studying mechanical engineering to being Sam's project manager?" Guin asked Rita, in an attempt to change the subject.

"I got bored working on buildings. I'd helped Sam out on a few of her projects. And when she started getting commissions for more complex pieces and said she could really use a project manager, I offered to come work for her."

"I told her she was crazy," said Sam. "But she was pretty persistent."

Rita smiled.

"And we've been working together ever since."

"I couldn't have pulled off this fountain, and many of my other works, without Rita's knowledge of mechanical engineering," Sam explained.

"Just doing my job," said Rita. "And we haven't pulled off the fountain yet."

"What about you, Marta?" asked Guin. "How did you become involved?"

"They said they needed help, so I help," replied the older woman, who was continuing to glue shells onto the fountain.

Guin detected a slight accent, but she couldn't place it.

"Don't sell yourself short," said Sam. "Marta here is an amazing shell artist. Even won some awards. Isn't that right, Marta?"

Marta gave a quick nod but didn't speak, just kept working on the fountain.

"In fact, we asked Marta if she would join our little team full time, but she turned us down," said Sam.

"Sanibel is my home," said Marta. "I have no desire to leave."

"Are you from here?" Guin asked.

"No," Marta replied. "But I've been here a long time now."

"What about you, CiCi?" asked Guin, looking over at the young woman.

"CiCi here's our Gal Friday," said Sam, smiling. "She does a bit of everything, including keeping us fed."

"Speaking of which, what do you guys want for lunch today?" CiCi asked. "I picked up some stuff on my way here, and I was thinking I'd make a seafood salad."

"CiCi is hoping to be a chef," said Sam, "and we are her guinea pigs."

"Do you go to school around here?" Guin asked. "I didn't think there was a cooking school near Sanibel."

"I'm in my last year at FGCU. I've been majoring in marine biology, but I realized I liked eating seafood more than studying it," she said, with an apologetic grin.

"I have a good friend who teaches marine biology over at FGCU," said Guin. "Maybe you've taken a class with him? Dr. Harrison Hartwick."

"Oh, Dr. Hartwick," said CiCi, smiling. "Yeah, I know him. He's awesome."

Guin was about to ask CiCi another question when Sam interrupted.

"So," said Sam, "I assume you have some questions for me?"

"I do," said Guin, turning to face her. "Is there someplace quiet we can chat?"

"Follow me," said Sam.

She stopped at the door.

"You good in here, Rita?"

"We'll be fine," she replied. "Have fun."

Sam made a face (she was not fond of interviews) and led Guin down the hall to the kitchen.

CHAPTER 2

"I meant it about helping you," Guin said, when she was done interviewing Sam.

"Thanks," Sam replied. "But we should be okay."

"Well, if you change your mind, here's my card," Guin said, reaching into her bag and pulling out a card from her card case.

Sam took it.

"And what's the best way to reach you, in case I have follow-up questions?" Guin asked her.

"Just text me, or Rita."

She gave her Rita's number.

"Will do," said Guin. "Is it okay if I take a few pictures of you and the fountain before I go? I promise, no one will see them, at least until the article is published. I'd also love to get .jpgs of some of your other projects."

"Talk to Rita about the .jpgs. She'll get you whatever you need. As for photos of me and the fountain…"

Sam looked apprehensive.

"I promise: No one will see them until the article comes out," Guin said.

"Okay," said Sam. "But if they show up online beforehand, Rita will kill you."

"Got it," said Guin. "The paper will send an official photographer to the unveiling. These are mainly for my reference, though a couple will probably appear in the article."

"That's fine. I'm just superstitious about people seeing my work before it's done."

"I understand," said Guin.

She followed Sam back to the master bedroom, where Rita, Marta, and CiCi were all busily working on the fountain.

"Ladies, Guin here would like to take some photos of the fountain."

"And all of you," added Guin, "with your permission."

"But I look horrible!" said CiCi.

"You look fine, Ci," said Rita. "I, on the other hand…"

She glanced down at her t-shirt and shorts.

"You all look fine," said Guin. "I just want to make sure we include a picture of the four of you in the article. Go ahead and continue what you're doing. I want the photos to look natural."

"Fine," said CiCi, clearly not happy.

Marta pursed her lips.

Guin dug out her camera from her bag and took several photos. The lighting wasn't the best, but hopefully Jasmine, the head designer for the paper, or one of her minions, could fix that in editing. She also took a few shots with her phone.

"I think I should be good," Guin said, a few minutes later. "The fountain is amazing. You should all be very proud. Everyone will be thrilled."

"I hope so," said Sam.

She and Rita exchanged a quick look.

"If you would excuse us, Guin," said Rita. "We still have a lot of work to do."

"Of course," said Guin.

"Rita, can you see Guin out?" said Sam.

"No prob," said Rita, taking a step toward Guin.

"That's okay," said Guin, stopping her. "I can see myself out."

Guin leaned against the Mini and checked her phone. There was a text from her friend, Shelly, wanting to know what she was up to.

Guin looked at the time. It was 11:30. She hadn't eaten much for breakfast and realized she was hungry.

Instead of texting Shelly back, Guin called her.

"Hey!" said Shelly. "What's up?"

"You want to meet for lunch over at Doc Ford's?"

"When?" asked Shelly.

"Now," said Guin. "I'm starving."

"Sure. Just give me a few. I'll see you over there. Where are you?"

"I'm over in…"

She was about to say "East Rocks." Then she remembered that Sam's location was supposed to be top secret.

"I just finished up an interview. Why don't I meet you at Doc Ford's at noon?"

"Perfect," said Shelly. "See you then."

Guin checked the rest of her messages. There was nothing urgent. She just needed to kill a little time before she met Shelly. Well, she could always go over to Lily & Co. Jewelers, which was next door to Doc Ford's. Ginny had asked her to do a piece on their upcoming jewelry show, which was to feature several local designers. May as well get a little work done while she waited.

Guin parked at Doc Ford's and then walked over to Lily & Co. She had only been in the shop a couple of times, not having much need for jewelry. Though they sold things besides jewelry, such as hostess gifts.

There were three main jewelry stores on the island—Lily & Co., Congress Jewelers, and the Cedar Chest Fine Jewelry—and they all advertised in the paper. So it was important that the editorial staff not be seen as playing favorites.

Guin walked around the store, gazing at all the beautiful pieces.

"May I help you?" asked a woman.

"I'm with the *Sanibel-Captiva Sun-Times*," said Guin, extending her hand. "Guinivere Jones."

"Guinivere," said the woman, shaking Guin's hand. "That's an unusual name."

"My mother had a thing for Arthurian legends," Guin explained.

"So, Guinivere Jones," said the woman, "how can I help you?"

"I'm doing a write-up on your upcoming show, the one featuring several local designers."

"Oh yes," said the woman. "We're very excited about it. I'm Barbara, by the way."

"Nice to meet you, Barbara," said Guin. "I'm meeting a friend for lunch next door. But I'd like to stop by afterward and learn a bit more about the show. Do you have some of the pieces that will be on display?"

"We do," said Barbara, "though not all of them. If I'm not here when you stop back, ask for Laurence. He's in charge of the show. He's out right now, but he should be back around one."

"Sounds good," said Guin. "Thank you, Barbara."

Barbara caught Guin eyeing a nearby case.

"Is there something I can show you?"

Guin sighed.

"Everything is lovely," said Guin. "I just don't have

much of an occasion to wear jewelry."

"Does one really need an occasion to wear jewelry?" asked Barbara. "I think jewelry should be worn all the time."

"Even to the beach?" Guin asked. "I'd be terrified of losing something in the sand or the water."

"Maybe not to the beach," Barbara replied, with a smile. "But I never leave my house without at least one piece of jewelry on."

Guin took a closer look at Barbara. She looked like she had stepped out of *The Official Preppy Handbook* or a Lilly Pulitzer catalog. She was wearing a simple yet stylish button-down shirt and a brightly-colored skirt, quite possibly from Lilly Pulitzer. On her fingers were several rings, and both wrists were encircled with bracelets. Adorning her neck was a necklace with what looked like little sea stars.

"Thank you for your help," said Guin. "I should probably get going, but I'll stop back after lunch."

"Very good," said Barbara. "And remember to ask for Laurence."

"Will do," said Guin.

She then made her way out of the store, glancing at the various displays as she left.

"Oh come on!" said Shelly, waving a french fry. "You can tell me. I promise, I won't tell a soul."

"Sorry, Shell, my lips are sealed," said Guin.

After telling her friend about her Australia trip, Guin had confided that she was working on an article about Sam Hutchins. And, of course, Shelly had immediately pressed her for details.

"Fine. Be that way," said Shelly, a bit huffily.

"Let's change the subject," said Guin. "Are you done with your entry for the Shell Show?"

Shelly immediately brightened. "I am!"

"And?" said Guin.

"I have to admit," she said, "I think it's pretty fabulous. You know how I was going to do this really cool mermaid necklace?"

Shelly made jewelry, most of it composed of shells and sea glass, which she sold on Etsy and locally. But she had recently branched out into making decorative objects: little jewelry boxes, picture frames, and tchotchkes.

"I remember," said Guin. "Did something happen? Did you change your mind?"

"No. Well, sort of. I added to it. Now it has a matching tiara and earrings!"

"Wow!" said Guin. "Where did you find the time? Don't you have to make jewelry for the Naples art show?"

"That's the thing," said Shelly. "I'm going to sell all three pieces at the Naples show after. I'm killing two birds with one stone, or set of shells!"

"Well, I'd love to see them," said Guin. "Maybe we could run a photo of them in the paper or online. I can ask Ginny, if you'd like."

"Oh, I'd love that!" said Shelly. "Do you think she would? It would be great publicity."

"I'll ask her. Do you have some pictures I can send her?"

"I'll take some and send them to you when I'm done. I have a few little tweaks to do first."

"Well, if you want them to run in the print edition, I need them this afternoon."

"But the paper doesn't come out until Friday," said Shelly.

"Yes, but it goes to press several days before. In fact, it's probably too late for this week's edition, but next week's paper is devoted to the Shell Show. I bet we could run it then."

"Can you believe the show is just over a week away?" said Shelly. "Let's just hope nothing goes missing this year."

Had it really been a year since the last Shell Show? So much had happened between then and now. Guin's mind flashed back to the year before, when the star attraction of the show, the Golden Junonia, the world's largest junonia shell, had disappeared during the preview.

"I'm with you," Guin replied. "I've had enough drama over the last year to last a lifetime."

"Though there's *always* drama at the Shell Show," said Shelly.

"Well, let's hope there's no extra drama," said Guin.

"I'll drink to that!" said Shelly, raising her iced tea.

Guin raised her Arnold Palmer and clinked Shelly's glass. She took a sip, then looked down at her watch.

"I should get going. Got lots of work to do. You okay if we get the check?"

Shelly ate another french fry.

"I'm good," she said.

Guin looked around, then signaled to their server. As she was waiting, she took a last bite of her crab cake.

"You ladies all done here?" asked their server. "Any interest in a little dessert?

"No thanks. Just the check," said Guin.

"You sure you don't want a slice of our key lime pie?" he asked them.

"We're good," said Guin. "Just the check."

A minute later he had returned with their check.

"You ladies have a nice afternoon," he said, placing the check on the table. "No hurry."

"Thanks. You, too," said Guin.

They settled up, then left.

"Remember to send me some pictures," said Guin, when they got to the parking lot.

"Will do," said Shelly. "And don't be a stranger!" she called. "We need to go shelling!"

Guin waved, then headed back over to Lily & Co.

Guin walked into the boutique and asked if Laurence was available. Fortunately, he was. Guin introduced herself and asked if he could show her some of the pieces that would be in the upcoming show.

As she followed him, she heard her name being called.

"Guinivere, is that you?"

Oh, great. It was Susan Hastings.

"Hey Suzy," said Guin, forcing a smile.

"Buying yourself a little something?"

Guin kept the smile plastered on her face.

"No, I'm working on a piece for the paper."

"Speaking of which," said Suzy, moving closer, "I heard you scored an interview with Samantha Hutchins. You know, I rented her the house they're staying in."

Guin continued to smile, though her cheeks hurt at the effort.

"I thought it would be perfect for her sculpture," Suzy continued.

Guin regarded her, wondering how much she knew about the project. She knew Suzy had been caught snooping around the place. Had she seen the sculpture?

"The sculpture is amazing, isn't it?"

"I'm afraid I can't talk about it," said Guin.

"Oh, come on, Guinivere. You can tell me. You know I'm the soul of discretion."

Guin stifled a laugh. Suzy was the gossip queen.

"Sorry, Susan, I can't. I signed an NDA."

Suzy grimaced.

"That's fine. I have plenty of other sources."

"Sam's helpers have all signed NDAs, too," Guin warned her.

Susan smiled, though it was not a friendly smile.

Guin felt uncomfortable. She didn't trust Suzy. Not one little bit.

"If you'll excuse me," she said, continuing to smile at Susan.

She looked over at Laurence, who was standing a few feet away and had clearly observed the exchange.

"Of course!" said Suzy. "I'm just here to pick up the gorgeous ruby ring Karl bought me for our anniversary. Had to have it resized, my poor fingers are too slender for such a big ruby."

Guin had to stop herself from rolling her eyes.

"Shall we?" she said, turning to Laurence.

"This way," he said, leading her back to his office.

CHAPTER 3

Susan parked her car a little way away from Sam's house and hunched down in the driver's seat, so no one could see her. She had continued to stake out the place, despite being told to stay away, and was now familiar with the three women who were helping Sam with the sculpture. She knew she wouldn't be able to pry any information out of Rita. And Marta, whom she knew a bit, was also unlikely to spill the beans.

No, her best shot at getting information was the little brunette, CiCi. Susan had done some poking around and found out she was living back at home with her folks and was an aspiring chef. With a little flattery and the promise of some private chef work, she was convinced she could get the girl to open up. She just had to find the right opportunity.

Fortunately, she didn't have to wait long. A few minutes after she had parked, CiCi came charging out of the house, jumped into a little white VW convertible, and headed off. Suzy followed her at a safe distance and smiled when she saw CiCi pull into the Bailey's parking lot.

She parked nearby, then followed CiCi into the grocery store, grabbing a basket on her way in. CiCi was clearly preoccupied, picking out fruit and vegetables. Now was Susan's chance.

"Oh, I'm sorry," Susan said, after accidentally on purpose bumping into her.

"That's okay," said CiCi.

"I'm at such a loss," sighed Susan, dramatically. "I'm hosting a small dinner party in a couple of nights, and I have no idea what to make."

CiCi immediately perked up.

"Do your guests like seafood or do they prefer meat— or are they vegetarians?" she asked.

Susan smiled.

"No vegetarians. And I'm sure they'd be fine with seafood or meat."

CiCi looked thoughtful.

"You could cook up some grouper. It's in season right now. Or you could make a roast. How many people are you having over?"

"Are you a chef?" Susan asked her.

"Not yet," said CiCi. "But I'd like to be. I've been doing some cooking for some people here on the island. They seem to like my food," she added, shyly.

"Who have you been cooking for?" Susan asked, innocently.

"Sam Hutchins, the artist," CiCi replied, then winced.

"Are you okay?" asked Susan.

"It's supposed to be a secret," said CiCi.

"Well, I promise not to tell. Besides, I know Sam."

"You do?" said CiCi.

"I rented her that house." Susan held out her hand. "Susan Hastings. And you are?"

"Caroline Rawlins," CiCi replied, shaking Susan's hand. "But everyone calls me CiCi. It's short for Caroline Clare."

"Charming," said Susan, smiling at CiCi. "Well, my husband Karl and I would love to have you cook for us."

"Sure," said CiCi. "But right now I'm kind of busy with

school and the fou—and stuff," she quickly amended.

Susan smiled. This was going to be easier than she had thought.

"I imagine the sculpture's nearly done," said Suzy, smoothly, "what with the show only a week away."

"Nearly," said CiCi. "Just needs a few more shells."

"Oh?" said Suzy. "I would have thought you had all the shells you needed."

"That's what Rita, she's the project manager, says. But I don't like this one Scotch bonnet we're using. I know I can find a better one, especially with the storm coming through."

"So you're a sheller?" Suzy asked.

"Oh yeah," said CiCi. "Since I was a little kid. I know all the spots."

"And where do you think you'll find this Scotch bonnet?" asked Susan.

"Over by Silver Key. Not a lot of people get over there. I figure if I get there real early, I'll get first dibs."

"I see," said Susan. "How early is 'real early'?"

"The tide's supposed to be real low around six-thirty Thursday. So around five-thirty or six. Though I've gone out even earlier."

"I bet you have," said Susan. "Well, I hope you find your Scotch bonnet."

"Me, too!" said CiCi. She paused and glanced down at her cart. "I should get going."

"By all means," said Suzy.

She reached into her handbag and pulled out her card case.

"Here's my card," she said, handing one to CiCi. "I meant what I said about hiring you to cook for me and Karl. We've always wanted a private chef."

"Thanks," said CiCi, pocketing the card.

"By any chance do you have a card?" Suzy asked.

CiCi looked sheepish.

"I don't. My mom's been getting after me to have some printed up. She says lots of snow birds would kill to have a private chef."

"Your mom's right. Would you give me your number then, so I can call you about cooking for us?"

"Sure," said CiCi.

She told Susan her number, which Susan entered into her contacts.

"Thanks," said Susan.

She smiled at CiCi, then waved goodbye. She was confident she would have no trouble getting the information she needed from the young woman, if she played her cards right.

CiCi placed the bags on the kitchen counter and started to unpack them.

"Can I give you a hand with that?"

CiCi jumped, then turned to see a good-looking man smiling at her.

"I'm Denny," said the man, extending a hand.

"The guitar player!" said CiCi, shaking Denny's hand. "But I thought you weren't arriving until this weekend."

"I decided to surprise Sam and flew down a little early. So, can I give you a hand?"

"I'm good," said CiCi, trying to hide a blush. She had been watching No Signal videos ever since she found out Sam's boyfriend played guitar for them, and she had developed a bit of a crush on Denny. He was just so charismatic.

Denny watched as she unloaded the groceries.

"I heard you were about to go on tour," CiCi said, not sure what to say.

"In a couple of weeks," he replied.

He continued to watch her.

"Let me guess: Your name is CiCi."

"How did you know?" she asked.

Denny continued to smile at her.

"I understand you like to cook."

"Uh-huh," she said, a bit starstruck.

"I'd love it if you made something special for me," Denny said.

CiCi was definitely blushing now.

"Just tell me what you like," she said, willing her cheeks to return to their normal color.

"Knock it off, Denny. Can't you see you're embarrassing the girl?"

It was Rita.

"You didn't tell me she was so cute."

"Keep it in your pants, Dennis."

"Just stating a fact," said Denny.

Rita glanced at CiCi, who was furiously trying to pretend she couldn't hear them.

"Whatcha making for dinner, Ci?"

"Gazpacho, followed by fish tacos with my special salsa and guacamole."

"I love fish tacos," said Denny.

"You get enough food?" Rita asked her. "Denny here eats like a horse."

"Yeah, you know me," said CiCi. "I always buy enough to feed a small army. Though you probably won't have any leftovers."

"That's fine," said Rita. "We can always get more stuff tomorrow."

"Is she any good?" Denny whispered to Rita.

"Oh yeah," Rita replied. "We're lucky to have her. She's studying to be a marine biologist, but her passion is cooking.

And she's been a big help with the project."

"A woman of many talents," said Denny, looking over at CiCi.

CiCi glanced up to see Denny smiling at her and felt herself blushing again.

Rita rolled her eyes.

"Come on and help me in the other room."

"You mean I'm allowed into the inner sanctum?" he asked, in mock surprise. "Sam told me to go amuse myself until dinner."

"Yeah, well, I don't think this is what she meant."

Denny glanced back at CiCi.

"Bye, CiCi. It was nice meeting you. I'm looking forward to dinner."

CiCi looked up. He was awfully good looking, in that scruffy, older rocker kind of way. She wondered if he cultivated that slightly unkempt look: the hint of stubble on his face, the wavy shoulder-length brown hair, the fitted t-shirt with strategically placed rips, and the faded jeans that hugged his hips.

"See you later," she said, unable to stop herself from smiling back at him.

He turned and headed down the hall. CiCi watched for several seconds, then continued to put the groceries away.

"So you should be all set," CiCi said to Sam. "Just follow the directions I left for you."

"You're not joining us for dinner?" Denny asked her.

"No," said CiCi. "I've got a paper due."

"Thanks for everything, CiCi," Sam said. "It looks delicious. And I promise not to screw up the tacos."

"Oh, and there's a key lime pie in the fridge," she said.

"My favorite," said Denny, smiling at her.

"That's what Sam said," said CiCi, blushing.

"Well, we don't want to keep you," said Rita, looking from Denny to CiCi.

"Right," replied CiCi. "Well, I'll see you tomorrow."

"Drive safely," said Sam.

CiCi smiled, then headed out.

"Cute kid," said Denny.

"Emphasis on the kid," said Rita, giving her brother a warning look.

"What's with the look?"

"You know perfectly well what the look is for."

"Play nice, you two," said Sam.

Rita glared at her brother, who stuck his tongue out at her.

Sam went over to Denny and put her arm around him. He looked down at her and smiled.

"How about a quick nap before dinner? Care to join me in the bedroom?"

Sam grinned.

"I think I just lost my appetite," said Rita.

"I need to finish fixing dinner," said Sam.

"Rita can do that," said Denny, a bit sulkily.

"Rita needs to go do some work before dinner," Rita informed him. "Unless you need me to help you?" she asked Sam.

"I'm good," said Sam. "Dinner in," she looked up at the clock, "say forty-five minutes?"

"Sounds good," said Rita. She then made her way down the hall.

"You sure I can't help?" Denny asked.

"I've got this," Sam said. "There really isn't much to do. I just figured I'd give Rita a break."

"Well, in that case," said Denny, walking over to her and kissing her neck, "how about a quickie?"

Sam giggled and allowed Denny to lead her back to the bedroom.

The next morning CiCi arrived at the house and nearly collided with Denny, who looked like he had just rolled out of bed.

"Oh, sorry!" said CiCi, blushing and turning away.

"Good morning," he said. "You know where I can get a cup of coffee around here?"

"I'll go make up a pot."

She headed to the kitchen, Denny following her.

"It'll just be a few minutes," she informed him.

"No problem, I can wait," he said, leaning against a counter.

CiCi tried to focus on making the coffee, but it was hard with Denny standing just a few feet away, dressed in a ripped t-shirt and a pair of loose-fitting shorts. She had gone home to work on her paper the night before, but her mind had kept going back to Denny, until she finally gave up and watched a few of his music videos.

"You from around here?" he asked her as she poured the ground coffee into the coffee pot and filled the carafe with water.

"Born and raised," said CiCi.

"Maybe you could give me a tour later."

CiCi didn't know what to say. She and Marta and Rita still had a lot of work to do on the fountain.

"So what do you take in your coffee?" she asked, when the coffee was done brewing.

"Milk and a little sugar."

CiCi poured some milk into a mug and stuck it in the microwave.

"What are you doing?" Denny asked her.

"Just heating up the milk a little bit. It tastes better that way."

CiCi could feel him watching her and tried to ignore him. But it was hard.

"Here you go," she said a minute later, handing him the mug.

"Aren't you forgetting something?" he asked her, placing a hand on top of the one that was holding the mug.

She swallowed.

"What?"

"I need some sugar."

CiCi swallowed but didn't move.

"For my coffee," Denny added, smiling.

"Oh," said CiCi. "Right."

She moved to where the sugar was.

"One teaspoon or two?"

"One's fine," said Denny.

"Hey, is that coffee I smell?" asked Rita, walking into the kitchen.

"It is," said CiCi. "Can I get you some?"

She handed the mug back to Denny.

"I can fix it myself," said Rita.

She glanced over at Denny.

"You have a good night?"

"Very good," he said, smiling up at her. "Hope we didn't keep you up."

"Please," said Rita.

CiCi poured some coffee into a mug and handed it to her.

"Here you go, Rita."

The front door opened, and Marta walked in.

"Good morning," she said curtly, giving a quick nod to Rita.

She glanced around the room, her eyes alighting on Denny.

"Marta, Denny. Denny, Marta," said Rita, making the introductions.

Marta had left before he had arrived the night before.

"I hear you play guitar," said Marta.

"You heard correctly."

"Marta here sings," said Rita.

"Oh?" asked Denny.

"She's in the local choir," Rita explained.

"Ah," said Denny.

"You want some coffee, Marta?" CiCi asked.

"Just some herbal tea," she replied.

CiCi immediately began boiling some water.

"Good morning!"

Sam walked into the kitchen, her blue-black hair sticking up in several directions.

"Is that coffee I smell?"

"It is," said CiCi. "Can I pour you a cup?"

"Make it a mug. We've got a lot of work to do this morning."

"Can I help?" asked Denny.

Sam looked at him.

"Do you really want to help?"

"I wouldn't have asked if I didn't."

Sam glanced at Rita, who shrugged.

"Okay, then. I'm sure we can find something for you to do. But first, coffee."

CHAPTER 4

No one else seemed to feel self-conscious around Denny. Just CiCi. She caught him looking at her several times over breakfast and could feel herself blushing. She wondered if Sam saw and would glance her way to check. But Sam seemed not to notice. Or maybe she was more interested in her yogurt and granola. Or she didn't care. Maybe that's what happened when you dated a rock star. Though CiCi knew she would be jealous if her good-looking rock-star boyfriend was flirting with another woman.

"Can I get a refill?" Sam asked.

CiCi looked momentarily confused.

"Some more coffee?"

Sam smiled at CiCi.

"Oh right. Sure," said CiCi, grabbing the coffee pot.

"Everything okay?" asked Sam, as CiCi refilled her mug. "You up late working on your paper?"

"Yeah," said CiCi, stealing a glance over at Denny.

Sam followed her gaze.

"Don't pay too much mind to Denny," she said. "He flirts with everyone. Now, let's finish up breakfast and get back to work."

CiCi sighed as she glued another shell on the side of the fountain.

They were almost done applying the shells. Just a few more hours. Then there would be the finishing work, which was Marta's specialty. Though CiCi had to admit, today hadn't been so bad. Denny had stuck around and had made them all laugh with stories about some of the crazy things No Signal's fans had done. And he had serenaded them on his guitar.

"Why don't you guys take off," said Rita, looking at the clock on her phone.

It was late afternoon, and they had been working on the fountain since morning.

"You sure?" asked CiCi. "I don't mind staying," she added, casting a quick glance at Denny, who grinned when he saw her looking his way.

"Nah, you and Marta go," Rita replied. "Between the three of us, we're good."

"Actually, I was hoping you or Sam could give me a tour of Sanibel and Captiva this afternoon," said Denny.

"Sorry, bro, Sam and I still have work to do," said Rita. "Maybe when we're done."

"I could take you," said CiCi.

Oh my God. Had she really just said that? She could feel her cheeks turning pink.

Denny smiled at her.

"That's a great idea," said Sam. "CiCi here's a native. She probably knows places that aren't even on the map."

She looked over at CiCi.

"You sure you don't mind? Denny can be a handful."

CiCi glanced over at Denny.

"It's fine," she said, as nonchalantly as she could, though her heart was racing. "But we should probably stick to the West End and Captiva. Traffic will be a nightmare heading to the Causeway. I can take you to see the rest of the island tomorrow, though. That is, if you want to," she added, feeling suddenly shy.

"Fine by me," said Denny, his violet-colored eyes twinkling.

Hold it together girl, CiCi told herself.

"You two have fun," said Sam.

"You sure you don't mind?" asked CiCi.

"Why would I mind?" asked Sam. "You're doing me a favor, getting Denny out of my hair. Besides, he could probably use a break. Some sea air will do him good."

Denny went over to Sam and gave her a kiss.

"You're the best, babe."

He turned to CiCi.

"Shall we?"

CiCi turned to Sam.

"What time should I have him back here?"

"I don't know, seven?" said Sam, looking over at Rita, who shrugged. "Whenever is fine," she said, looking back over at CiCi. "Have fun!"

She turned back to Rita, asking her a question about the lighting mechanism for the fountain.

"Let's go, before they change their mind and put us to work," Denny whispered into CiCi's ear.

His warm breath tickled. She glanced back at Rita and Sam. They were totally absorbed in the sculpture. It was as if she and Denny weren't there. She glanced around the room for Marta. There was no sign of her. No doubt she had left while they were chatting. CiCi always thought that Marta would have made a good spy, the way she could slip in and out of a room without being seen.

"That's my car there," said CiCi, pointing to the white Golf convertible.

"It's cute," said Denny. "It suits you."

CiCi smiled.

"It's pretty basic, but it gets me from here to there."

They got in the VW and headed toward West Gulf Drive.

"I figured we would drive down to Captiva, by South Seas, that's the big resort at the end, then come back and check out the sunset on the beach."

"Sounds good to me," said Denny.

CiCi smiled and put the car in gear.

They parked by Beach Access #5 and walked down to the water to watch the sunset. CiCi had taken Denny up to Captiva, where he had grabbed a green tea at the Starbucks and bought CiCi a mocha. Then they had headed back to Sanibel. Along the way, CiCi pointed out various landmarks: the 'Tween Waters Resort and Castaways; the Mad Hatter restaurant and the Sunset Grill and the Lazy Flamingo; and the J. N. "Ding" Darling National Wildlife Refuge, before turning onto Rabbit Road and heading to West Gulf Drive.

They made their way down to the beach, where a number of people were waiting for the sun to set.

"I can see why people like it here," said Denny, a few minutes later. "It's very peaceful."

"Yeah, Sanibel's a pretty magical place," said CiCi.

They stood on the beach for several minutes, neither saying a word, as the sun gradually faded from view, turning the sky shades of red, orange, and pink.

"I should get you back," CiCi said with a sigh. "Sam's probably wondering what happened to you."

"Knowing Sam, I doubt it," he replied.

"Well, I need to get going," said CiCi, thinking about the paper she still had to finish.

They made their way back to the car, neither saying

anything. As CiCi was about to turn the key in the ignition, Denny placed a hand on her arm. CiCi froze.

"Thank you for showing me around this afternoon," he said, his breath caressing CiCi's ear.

She could feel her heart racing.

"One of the many services I offer!" CiCi replied, a bit too cheerily.

Denny smiled at her.

"Do I make you nervous, Caroline?" he asked her, taking a lock of her hair and gently placing it behind her ear.

"You? No," she replied, trying desperately to hide her nervousness.

"You're very beautiful," Denny continued, gently turning CiCi's face towards him.

CiCi tried to swallow.

"Very beautiful," he said, moving his face closer to hers.

The next thing CiCi knew, Denny was kissing her. And, heaven help her, she was kissing him back.

"Stop!" she yelled, a minute later, pushing him away. "This is wrong."

She hated herself for allowing him to kiss her. But she hated herself more for not wanting him to stop.

"What would Sam say?"

"I doubt Sam would care," he replied.

CiCi found that hard to believe.

"Well, I care," she said.

"I'm sorry," said Denny. "I just felt that you wanted to be kissed. Clearly, I was wrong."

CiCi started the car, a flood of conflicting emotions running through her brain.

"Look, I'm sorry," said Denny.

He ran a hand through his hair.

"I'm just so used to women throwing themselves at me…"

CiCi glared at him.

"I'm not saying you were throwing yourself at me," he said. "I…" He ran a hand through his hair again. "Look, I'm sorry," he said again. "I don't know what else to say. I promise it won't happen again."

"It better not," said CiCi, turning to look at him. Though even as she said it, a part of her felt disappointed.

"We're back!" CiCi called.

She could hear music playing but didn't see Rita or Sam. She walked down the hall to the master bedroom.

"We're back!" she said again, a bit louder, to be heard over the music.

It was as if Sam and Rita hadn't moved.

"Oh, hey, Ci!" said Sam, looking up and smiling at her.

Rita also turned to look.

"You guys have a good time?" asked Sam.

"Can you turn down the music?" CiCi asked, practically yelling.

"Sorry," said Sam. "They were playing one of my favorite songs."

She turned down the volume.

"So, you guys have fun?" Sam repeated. "CiCi show you around?"

"CiCi here's an excellent guide," said Denny, smiling. "I'm hoping she can show me the rest of the island tomorrow."

"I have to get to Silver Key first thing," CiCi quickly replied. "Maybe after."

"Just make sure you get some sleep," said Rita. "We've got a big day tomorrow."

"Don't worry," said CiCi. "I'll be fine."

"What's Silver Key?" asked Denny.

"It's a little strip of beach between Blind Pass and Bowman's," explained CiCi. "There's a nature trail nearby, where lots of birds like to hang out."

Denny seemed nonplussed.

"I'll show you on the map, later," said Rita, getting up. "I don't know about all of you," she said, stretching, "but I could use some food. How about we take Denny here to the Lazy Flamingo?"

"An excellent idea," Sam replied.

"The Lazy Flamingo?" said Denny. "Did we pass that?" he asked CiCi. "Sounds kind of familiar."

"It's a dive bar over by Blind Pass," explained Rita. "They serve beer on tap and have the best conch fritters this side of Key West; oysters, too."

"I'm sold," said Denny. "CiCi, you want to join us?"

"I need to go work on that paper," she replied.

"You sure?" asked Sam. "You're welcome to join us."

CiCi glanced over at Denny.

"No, you guys go," she replied. "I'm good."

"Suit yourself," said Sam. "I just need to freshen up. Then let's scoot."

CHAPTER 5

Sam yawned as she walked into the kitchen. Rita was nursing a mug of coffee.

"Where's CiCi?" Sam asked, looking around.

"Not here," said Rita.

Sam looked up at the clock. It was almost 8:30.

"She must have gone out shelling early and fallen asleep again," said Sam.

"Probably," said Rita. "She said she wanted to get over to Silver Key first thing."

"You make the coffee?" asked Sam, looking at the nearly full coffee pot.

"I did," said Rita.

Sam grabbed a mug and helped herself.

"You see Denny this morning?" she asked, after having taken a couple of sips.

"No, why? You kick him out of bed for snoring or something?" Rita asked.

"No, he wasn't there when I got up," Sam replied.

"He probably couldn't sleep and went for a walk. Is his guitar still there?"

"I didn't check," said Sam.

They stood in the kitchen sipping their coffee.

"We got anything to eat?" Sam asked a minute later.

"Go look," said Rita.

Sam made a face, then started opening cabinets.

"Is there something in particular you're looking for?" asked Rita.

"CiCi usually has stuff lying around," Sam replied, opening the refrigerator.

"Well, CiCi's not here," said Rita.

"I was hoping maybe she left us something," Sam said, peering into the refrigerator.

"Anything?"

Sam sighed and shut the fridge.

"No."

"There's always cereal, or toast," said Rita.

"I'll stick with coffee," said Sam.

"Suit yourself," said Rita. "But don't snap at me later when your blood sugar crashes."

Sam made another face.

"Well, hopefully CiCi will be here to fix lunch."

"Otherwise, what, you'll starve?"

"Probably," said Sam. "You know I hate to cook."

"Oh, I know," said Rita. "Here, have a protein bar," she said, reaching into an open box next to her.

She tossed a bar to Sam, who caught it.

"What's in it?" Sam asked, holding it up.

"I assume you can still read," said Rita. "Look at the wrapper."

Sam read: "Peanut Butter Banana Dark Chocolate Breakfast Protein Bar. That's a mouthful."

She looked up at Rita.

"Any good?"

"It's all right."

She was about to unwrap the bar when Marta entered, bearing a plate of muffins.

"Oh, thank God!" said Sam, practically lunging at the plate.

"Good timing," said Rita.

"I had a feeling you might need a little something," said Marta, placing the plate on the counter.

Sam grabbed a muffin and took a bite.

"Mmm…" she said, closing her eyes.

Marta smiled.

"What kind?" asked Rita.

"Blueberry lemon," said Marta. "Old family recipe."

"They're delicious," said Sam, finishing up the little muffin and reaching for another one. "Rita, have one."

Rita took one and popped it in her mouth.

"Hey, these are good," she said, chewing.

Marta beamed.

"Glad you both like them."

"Why didn't you tell us you could cook?" Sam asked.

Marta shrugged.

"By any chance did you see Denny wandering around when you drove in?" Sam asked.

"No," said Marta. "Why?"

"No reason," said Sam, finishing off the second mini muffin and contemplating a third.

The storm the night before had awakened Guin and the cats, one of whom, no doubt Fauna, had been asleep on Guin's head. She had shooed her off and had gone into the bathroom. But when she got back into bed, she couldn't fall back to sleep. Finally, a little before 6:30, she decided she might as well get up and go shelling.

She went back into the bathroom, pulled her hair back, splashed some cold water on her face, then got dressed and headed to the kitchen.

"Coffee now or coffee later?" she mused. She glanced at the French press. "Probably best to wait till later."

She opened the fridge and poured herself a glass of water instead.

She made to leave, but the cats blocked her path. Fauna started to meow.

"Fine, I'll give you guys some food."

She headed back to the kitchen and opened a can of cat food. A few minutes later, she was in the Mini, headed to Blind Pass.

It was still dark when she parked her car, though the sky was just starting to lighten. She turned on the flashlight on her phone and made her way down to the shoreline. She could hear the waves before she could see them. Hopefully that was a good sign. She saw a few people with headlamps and flashlights searching for shells, along with a few fishermen. She smiled and said good morning to those she passed, making her way down to Silver Key, the stretch of beach to the east of Blind Pass, just before you got to Bowman's.

As she made her way east, she gazed downward, searching for shells. The storm had washed ashore hundreds of them, most of them common ones. There were arks, clam shells, pen shells, Florida fighting conchs, and several varieties of scallops, as well as hundreds of little shells and shell fragments. Personally, Guin was hoping to find a Scotch bonnet. Glancing at the posts in the various shelling groups on Facebook, Guin felt like she was the only one on Sanibel who hadn't found one.

She would happily settle for a true tulip or an alphabet cone, though. Or a nice, big horse conch. (She didn't even bother hoping for a junonia, though you never knew. Maybe she would get lucky.)

By the time she reached the beginning of Silver Key, her shelling bag contained a few lettered olives, a couple of small horse conchs, a handful of pink and orange scallops, a couple of shark eyes, and a gaudy nautica (also known as a colorful moon snail), one of her favorites.

The sun was now just over the horizon, and Guin stopped to watch. It never got old, being on the beach and watching the sun rise over the dunes. She took a deep breath and raised her arms, once again thanking God, or the universe, that she was able to live in such a beautiful place. She turned and stared out at the sea, watching as some brown pelicans dove for fish. Then she continued on.

When she made it to the end of the beach, she stopped and glanced around. There was no one in sight. Just some birds. She watched as they flew toward the nature preserve. Then she spied a large pile of shells a few feet away.

Normally, Guin avoided shell piles, especially ones that far from the wrack line. But this one beckoned to her.

"May as well go check it out," she sighed.

She walked the short distance to the pile and gazed at it. There must have been thousands of shells. Maybe tens of thousands.

Overhead an osprey was squawking. She looked up to watch. The osprey had a fish clutched in its talons and was flying right by her. She took a couple steps, climbing atop the pile of shells to get a better look, and nearly went flying herself. She looked down to see what had caused her to stumble and screamed.

It seemed to take the police forever to get to Silver Key, and Guin had had to duck into the bushes to relieve herself. Finally, she spied an SUV making its way down the beach.

A couple of minutes later, it had parked. A man and a woman got out.

"Ms. Jones, why am I not surprised to find you here?"

It was Detective O'Loughlin. Of course he would be the one to investigate.

"Detective," said Guin. "The body's just over there," she said, pointing.

The detective and Officer Rodriguez, a female cop Guin knew from her previous investigations, made their way over to the body.

"Where're the EMTs?" asked Guin.

"They're on their way," said the detective.

Guin led him to where she had found the body. It was a woman, with brown curly hair, around Guin's height. She was lying face down. There was a bloody gash on the back of her head.

"Take some pictures of the scene," the detective ordered Officer Rodriguez.

"Yes, sir," she replied, taking out her phone.

Guin watched as Officer Rodriguez took several photos, being careful not to touch or disturb anything.

"She was dead when I found her," Guin informed the detective, as he knelt to take the woman's pulse.

"And what time was that?" asked the detective, getting up.

"Around seven-thirty?" said Guin. "Maybe a bit later. I wasn't wearing a watch."

The detective pulled out the little notepad and pen he always kept on him and made some notes. A minute later, they saw another vehicle coming towards them. The EMTs.

"The body's over there," said the detective to the two men who had jumped out of the vehicle.

He walked with the two men back over to where the body lay and watched as they carefully examined it. Just then another SUV appeared.

"You call in the cavalry?" Guin asked.

She watched as the new SUV drove over the beach,

crushing who knew how many shells.

"The shellers are not going to be happy," said Guin.

The detective shot her a look.

"Bill."

The detective turned to the man who had called his name. It was Mike Gilbertie, a Lee County medical examiner. Guin had met him before, after she found her first dead body.

"Mike," replied the detective.

He walked him over to where the EMTs were examining the dead girl's body.

"So what have we got here?" the medical examiner asked.

"From the looks of it," said the detective, "it seems like someone clubbed her on the back of the head."

Guin watched as the medical examiner put on a pair of latex gloves and squatted down to examine the body, exchanging a few words with the EMTs.

"What's your verdict?" asked the detective, a few minutes later.

"Blunt force trauma to the back of the skull," the medical examiner replied. "Looks like she was hit with a heavy object."

He moved aside some of the dark brown hair surrounding the gash.

"What do we have here?" he said, holding up what looked to Guin like a piece of shell.

"May I see?" she asked.

Mike looked over at the detective, who nodded.

Guin took a step closer.

"It looks like a piece of shell," she said, eyeing the black sliver. "Possibly from a big horse conch."

The medical examiner looked at her.

"Could she have been conked over the head with a horse conch?" she asked him. "It would have to have been a large one. Though I've seen some pretty big ones."

She looked down at the pile of shells. She didn't see a big horse conch anywhere, but… Just a few feet away was some brush. She quickly ran over and peered through the dense foliage, moving aside some branches.

"I think I found something!" she called.

"Don't touch anything!" shouted the detective and the medical examiner.

A few seconds later, they were standing next to Guin.

"There!" said Guin, holding aside some branches.

The detective and the medical examiner looked down.

"Hold these," she said to the two of them, indicating the branches.

They held them aside while Guin shone the flashlight app on her phone on the ground. There, hidden amongst the leaves, twigs, and shells, was a large horse conch, covered with blood.

CHAPTER 6

The medical examiner, still wearing latex gloves, bent down and carefully retrieved the horse conch from beneath the brush.

"You think that's the murder weapon?" Guin asked, looking from the medical examiner to the detective.

"The lab will need to run some tests," said the medical examiner.

"What about the female? Were you able to ID her?" Guin asked.

She followed them back over to where the body was now lying face up, about to be placed on a stretcher.

"Oh my God!" said Guin, clearly shaken. "That's CiCi! She's one of Sam Hutchins's volunteers."

Guin felt sick. She had just seen the young woman, who couldn't have been more than 22 or 23. She had seemed so alive. Guin felt as though she would throw up.

"You okay?" asked the detective.

"No," said Guin. "Why would someone do this? That girl wouldn't hurt a fly."

She gazed down at CiCi.

"What's that clasped in her hand?" she asked.

The detective and the medical examiner looked where Guin was pointing. The medical examiner lifted CiCi's clenched hand and gently pried back her fingers.

"It's a Scotch bonnet!" said Guin.

The medical examiner looked over at her.

"One of the nicest ones I've ever seen," she continued. "CiCi was hot to find one, to put on that sculpture they've been working on."

Guin continued to stare down at the shell and sighed.

"What a shame."

The detective was looking at the shell.

"I know a lot of people who'd kill for a shell like that," said Guin.

The detective raised an eyebrow.

"Figuratively, not literally," Guin quickly added.

She watched as the EMTs covered CiCi and placed her in the back of their vehicle.

"Someone needs to tell the girl's parents, and Sam and Rita. They'll be devastated."

"She live on the island?" asked the detective.

"Yes. She was going to school at FGCU. I think she was commuting. And she was helping Sam Hutchins. She's the artist creating that sculpture for the city. I'm covering it for the paper."

"I'll need to speak with her."

"Can I go with you?" Guin asked.

"Why?" asked the detective.

"Well, I was the one who discovered the body. And you know Ginny is going to want me to cover this story."

The detective ran a hand over his face.

"We're heading out, Bill," the medical examiner informed the detective. "We'll let you know what we find. Might take a few days as it's nearly the weekend."

"That's fine," said the detective.

"See you Sunday?"

"Unless I have to work," replied the detective.

"You wouldn't want to disappoint the fish," said the

medical examiner, who was smiling at the detective.

Guin watched as the ambulance and the medical examiner's SUV made their way down the beach. Then she turned to the detective.

"Fine, you can accompany me to see the artist," he said to her. "But you are not to say a word, you understand?"

"I'll be as quiet as a mouse," she promised.

"You ever hear mice?" said the detective. "They're not quiet. They squeak and drive me crazy."

"Well, I promise not to squeak," said Guin.

The detective made a face.

"Just let me do the talking. You can ask your questions later."

"Fine," said Guin.

He looked around.

"You want a lift?"

Guin looked down the beach. It was a long walk back to where she had parked the Mini, and she wasn't in the mood to shell anymore.

"Sure, if you have room. I'm parked down by Blind Pass."

"Hop in," said the detective.

Guin followed the detective and Officer Rodriguez back to their SUV and got in the back.

"So you'll call me when you're headed over to interview Samantha Hutchins?" Guin asked when they had reached the Blind Pass parking lot. "You can just text me if it's easier."

The detective grunted.

"Thanks for the lift!" Guin called as they pulled away.

As soon as she got back to the condo, Guin phoned Ginny.

"What's up, buttercup?"

"We've got trouble," Guin said.

"With a capital T, that rhymes with P, and that stands for pool?"

"Excuse me?" said Guin.

"Never mind," said Ginny, sighing. "Just don't tell me you found another dead body."

There was silence for several seconds. Then Guin heard Ginny sigh again.

"This used to be such a peaceful island, until you showed up. Not that I don't appreciate the big boost in circulation your and Craig's stories have garnered. But you keep finding dead bodies and no one's going to want to come to Sanibel anymore."

"I doubt that," said Guin. "Now if the birds stopped coming and there were no more shells…"

"Point taken," said Ginny. "So, who'd you find this time?"

"A young woman by the name of CiCi Rawlins. Found her lying face down over by Silver Key early this morning. She was probably out shelling."

"Or someone could have dumped her there," said Ginny.

Guin hadn't thought about that, though the detective and the medical examiner probably had. She would have to ask the detective later.

"We think she was killed by a blow to the back of the head."

"Sounds nasty," said Ginny.

"It was," said Guin, shivering at the memory.

"Any idea who did it?"

"Not yet," said Guin. "I just found her a little while ago. Sam and Rita are going to be very upset. CiCi was one of their volunteers."

Ginny whistled.

"I assume you want me to write about the murder."

"Unless you want Craig to," Ginny replied.

Craig was Craig Jeffers, an award-winning crime reporter from Chicago who had retired to Sanibel with his wife Betty. That is until Ginny convinced him to come out of retirement to be the paper's fishing reporter.

Craig had also helped Guin cover a number of crimes on the island, and the two had become friends. More than friends. Craig and Betty had become almost like parents to Guin, or an uncle and aunt. And they were always inviting Guin over for dinner.

Guin had a lot on her plate, but there was no way she was going to give this particular story to another reporter, not even Craig.

"I can handle it," Guin replied. "But I'll see if Craig wants to help."

Ginny smiled.

"Good. Well, you two get on it, and keep me posted."

Guin could hear Ginny's phone beeping.

"I need to take this. Talk to you later."

Guin said goodbye, but Ginny had already hung up.

CHAPTER 7

"Nice of you to join us," said Rita, as Denny sauntered into the bedroom.

Sam and Marta stopped what they were doing and looked up at him.

"There's no coffee in the coffee pot," he reported.

"Well then, why don't you go make some?" suggested Rita.

He scratched his head.

"Never mind," she said, getting up. "I'll go make another pot. I could use more anyway."

She paused by the door. Denny looked like he hadn't slept. Though that was kind of his default look.

"As you're here, why don't you make yourself useful and give Sam and Marta a hand," Rita said.

"Sure," Denny replied. "What do you need me to do?"

Rita returned a short time later, bearing two mugs of coffee.

"Here," she said, handing one to her brother, who was leaning against the wall, staring across the room.

"Thanks," he said, turning his gaze to her and taking a sip.

"You're welcome," she said. "So, you going to stand there all day or are you going to help?"

"Sam said to wait for you," Denny replied.

Rita looked over at Sam, who shrugged.

"Fine," said Rita. "You can help me check the dolphin."

"Check the dolphin?" said Denny, confused.

"Yes, the dolphin. Go examine the top of its head and make sure nothing's exposed."

Denny looked at the fountain, then back at Rita.

"Go on," said Rita.

Denny walked to the edge of the fountain, then hesitated.

"What's the problem?" asked Rita.

"I don't want to break anything."

"Oh for God's sake," said Rita. "Just watch your step—and be careful."

Denny looked from Rita to Marta to Sam. They were seated on the floor, looking up at him.

"Fine," he said. "But if I trip and break something, don't say I didn't warn you."

Rita rolled her eyes.

"Pretend it's a guitar."

Denny gingerly stepped into the fountain.

"There now. That wasn't so hard, was it?" said Rita.

Denny made a face.

"Now check the dolphin's head."

Denny took two steps, then stopped.

"What's the problem now?" asked Rita.

"I'm not tall enough," he said.

Denny was around 6'2", but the dolphin's rostrum, or nose, was still several inches above him.

"Stand on your toes."

"What if I lose my balance?"

Sam got up and grabbed a small stepladder from the corner. She walked back to the fountain and placed it inside the fountain.

"Now try," she said.

Denny stared at the stepladder.

"Go on," said Rita.

He climbed up the little ladder.

"Okay. I can see the top of the dolphin's head. What exactly am I looking for?"

"Just let me know how the blowhole looks."

He snickered.

"Seriously?" said Rita.

"Come on, 'blowhole' is funny."

"Maybe to you," his sister replied. "Just do me a favor and take a look. Then let me know what you see."

Denny looked at the blowhole.

"It looks like a hole."

Rita sighed.

"Hold on. I'm going to turn the fountain on. Don't move."

"Won't I get wet?" Denny asked.

"I'm just checking the lights, not the water. That's not hooked up yet."

Sam and Marta watched as Rita plugged in the cord.

"I still don't see anything," said Denny.

"Hold your horses," said Rita.

She turned off the overhead lights, then walked over to the side of the fountain. There was a hidden panel, which she opened. Then she flipped a switch. Suddenly the fountain was aglow.

"Cool," said Denny.

There was a light shining from inside the dolphin's blowhole as well as several lights shining up from the base.

"Nice."

"You've outdone yourself, Rita," said Sam, standing up and looking at the fountain.

Rita smiled.

"It was a team effort."

"Speaking of team, you didn't happen to see CiCi this morning, did you?" Sam asked Denny, who was still standing on the stepladder, staring up at the ceiling, where the blue of the lights created sea-like patterns.

"No, why?"

"She hasn't shown up or called," Sam replied.

"Probably overslept," said Denny.

He looked down at Rita.

"Can I get down now?"

"How does the blowhole look?" Rita asked. "Any cracks?"

Denny peered at the blowhole again.

"It looks fine to me."

"Run your finger around the edge of the hole, just to make sure."

Denny looked down at his sister.

"What if I get electrocuted?"

"Seriously?" asked Rita.

"Fine," said Denny. "But if I die, there are witnesses."

"Oh, for Pete's sake," said Rita. "Get down. I'll do it."

Denny climbed down and Rita was about to take his place when the doorbell rang.

"I wonder who that could be?" said Sam.

"Maybe it's CiCi," said Rita. "I'll go let her in."

"Saved by the bell," said Denny.

A minute later, Rita returned, accompanied by Detective O'Loughlin and Guin.

Much to Guin's surprise, the detective had let her know, via text, that he was headed over to Sam's place. He hadn't given her much notice. He was probably hoping she wouldn't receive his text until later or was too busy, Guin thought. But Guin happened to have had her phone on her desk and had heard the telltale beep.

"I'll be right there," she had texted him back.

And twenty minutes later, she was bolting from the Mini to Sam's front door, where the detective was standing.

"You are not to say a word," he had warned her, as they made their way down the hall to the master bedroom.

Denny, Marta, and Sam were all staring at the detective.

"This is Detective O'Loughlin of the Sanibel Police Department," Rita announced.

"Is there a problem, detective?" Denny asked.

The detective glanced at him.

"And you are?"

"Dennis Sumner," said Denny.

"You staying here?" asked the detective.

"He's with me, detective," said Sam.

She moved towards the detective and held out her hand.

"I'm Sam… Hutchins. I'm renting this place."

"The artist," said the detective, looking from Sam to the fountain.

"That's me," said Sam, sounding cheerier than she felt.

The detective turned his gaze on Marta.

"Detective," said Marta.

"Ms. Harvey," replied the detective, giving her a brief nod.

"You two know each other?" Guin asked the detective in a hushed voice, looking at Marta.

"The detective is a regular at our choral concerts," Marta replied, somewhat imperiously, Guin thought.

Guin was surprised. The detective didn't seem to be the choral concert type. Then again, what did she really know about him?

"So, why are you here, detective?" Denny asked him. "One of the neighbors complain about my guitar playing?"

"No," said the detective, glancing over at him.

"It's CiCi," said Guin, unable to contain herself.

"What about CiCi?" asked Sam, looking from Guin to the detective.

"Her body was found on the beach this morning," replied the detective.

Sam's hand flew to her mouth.

"Is she...?" Sam asked. Her face had gone pale.

Rita moved to Sam's side and put an arm around her friend.

"I'm afraid so," said the detective.

"Oh my God," said Sam, her eyes wide.

She looked at the detective.

"But she was just here. I don't understand. What happened?"

The detective glanced around the room at the others. Then his gaze rested back on Sam.

"When was the last time you saw her?" he asked.

"Last night. I think it was around seven," she replied.

"And that was the last time any of you saw her?" he asked, glancing around the room.

They each nodded their heads.

"You say you found her body on the beach?" Rita asked.

Guin looked over at the detective, mentally pleading with him to let her speak. He gave her a quick nod.

"I found her, over by Silver Key," Guin replied.

"Hell," said Rita.

The detective regarded her.

"She insisted on going over there, though we told her it wasn't necessary," explained Rita. "She was determined to get one more Scotch bonnet, though, as you can see, we don't really need more shells."

"Well, she got that Scotch bonnet," said the detective.

They waited for the detective to continue. When he didn't, Guin spoke up.

"When I found her, she had a Scotch bonnet clenched in her hand. It was a beauty."

"So what happened?" asked Denny. "Did she drown?"

Guin looked at Denny.

"No, she didn't drown," replied the detective.

"Then what happened to her?" asked Rita.

"She was murdered," said the detective.

CHAPTER 8

"Murdered?" said Sam, staring at the detective. "Who would want to murder CiCi?"

"It was probably one of those crazy shellers she was telling me about," said Denny.

Everyone turned to look at Denny.

"What?" he said. "She just told me that people around here would kill to find certain shells. I thought she was kidding, but…"

Guin used to think the same thing, but she had learned. She was dying to say something, to ask them about CiCi and where they all were earlier that morning, but she had promised the detective she would keep quiet, for now, and just observe. It was taking all of her willpower, however, to keep her mouth shut.

As if reading Guin's mind, the detective asked where everyone had been earlier that morning.

"I was in bed here until after eight," said Sam.

"I was here, too," said Rita.

The detective glanced at Marta.

"I was at home, making muffins," said Marta. "Then I drove over here a little before eight-thirty."

The detective looked at Denny.

"I was here, too," said Denny.

Sam and Rita exchanged quick looks but didn't say anything.

"Can anyone verify your whereabouts?" asked the detective, glancing around the room.

"I live alone," said Marta. "And I doubt my cat would be of much help."

Guin grinned, then wiped the smile off her face. This wasn't funny.

"I can vouch for Sam," said Rita.

"Rita was in the kitchen making coffee when I got up," Sam added.

The detective looked over at Denny.

"I was in bed."

Denny was smiling and had placed an arm around Sam.

Sam did not look happy but didn't say anything.

"I'd like to speak with each of you individually," said the detective, many seconds later.

He had been scribbling notes in the little notebook.

"Is there someplace private we can talk?"

"You can use my room," said Rita. "And there's the kitchen and the lanai."

"Ms. Hutchins," said the detective, gesturing towards the door.

Denny gave her shoulder a squeeze.

She extricated herself from Denny and headed to the door. As she exited the room, she glanced back at him.

Guin had made to follow Sam and the detective, but the detective had stopped her.

"But," Guin protested.

But one look from the detective and she knew not to bother.

"Fine," she said, stopping.

She returned to the bedroom and was immediately met with questions.

"So you found the body?" asked Denny.

"I did," said Guin.

"Must have been quite a shock."

"It was," said Guin.

She looked at Denny. He had aged since that poster she had of him in college, but he was still good looking.

"What happened to her?" he asked.

"I'm not at liberty to say," said Guin.

"Come on, you can tell us," he said with a smile. "We won't breathe a word to the detective."

Guin bet he got a lot of women to tell him all sorts of things with that smile.

"So, are you staying here?" Guin asked.

"I just flew in for a quick visit. I'm going back out on tour in a couple of weeks. I play guitar in the band No Signal."

"And you knew the dead girl, CiCi?" Guin asked him, ignoring her fan-girl impulse to ask him about the band.

"Not really. I had just met her. She volunteered to give me a tour of the island."

"When was that?"

"Yesterday afternoon," said Denny. "She drove me up to Captiva and then back here. Said she would show me the rest of the island today or tomorrow."

"Did she say anything about going to Silver Key this morning?" asked Guin.

"She mentioned it," said Denny. "Though I had no idea where Silver Key was."

"Had she mentioned to either of you that she planned on going to Silver Key early this morning?" Guin asked Rita and Marta.

"Yeah," said Rita. "She said she wanted to get a Scotch bonnet for the fountain. Didn't like the one we had used for the turtle's eye. And she thought, with the storm coming through, she'd find one over by Silver Key. She said it was a good place to find them, 'cause not that many people knew about it."

Guin knew about Silver Key, but she had never found a Scotch bonnet there.

"I told her we were good," said Rita. "That she didn't have to bother. But CiCi could be pretty stubborn when it came to shells."

"She liked pretty things," said Marta, looking over at Denny.

Guin followed Marta's gaze, or was it a glare? Interesting.

"Any idea how she got there?" Guin asked. "Did she have a car?"

"She had a little white convertible, an old Volkswagen," Denny replied.

"A Beetle?" asked Guin.

"No, a Golf," said Rita. "Must have been at least ten years old."

Guin tried to remember if she had seen a white Golf convertible in the parking lot over by Blind Pass that morning.

"Would she have driven it over there?"

"It's possible," said Rita. "Though I think her family's place wasn't too far from there. She could have biked or maybe even walked."

She turned back to Denny.

"And you said CiCi dropped you back here around seven last night?"

"That's right, though I couldn't swear to the exact time," said Denny. "I wasn't wearing a watch."

"Did any of you see or hear from her after that?" Guin asked.

"Why all the questions?" Denny asked.

"Sorry," said Guin. "Occupational hazard. I'm a reporter for the local paper, the *Sanibel-Captiva Sun-Times*. I'm covering the story for the paper."

"I thought you were doing a profile of Sam and the sculpture," said Rita.

"It's a small-town paper. I write about a lot of things," said Guin.

She paused.

"So is it okay if I ask you some more questions?"

"Ask us anything," said Rita. "We've got nothing to hide."

Guin smiled.

"Thank you. So do any of you know if CiCi told anyone else she'd be at Silver Key this morning?"

Guin glanced around the room.

"No one?" she asked.

"She may have told someone," said Rita. "She'd been talking about it for days. But I couldn't name names."

Guin looked back over at the fountain.

"Looks like you're done."

"Almost," said Rita. "Just need to polish her up and check a few things. Then we should be good to go."

"I'd be happy to help, if you could use an extra set of hands," said Guin.

"Thanks," said Rita. "But we should be fine."

Guin continued to stare at the fountain. Then she caught herself and turned back to Rita.

"One more question," she began.

But just then Sam came back.

"You're next, Rita."

"Oh goody," Rita replied.

She sighed and headed down the hall.

Denny was the last one to be interviewed by the detective, and it took longer than the others.

"I wonder what he's asking him," said Sam.

"Probably where he was early this morning," said Rita.

"I thought you said he was here with you," said Guin.

Sam and Rita exchanged a look.

"Was he not here when you got up?" she asked Sam.

Sam looked over at the fountain.

"You think we can apply polyurethane today, or should we wait until tomorrow?" Sam asked Rita.

"You should wait until morning," said Marta. "Give the glue more time to dry."

"Rita?" asked Sam.

"I'm fine waiting until tomorrow morning," she replied. "I still want to do one more check, to make sure we didn't miss a spot."

Guin looked over at the fountain. Even if they had missed a spot, she doubted that anyone could tell.

"So how are you going to get the fountain to the museum?" Guin asked.

The fountain took up at least half of the room and looked heavy.

Rita smiled.

"It comes apart."

"Ah," said Guin.

"The base and the pedestal and the dolphin are separate pieces," Rita explained. "The city hired movers to help us get the pieces safely over to the Shell Museum. Then we'll reassemble and test it on site."

"Sounds like a lot of work," said Guin, eyeing the fountain.

"Nah," said Rita. "Once you've done a few of these installations, you get used to it. Just wait until you see it all set up."

Everyone was looking at the fountain.

"So when do you move it?" asked Guin.

"The movers are coming Tuesday. The museum is closing early, so we can set it up and test it without anyone trying to sneak a peek."

"Good idea," said Guin. "Would it be okay if I stopped by? I'd love to see it being put together."

"As long as you don't tell anyone," said Rita.

"Mum's the word," said Guin. Though it would take a Herculean effort to keep it from Shelly.

"Then you can come," said Rita, smiling.

"Excellent!" said Guin. "I'll swing by late that afternoon."

Guin was staring at the fountain again. It really was amazing. There must have been thousands of shells covering it. It was like a mosaic.

Just then Denny returned, accompanied by the detective. He looked tired.

Guin glanced at the detective. His face was difficult to read. Guin always thought he would have made a great professional poker player.

"You done here, detective?" she asked him.

"For now," he replied.

Guin debated whether she should stay and ask more questions or go with the detective. She had several questions for him, too.

She turned to Sam.

"Okay if I follow up with you tomorrow or the day after? I may have some more questions."

"Sure," Sam replied. Though her attention was focused elsewhere.

Guin followed Sam's gaze. She was looking at Denny, who had his hands thrust into the pockets of his ripped jeans, like a kid who'd been caught misbehaving.

CHAPTER 9

"So?" said Guin, looking at the detective.

They were standing next to the detective's car.

"Did you discover anything? Did one of them know something? I'll bet you a pair of Spring Training tickets that the boyfriend's hiding something," Guin said.

Was that a slight twitch of the detective's lips? Guin knew the detective, a devout Boston Red Sox fan, liked attending Spring Training games at JetBlue Park in Fort Myers. (Guin herself was a New York Mets fan but didn't have a problem with the Red Sox.)

"As tempting as your offer is, Ms. Jones, you know I can't answer your questions," he replied.

"Fine," said Guin. "I'll find out for myself. I was planning on going back there and asking them more questions tomorrow anyway. Though it would save everyone a lot of time and grief if you would just share what you knew," she grumbled.

"You mean it would save *you* a lot of time and grief," the detective said. "Besides, I wouldn't want to deprive you of the chase," he added. "What fun would it be if I just *gave* you information, Nancy Drew?"

Guin glared at him.

The detective turned and opened the door to his car. He was about to get in when Guin stopped him.

"You know I'm going to have to interview you at some point."

The detective turned his weather-worn face to her, his freckles barely visible under his tan. Guin could imagine him as a boy: his hair redder, his skin fairer, with a smattering of freckles, his tawny eyes full of mischief. She wondered if he had been skinny. In his current form, he reminded Guin of a boxer, or former boxer, with his solid physique, square jaw, and slightly off-kilter nose (no doubt broken, at least once, in a fight).

"I look forward to it," he replied.

Guin suspected that was sarcasm. Getting information out of William O'Loughlin was like trying to pill her cats. Not impossible, but it required perseverance and determination. And you might get bitten in the process.

The detective made to get in his car again when Guin stopped him once more.

"So you'll send me the results of the autopsy?" Guin asked.

The detective straightened and gave Guin a look.

"Anything else?" he asked her.

"Just one more thing."

He waited for her to continue.

"Did you find CiCi's car at Blind Pass? It's a white VW Golf convertible."

"Why do you want to know?" asked the detective.

"I have my reasons."

The two of them stood there, regarding each other, for several seconds.

"So you'll let me know about the autopsy and the car?" Guin asked.

"I'll think about it," the detective replied. He paused. "Now I have a question for you."

"Yes?" Guin answered.

"You want to have lunch?"

"So you go to any games yet?" Guin asked him as they were eating their fried chicken.

The detective had suggested they eat at the Pecking Order, which had the best fried chicken and sides on Sanibel. It was a hole in the wall, with no formal seating. But there were a handful of stools at the outside counter.

"Just one. Been busy," said the detective, taking a bite of coleslaw, then a sip of his Coke. "What about you? You go to any Mets games?"

"Not yet," said Guin. "No one to go with."

She glanced at the detective. The summer before they had gone to a couple of ball games, a Red Sox game in Tampa and a Mets game in Miami. But since then, nothing. And Guin missed their baseball outings.

They finished their meal in silence.

"So you'll send me the results of the autopsy?" Guin asked him as they were getting ready to leave.

"Yeah, yeah, yeah," said the detective.

"And when can I interview you? You know Ginny is going to want me to get a quote."

The detective sighed.

"Do I have a choice?"

"Not really, no," said Guin, smiling.

The detective looked at his watch.

"I've gotta go," he said. "I'll get back to you."

Guin opened her mouth to say something, then shut it. She knew she would need to follow up with the detective, that he wouldn't automatically get back to her. But she was getting used to it.

They tossed their empty boxes into the nearby garbage can and walked to their cars.

"Thanks for lunch," said Guin.

As usual, the detective had insisted on paying.

"Gotta eat," he replied.

"Well, goodbye," said Guin.

The detective raised a hand in farewell, then got into his car.

Guin heard her cell phone beeping as she drove back to her condo, but she waited until she had parked to see who had left her a message. Ris.

"Looking forward to seeing you this weekend!" he had typed.

Guin smiled. She had been so busy she had forgotten that Ris would be flying back to Fort Myers that weekend.

"Send me your flight info and I'll pick you up at RSW," she replied.

"Will do," he wrote. "Everything good?"

Guin paused. He would not be happy to hear she had found yet another dead body.

"Everything's great!" she typed back, mentally crossing her fingers. "Just busy."

At least that part wasn't a lie.

"Hope you'll make some time for me," he replied with a smiley face.

"Gotta go," she wrote him. "Send me your info. Bye!"

Guin didn't mean to be rude. She just wasn't in the mood to text with him.

She got out of the Mini and headed up the stairs. No sooner had she opened the door when she was greeted by her two cats.

"You sure you guys aren't part dog?" she asked them, bending down to scratch their heads.

Flora and Fauna purred.

Guin got up and headed to the kitchen, the cats following after her. Fauna meowed.

Guin looked over at their bowls.

"You guys still have food. I'll give you some more when you're done with what's there."

Fauna gave her a baleful look and loudly meowed.

"Sorry, kitty cat."

Guin turned and walked to her bedroom/office and booted up her computer. She wanted to type up everything she knew about CiCi's death, while it was fresh.

She opened a new Word doc and began to type. When she had finished typing, she reviewed what she had written. She needed to learn more about CiCi, find out if she had any enemies (though that seemed hard to imagine, at least from what she knew about her) and who knew she would be shelling by Silver Key that morning.

"I should call Craig," she announced.

Knowing Craig, he had probably already heard about the body. She just hoped that word hadn't gotten out to the general public. Sanibel was known for its beaches, and for being a safe place. If people heard that someone had been murdered on Silver Key, it would be bad for tourism. Very bad. She just hoped Susan hadn't heard about it. Though surely Suzy Seashell would realize that blogging about a young woman being found dead on one of Sanibel's beaches would be bad for business.

Should she call Susan, to see if she knew anything? Of course, if she didn't know about the body, she would after Guin called her. Guin sighed. What to do?

She picked up her phone and speed-dialed Craig.

CHAPTER 10

"So, have you heard?" asked Guin.

"About the dead girl?" Craig replied.

Of course Craig knew. Sanibel was a small island, and he had friends in the police department and in the medical examiner's office. And Ginny had no doubt phoned him to let him know Guin had found yet another dead body.

"Yeah," said Guin. "Who told you?"

"I cannot reveal my sources."

Guin rolled her eyes.

"Yeah, yeah, yeah. So will you help me?"

"Of course," he replied. "You want to come over? Betty just made some oatmeal raisin cookies. Better yet, come for dinner. You can tell us all about your trip to Australia. Betty's been bugging me to have you over. She always wanted to go to Australia."

Guin smiled. She could just picture Betty trying to persuade Craig, who wasn't a fan of travel, to go to Australia.

"You sure I wouldn't be imposing?"

"You? Never! Just be prepared to be peppered with questions."

"Can I bring anything?" Guin asked.

"Nah, just yourself. You know Betty. She cooks enough for a small army."

"What time should I come over?"

"How's five? That way we can talk before dinner."

"Sounds good," said Guin. "I'll see you at five."

She ended the call and wandered over to her computer.

"Let's see what Google has to say about you, Ms. CiCi Rawlins."

She typed "CiCi Rawlins" into her browser.

She got a handful of results.

Then she typed in "Caroline Rawlins Sanibel." That yielded far more.

Guin learned that Caroline Clare Rawlins was a student at FGCU, majoring in marine biology. She was a member of the Kappa Delta sorority and the FGCU Culinary Club. She had made Dean's List every year, and she was scheduled to graduate that April.

How devastating for her family and friends, Guin thought. A young woman with everything to live for. Struck down, literally, in the prime of her life.

Guin shook her head. Then she continued to search for information.

She found CiCi's Facebook page, but it was private. However, her Instagram page was not. Guin scrolled through CiCi's photos. She clearly loved food and nature. Almost all of her recent pictures were of some dish she had made or eaten, or else photos of shells and sea life. (CiCi, like many people who lived on or visited Sanibel, loved dolphins and manatees.)

Guin continued to scroll through CiCi's photos. There were only a handful of people shots: photos of CiCi with some of her sorority sisters, a few from the Culinary Club, and a couple with a boy.

Guin clicked on the tag on one of the photos of CiCi with the boy, a good-looking redhead. The boy's Instagram handle was HotScot. She went to his Instagram account. HotScot, real name Scott Murray, seemed to be quite popular with the ladies, at least according to his feed. The majority of pictures showed him cheek-to-cheek or hanging out with one or more attractive woman.

"So how did you know CiCi?" Guin wondered, aloud.

She clicked around and discovered HotScot was also a student at FGCU. Were the two of them friends? Dating? She thought about messaging him, then changed her mind.

What about CiCi's family? No doubt the detective had broken the bad news to them.

Guin did a search. There was a Jack and Kimberly Rawlins over on Pine Tree. That must be them, Guin thought, after doing a bit more research. And it seemed as though CiCi had an older brother.

Guin did some more poking around. She was always amazed at what you could find online about people with a little digging: their address, political affiliation, age, relatives, criminal records.

It appeared that CiCi's mother sold insurance and her father ran a charter fishing business, Rawlins Reel Good Fishing Charters.

"I wonder if Craig or the detective know him?" Guin mused. Probably. She would have to ask them.

As for CiCi's brother, John Jr., he appeared to work for his father, at least according to the Rawlins Reel Good website. And CiCi likewise worked in the family business, as a naturalist. Though where she found the time, Guin didn't know.

Guin made notes to reach out to CiCi's family, HotScot (she would need to remember to refer to him as Mr. Murray when she contacted him), CiCi's sorority, and the Culinary Club, as well as Sam, Rita, Marta, and Denny.

Yikes. That was a lot of people. Hopefully Craig could help. She was counting on him to find out about the autopsy report, in case the detective didn't share the results with her.

And he would no doubt have some theories and advice.

Despite being an award-winning crime reporter, Craig seemed content to let Guin do most of the investigating, helping out only as and where needed. Indeed, if left to his own devices, he would spend his days fishing and his nights, or some of them, playing poker with his buddies.

Guin did a little more research, searching for images of CiCi online and finding out whatever she could about the young woman. But there was not a whole lot to be found. If she wanted to find out who might wish to harm CiCi, she would need to speak with her friends and family.

Guin arrived at Craig and Betty's promptly at five and rang the doorbell.

"Coming!" called Craig.

"Hi," said Guin, when Craig opened the door.

"Come in, come in," he said, ushering her inside. "Can I get you something to drink?"

"I'm good," said Guin.

"Guin!"

It was Betty. She came over and gave Guin a kiss on the cheek and a hug.

"How was Australia? Tell me all about it. Did you take pictures? Of course you did."

She ushered Guin over to the sofa and indicated for her to sit.

"Australia was good," said Guin. "I still need to sort through and edit my photos. But I'd be happy to show you some of the ones on my phone."

"I'd love that," said Betty.

She sat next to Guin on the couch and Guin proceeded to show her some of the photos she took on her trip, narrating as she went along.

"It sounds wonderful," Betty said with a sigh, after Guin had finished. "If only I could get Craig to go," she said, glancing over at her husband, who was in the kitchen.

She got up.

"Well, I need to go finish fixing dinner. And I know you and Craig have a lot to talk about. Did I hear right, that you found another dead body?"

"Unfortunately, yes," said Guin.

"How horrible!" said Betty, covering her heart with her hand. "And it was a young woman?"

"Yeah," said Guin. "I actually met her. She was in her early twenties."

Betty shook her head.

"Who would do such a thing?"

"I don't know," said Guin. "But I'm hoping to find out."

"Just be careful," said Betty. "What do the police think?"

"I don't know," said Guin. "Too early to say."

Craig came over and gave Betty a kiss on the cheek.

"Guin and I are going to go sit out on the lanai. Give us a call when dinner's ready."

"Can I help with anything?" Guin asked Betty.

"You go chat with Craig. I've got it."

Guin always felt a bit guilty about not helping out, but Betty seemed to enjoy cooking, or feeding people, and Craig always helped with cleanup.

"Okay," said Guin. "But come get us if you need anything."

Betty smiled and shooed them away.

"And that's everything," said Guin, after sharing what she knew with Craig.

Craig looked thoughtful.

"I'll need to see the autopsy report, but if she was killed

by that horse conch, the killer would have needed to be pretty big and strong."

"That's what I thought," said Guin. "So most likely it was a man. Though I guess it could have been a woman," she added, her brain flashing an image of Rita, who had to be at least 5'9" and was solidly built. She shook her head. Why would Rita want to hurt CiCi? Besides, she was supposedly at the house when CiCi was killed.

"Penny for your thoughts," said Craig.

"Sorry. I was just imagining what the killer might have looked like."

"So," said Craig. "What do you want me to do?"

"Well," said Guin, "I was thinking you could reach out to your buddy in the medical examiner's office. See if you could find out anything from him. And what do you know about Rawlins Reel Good Fishing Charters?"

"I know Jack. Good guy. I've gone out with them a few times. Son's kind of quiet. Didn't know the daughter. Think she only went out on their eco cruises."

"Would you be okay asking Jack about CiCi, see if she had a boyfriend or ex-boyfriend, or if there was anyone who might have wanted to harm her?"

"I'll give Jack a buzz later, pay my condolences. No parent should lose a child, especially like that."

"Thanks Craig."

"Dinner!" called Betty.

Guin and Craig continued to chat.

"Come along, you two," said Betty, going out onto the lanai and ushering them to the dining table. "Don't want dinner to get cold."

"What are we having?" asked Guin.

Betty was always after Craig about his diet. So she insisted on making healthy, simple meals when they ate at home.

"Roast chicken with carrots and onions, served with brown rice and roasted broccolini."

"Sounds delicious," said Guin.

"I miss having fried chicken," grumbled Craig.

"You can go to the Pecking Order on your cheat day," Betty said. "Personally, I prefer a good roast chicken," she said to Guin.

"I agree," said Guin, gazing at the nicely browned bird Betty was carrying to the table.

"Craig, would you like to do the honors?"

Craig cut up the roast chicken, giving Guin a thigh and a drumstick, along with plenty of veg and some rice.

"That was delicious," said Guin, as she brought her plate into the kitchen.

"I'm glad you liked it," said Betty. "And I have a special treat for dessert."

Guin and Craig helped clear the rest of the table.

"Am I allowed to have a little ice cream with my cookie?" Craig asked, taking one of the oatmeal raisin cookies.

"Yes, you may," said Betty, giving him a smile.

"Betty here makes the best oatmeal raisin cookies you've ever had," said Craig.

"You're just saying that," said Betty.

"It's true!" said Craig. "You have one and tell me, Guin."

Betty placed a container of vanilla ice cream on the counter, along with three bowls and some spoons.

"Help yourself," she said to Guin.

Guin scooped some ice cream into the bowl, then placed a cookie on top. Craig and Betty followed suit. Then they took their bowls back to the dining table.

"I forgot to ask, would you like some coffee?" asked Betty. "Or maybe some herbal tea?"

"I'm fine," said Guin.

She took a bite of the cookie and closed her eyes.

"Mmm…" she said.

She opened her eyes to see Craig smiling at her.

"Told you so!"

"These are delicious, Betty. You have to give me the recipe."

Betty beamed.

"I would be happy to. Now eat up."

Craig walked Guin to the door.

"Thanks for coming over."

"I should be thanking you," said Guin. "I think I would starve if it wasn't for the two of you."

It was a bit of an exaggeration. But since Ris had gone off to the South Pacific on sabbatical, Guin had been cooking much less.

"We love having you here," said Craig.

Guin knew that Craig and Betty missed their three children, none of whom lived close by and only came to visit a couple of times a year, if that.

"Well, I love hanging out with the two of you. So," she said, changing topics, "you'll check in with your buddy in the medical examiner's office and speak with Jack Rawlins?"

"I hear and obey," he said, standing at attention.

Guin laughed.

"At ease. And thank you. Let's catch up this weekend. Though…" she said, remembering Ris would be arriving on Saturday.

"You got plans?" Craig asked.

"Actually, Ris will be here."

"He will? Is everything okay? I thought he wasn't due back for at least a couple more months."

"Everything's fine," said Guin. "He's coming back to interview for the chairmanship of the Marine & Ecological Sciences department at FGCU and helping out with the Shell Show. Then he's off to Japan to continue his sabbatical."

"Well, I hope you two enjoy your time together," said Craig.

"Me, too," said Guin. She realized she had said it aloud and looked a bit sheepish. "Well, goodnight," she said, giving Betty a final hug. "Talk to you this weekend, Craig."

"Goodnight," they said in unison. Then they watched as Guin made her way to her car.

CHAPTER 11

Even though she was normally up early, Guin had set her alarm for six. She wanted to get to Silver Key before dawn, before a lot of shellers got there. Though few people typically walked all the way from Blind Pass to Silver Key, preferring to look for shells around Blind Pass bridge, or by Castaways, or the area just across from the Sunset Grill and the Lazy Flamingo.

Guin hurriedly got dressed, splashed some cold water on her face, and pulled her hair into a ponytail. Then she made her way to the kitchen. She thought about making coffee to take with her, but as there were no restrooms by the Blind Pass parking lot, she decided to wait until she got back home. Instead she poured herself some water and took a sip.

"Meow!"

Guin looked down to see Fauna looking up at her.

"Meow!" the cat repeated, followed by several more vocalizations.

"Yeah, yeah, yeah," said Guin.

She went over to the pantry and took out a can of cat food. Then she divided it between the two cat bowls.

"Special treat," she said. "Enjoy."

Fauna didn't need to hear any more. She ran over to her bowl and eagerly began consuming the wet food.

"Slow down!" Guin admonished her. But the cat paid her no mind.

Guin sighed and stood there watching the cats eat for several seconds. Then she grabbed her little backpack, which she had packed the night before with her camera, a notebook, a couple of pens, and a pair of latex gloves, wrapped her fanny pack around her waist, and took her keys off their hook. She stopped at the closet by the front door and grabbed her shelling bag (because you never knew when you might come across a Scotch bonnet, an alphabet cone, or, praise be to Poseidon, a junonia), threw on a baseball cap and a windbreaker, and headed out the door.

It was still dark when Guin parked at the Blind Pass lot, though there were already a few cars there. Hopefully, they belonged to fishermen, Blind Pass being a popular fishing spot.

She made her way down to the beach, flashlight in hand, resisting the urge to look for shells, which was difficult. But she was on a mission.

She made her way to Silver Key, only occasionally looking down. As she had hoped, the beach was empty. Though as she got closer to Silver Key, she saw someone with a flashlight ahead of her. Suddenly Guin began to feel nervous. What if it was the killer?

Guin stopped in her tracks, took a deep breath, and pulled her phone out of her pocket. She thought about texting Shelly or the detective, to let them know where she was, in case she didn't make it back. Then she decided against it. Shelly would only freak out, and the detective would only lecture her. She sighed and put her phone back in her back pocket.

"Come on, Guin," she said to herself. "If the person wanted to prey on unsuspecting shellers, he wouldn't be waving around a flashlight."

She had started to walk when suddenly her phone started to vibrate, making her jump.

She grabbed it and looked down at the screen. It was a text from Ris. He had sent her his flight information.

"Got it!" she quickly replied. "See you tomorrow!"

She put her phone back in her back pocket, ignoring its vibrations.

She looked down the beach. The person with the flashlight was still there. Had he seen Guin?

"All right, whoever you are," Guin said, under her breath. "Just please don't kill me."

She took a deep breath and slowly exhaled. Then she continued walking toward Silver Key.

The sky was turning from dark to light blue, and soon the sun would peek over the dunes. Guin turned off her flashlight and made her way to the end of the beach.

"Susan?"

There, standing on the pile of shells where she had found CiCi's body, was Susan Hastings.

The area had been cordoned off with police tape, but Susan had climbed over it and appeared to be searching for something.

"What are you doing here?" Guin asked her.

"Guin, you startled me!"

"What are you doing here?" Guin repeated. "Did you not see the police tape?"

Susan glanced around.

"I didn't see it in the dark."

Guin found that highly unlikely.

"You know this is a restricted area," Guin said.

"Oh?" said Susan, innocently.

Guin looked skeptical. She had seen Susan's flashlight

waving around. It was hard to believe she hadn't noticed the yellow police tape and the poles ringing the area.

"You looking for something?" Guin asked her.

"Looking for something?" Susan repeated, as if she hadn't understood Guin.

"Yes," said Guin.

"Just shells," said Susan.

Guin was dubious, especially as Susan wasn't carrying a shelling bag. Though she could have stashed it in her pocket.

"You find anything?" Guin asked.

"Oh, you know," said Susan, airily.

Guin knew Susan was hiding something. It was evident from her body language.

"You should probably get down from there," Guin said.

Susan had remained on the shell pile while they were talking.

The two women stared at each other for several seconds. Then Susan sighed and made her way to where Guin was standing, neatly stepping over the yellow police tape.

"Happy now?" she asked Guin.

Guin glanced over at the shell pile. Then back at Susan. So much for investigating the scene of the crime. Frankly, Guin was surprised that the detective hadn't posted someone to watch over the area.

They continued to stand there, eyeing each other, for several seconds.

"Well, I should get going," Guin finally said.

"Don't let me keep you," said Susan.

"You know this area is off limits," Guin said.

"What are you, the turtle police?" Susan retorted.

Though they both knew turtle nesting season was a couple of months away.

Guin was about to say something in reply when she heard a noise. She turned to see an SUV coming towards them.

"This is a restricted area," came a voice over a bull horn. The detective.

She watched as the SUV made its way to where she and Susan were standing. At the wheel of the police vehicle was Officer Pettit, a young policeman Guin had encountered on several occasions.

Officer Pettit and the detective got out.

"And what, may I ask, are the two of you are doing here?" asked the detective.

"Why looking for shells, of course," Susan replied, smoothly.

Guin had to hand it to her. She acted a lot cooler than Guin was feeling.

"This is a restricted area," the detective said, looking at the two women.

"Is it?" Susan answered, innocently. "It was so dark when I got here. I couldn't tell."

Guin looked at the detective's face, trying to read his expression. But it was impossible. Though she doubted he believed Susan.

"And you, Ms. Jones. What brings you to Silver Key this morning?"

Guin thought about lying, but what was the point?

"No doubt the same as you, detective."

The detective grunted.

"What is all this about?" asked Susan. "Why is this area restricted? Turtle season doesn't begin for another two months."

Guin and the detective both looked at Susan.

"This is a crime scene, Mrs. Hastings," said the detective.

"A crime scene?" said Susan. "Did someone steal a shell?"

Guin snorted, and Susan glared at her.

"A body was found on the beach yesterday morning,"

replied the detective. "A young woman."

"A young woman," said Susan. "How awful! What happened to her?"

"She was murdered," said the detective.

Susan placed a hand over her heart.

"Murdered? How dreadful."

Guin thought she was laying it on a bit thick.

"Had I known, I would have never crossed that police line," she said. "You really should have marked it better, detective. It was quite difficult to see in the dark."

Guin rolled her eyes. She had no doubt Susan had seen the police tape and had ignored it.

"Well, I should get going," Susan said. "I hope you catch whoever did it."

"A minute, Mrs. Hastings," said the detective.

"Yes?" said Susan, stopping.

The detective reached into his pocket and pulled out a necklace.

"Can you tell me how this wound up near the body?"

CHAPTER 12

Susan froze.

"My necklace," she said, unconsciously placing a hand just below her neck.

Was that what Susan had been looking for? wondered Guin.

"Where did you find it?"

"Over there," said the detective, pointing up at the shell pile.

"I wonder how it could have gotten there," said Susan.

Guin had to hand it to her, she was a good actress. She had seen Susan poking around the shell pile, looking for something, just a few minutes ago. No doubt it was the necklace.

"Of course, it may not be *my* necklace," she said, recovering. "I'm sure lots of people have necklaces just like that."

"With your initials and a picture of you and your husband inside?" said the detective.

Susan took a step closer and reached up to take the locket from him.

"Sorry, Mrs. Hastings," he said, placing the necklace back in his pocket. "Evidence."

Susan moved her right hand to just below her neck again, as if feeling for the necklace.

"So, you want to tell me how it got there?" asked the detective.

Susan sighed.

"I lost it the other day."

"When?" asked the detective.

"I don't know," said Susan.

Guin and the detective both looked skeptical.

"It's the truth," she said.

"If you don't know when or where you lost it, why were you poking around the shell pile before dawn this morning?" said Guin.

She turned to the detective.

"When I got here this morning, Susan was up there with her flashlight, searching for something."

If looks could kill, Guin would have been dead.

"Fine," said Susan. "I thought I might have lost it here the other morning."

"Go on," said the detective.

Susan looked distinctly uncomfortable.

"You were here yesterday, weren't you?" said Guin.

"I didn't kill that girl," said Susan. "I swear to you, detective."

The detective's face was impassive.

"She was alive when I saw her."

"So you saw CiCi, here?" Guin asked.

The detective shot Guin a warning look.

"Yes," Susan said.

"Did you speak with her?" Guin asked.

"No, she was with someone."

"Did you recognize the person she was with?"

"No, it was dark," Susan replied. "But I heard them arguing."

"What were they arguing about?" asked the detective.

"I wasn't close enough to hear," said Susan.

"But you were close enough to spy on them," Guin said.

Susan glared at her.

"I wasn't spying."

Guin found that difficult to believe.

"Could you describe the person you saw with Ms. Rawlins? What was he wearing?" asked the detective.

Susan thought for several seconds.

"I couldn't see his face, like I said. But he was tall. And he was wearing one of those hooded sweatshirts."

"Anything else?" asked the detective.

"No. Like I said, it was dark, and I didn't want to eavesdrop."

Guin snorted.

"So if you were standing far away, how did your necklace wind up near CiCi's body?" Guin asked.

Susan looked uncomfortable again.

"Answer the question," said the detective.

"Well…" said Susan.

The detective and Guin waited for her to go on.

"Like I said, the two of them were arguing. And when I didn't see either of them walk past me, I got worried."

"Go on," said the detective.

"Of course, they could have walked over to Bowman's, but the tide was coming in," said Susan, rambling a bit. "And the girl wasn't exactly tall."

"So you what, went back to check to see if she was all right?" asked Guin.

"Yes," said Susan.

"And?" said Guin.

"And I didn't see them. I figured they must have cut over to Bowman's after all or left some other way."

"So how did your necklace wind up on the shell pile?" Guin asked again.

"I was getting to that," Susan snapped. "As I was about to say, when I didn't see them, I figured they had left. So I continued to look for shells. I saw the big shell pile over there and went over to it. That's when I stumbled across the body. I must have been startled and reached for my necklace. Nervous habit. And it must have fallen off. I didn't realize it was gone until later."

"You say you stumbled across Ms. Rawlins," said the detective.

"Yes," said Susan.

"So the victim was dead when you found her?"

"I…" said Susan, reaching again for her throat.

The detective regarded her.

"She was just lying there, face down, not moving. And there was blood."

She was looking off into the distance, as if envisioning the scene.

"Why didn't you call the police?" Guin asked her.

"I should have. I know that," said Susan, turning back to face them. "But I was scared. Seeing the body like that…. I'd never seen a dead body before."

Her right hand reached once again for the missing necklace.

"So you just left the body there?" Guin asked.

"I was terrified," Susan replied. "I just wanted to go home and take a shower. But then I saw you."

"You saw *me*?" said Guin.

She didn't recall seeing Susan on the beach that morning.

Susan smiled.

"You were so busy looking for shells, I doubt you noticed me. And I wasn't in the mood to chat."

"So you just assumed I would find the body and what?"

"I didn't assume anything," said Susan, defensively.

"And what time was that?" asked the detective.

"I told you, I wasn't wearing a watch," said Susan.

"Approximately," said the detective.

Susan sighed.

"It must have been around seven-thirty as it was getting light out."

"That sounds about right," said Guin, looking over at the detective.

"I'd like you to come to the Sanibel Police Department," the detective said to Susan.

"Are you arresting me?"

"No," said the detective. "I'd just like you to make a formal statement."

Susan looked visibly relieved.

"Of course, detective. I'd be happy to. What time would you like me to stop by? I need to show a house at nine-thirty, but I'm all yours after that," she said, sweetly.

Guin made a face.

"Fine. Be at the police department at ten-thirty," said the detective.

"I'll be there, detective," she said, smiling at him.

Ugh, thought Guin.

"Now, if you'll excuse me, ladies," said the detective. "Officer Pettit and I have some work to do."

"About my necklace…" said Susan.

"It's evidence, Mrs. Hastings. We'll return it to you when the case is closed."

She opened her mouth to say something but quickly closed it at one look from the detective.

"I understand, detective," she meekly replied.

The detective turned and headed to where Officer Pettit had been standing. Then the two of them headed over to where Guin had found CiCi's body.

"Well, shall we?" said Susan.

"Shall we what?" asked Guin, who had been following the detective with her eyes.

"Head back to the parking lot," replied Susan.

"You go ahead," said Guin, still watching the detective.

Susan made a tsking noise.

"What?" said Guin, whipping around to face her.

Susan had a smug look on her face.

"Poor Dr. Hartwick. If he only knew."

Guin could feel her cheeks flushing.

"Knew what?" demanded Guin.

"About you and the detective," said Susan.

"There is absolutely nothing going on between me and Detective O'Loughlin," said Guin, a bit too vehemently.

"Uh-huh," said Susan, still looking quite smug.

"It's strictly professional," said Guin.

"Keep telling yourself that," said Susan. "I see the way you two sneak little glances at each other."

Was the detective sneaking glances at her? Guin was ashamed to admit that the thought thrilled her just a little bit. But she immediately shut it down.

"Don't you have a house to show?" Guin asked her.

"I'm going," said Susan, still smiling.

"Well, don't let me keep you," said Guin.

She waited as Susan began to slowly walk back down the beach. When she was out of earshot, Guin turned and walked to where the detective and Officer Pettit were working.

She cleared her throat.

"Yes," said the detective, looking down at her. "I thought we were done."

"I never said I was done," replied Guin. "And I have a few more questions I'd like to ask you."

Officer Pettit was smiling, but he wiped the smile off his face as soon as the detective shot him a look.

"Come by the department later."

"But," Guin began.

The detective shot her the same look he had given Officer Pettit.

"Fine," Guin huffed. "What time?"

"Come around noon."

"Great. I'll bring lunch," she said.

Officer Pettit was watching the exchange and smiling again.

"You don't have to do that, Ms. Jones."

"It's my pleasure, detective. I'll just stop at Jean-Luc's and pick up a couple of sandwiches."

"I don't suppose there's any way I can stop you," said the detective.

"Nope," said Guin, smiling.

"Now if you'll excuse me," said the detective, turning back to the shell pile.

"Of course," said Guin.

She then made her way back down to Blind Pass, humming softly to herself.

CHAPTER 13

Guin arrived back at the condo a short time later and immediately wrote down everything that had transpired on the beach that morning. Then she stared out at the golf course, where two couples were taking turns hitting balls. The course was next to the J.N. "Ding" Darling National Wildlife Refuge. And while there were signs posted all around the course proclaiming "Members Only" and "No Trespassing," the birds came and went freely. Indeed, there were typically more birds on the course than golfers.

She continued to watch the golfers, her mind drifting, when she felt something brush against her leg. Flora.

"Hey, girl," Guin said, bending down and stroking the multicolored feline.

Flora purred.

"I need to take a shower and make some calls," Guin said, straightening up a minute later.

Flora tapped her leg with her paw.

"Sorry, girl. I promise to pet you later."

Guin then made her way to the bathroom, Flora mournfully watching her go.

Guin stopped at Jean-Luc's on her way to see the detective. She was staring at the menu, trying to decide what to get, when Jean-Luc emerged from the back.

"Guinivere!" he beamed, leaning across the counter to give her a kiss on each cheek. "And what can I get for you today?"

Guin smiled at the French proprietor.

"What do you recommend? I have a meeting with Detective O'Loughlin over at the police department, and I said I'd bring lunch."

Jean-Luc looked thoughtful.

"The detective is very fond of our *jambon beurre*."

"That's ham and butter on a baguette, yes?" said Guin.

"*Oui!*" said Jean-Luc. "And a better *jambon beurre* you will not find between here and France," he said, proudly.

"Then I will take one of those for the detective, and I will have the baguette with turkey, brie, and Granny Smith apples," said Guin.

"*Très bien*," said Jean-Luc.

He fixed the sandwiches himself and placed them by the cash register.

"And for dessert?"

Guin looked at the case. As usual, everything looked delicious—and very caloric.

"I really shouldn't…" she said, gazing down at the pastries.

"Phht!" said Jean-Luc. "A man likes a woman with an appetite." He reached for the tongs. "One mocha eclair and one fruit tart," he said, placing the pastries in a little box.

"*Merci*," said Guin, smiling at him.

"And to drink?" asked Jean-Luc.

Guin was about to open her mouth, but Jean-Luc cut her off.

"I know: one bottle of water for you and a LaCroix for the detective."

Guin laughed.

"Do you know all your customers so well?" she asked.

"*Bien sûr!*" he replied. "It is a small island, and I am not so old, eh?"

He said it with a twinkle in his eye.

Guin smiled back at him.

"Actually, make that two LaCroix," she said.

As he went to retrieve the sparkling waters, Guin glanced around. There were several women in the bakery, and Jean-Luc had a smile for each of them. No surprise that they liked coming to Jean-Luc's. Not only was his food delicious but Jean-Luc was rather yummy, too. That is if you liked forty-something Frenchmen who loved women and knew how to cook.

Guin thanked Jean-Luc and paid.

"*Au revoir, cherie!* Come back again soon!" he called as she exited the bakery.

Guin carefully placed everything on the passenger seat. Then she headed to the police department.

Guin announced herself at the window, telling the officer on duty she had an appointment with Detective O'Loughlin, and was buzzed back a minute later. She had been to the detective's office so many times over the last year that she could have found it blindfolded. Though as she had her hands full, she decided to keep her eyes open, so she didn't accidentally bump into anyone.

The detective's door was ajar, and she could hear him talking on the phone. She poked her head in, and he gestured for her to come in and take a seat.

She placed the bag of sandwiches and the box of pastries on his desk, then sat down. As she waited for him to finish his call, she glanced around the room, taking in his Boston Red Sox paraphernalia.

The detective, like many, if not most, Massachusetts transplants, was a devout Red Sox fan, and his office was littered with photos of past players, pennants, signed balls, and even a glove, in addition to stacks of folders and papers. Guin shook her head. For a man who seemed so orderly, his office was a mess. Though the detective swore that he could find whatever he needed at a moment's notice.

"Okay, Mike," said the detective. "I'll check in with you later. Thanks."

"Mr. Gilbertie, I presume?" said Guin, after he had hung up.

"You know what happens when you presume…" said the detective.

"No, what?" said Guin.

The detective opened his mouth to speak, then shut it again, looking frustrated.

"I think you meant *assume*," said Guin.

The detective looked at her, then glanced over at the bag and box Guin had placed on his desk.

"That lunch?" he said.

"It is," said Guin.

She reached into the bag.

"One ham sandwich," she said, placing the wrapped baguette in front of the detective. "And one LaCroix," she added, placing it next to the sandwich.

"What did you get?" he asked her.

"The turkey, brie, and Granny Smith apple baguette," she said, removing it from the bag.

The detective regarded her sandwich.

"Did you want to switch? I'm fine with either," she said.

"How 'bout we share?"

"I'd be happy to."

Fortunately, the baguettes came in two pieces, so it was easy to share them.

"No chips?" asked the detective.

"Sorry, no," Guin replied. "But I have something even better," she said, opening the box with the pastries.

"I'd've been fine with chips," said the detective.

He took a bite of the ham sandwich and Guin did the same.

"So," said Guin, a minute later. "You think Suzy's telling the truth?"

The detective took a sip of his sparkling water.

"About?" he asked.

"About how her necklace came to be next to the body?"

The detective took another bite of his sandwich.

"You get the autopsy results?" Guin asked him.

The detective took another sip from his can.

"Next week," he said.

"And you'll share them with me?" Guin asked, hopefully.

The detective took a bite of the turkey and brie sandwich and Guin did the same.

"Any idea who killed her?" Guin asked, a couple minutes later, after they had both taken another bite of their sandwiches.

"We're investigating," replied the detective.

"I know," said Guin. "But surely you must have some suspects…"

"Some," said the detective. "And stop calling me Shirley," he added, grinning at her.

Guin groaned. Was that an attempt at humor? (She had seen *Airplane!* and knew the reference. But she hadn't heard the detective joke before.)

"Love that movie," he said, taking another bite of his sandwich.

"What about that big horse conch we found?" Guin asked him a minute later. "Do you think it was the murder weapon?"

"We're having it tested. Results should be in next week."

Getting information from the detective was like getting blood from a stone.

"What about her family and friends?" Guin asked.

"What about them?" said the detective.

"Have you spoken with them? I assume you informed CiCi's family. Did they have any idea who might have done it? Did she have a jealous boyfriend?"

"No jealous boyfriend, at least according to her family," replied the detective. "Though the mother did mention something about some girls being jealous and causing trouble at school."

"Oh?" said Guin. "Jealous of what?"

"The usual girl stuff," said the detective. "Something to do with a man."

"Is that why she moved back home?"

The detective finished his sandwich, then took another sip of his water.

"Have you spoken with any of her sorority sisters?" Guin asked.

"It's on my list."

Guin wondered what else was on his list.

"Anything else you learn from the family?" Guin asked.

"No," said the detective. "According to the mother, she was a good student. A bit shy. Didn't have a lot of friends, though she was friendly with lots of people. Kind of kept to herself. Her passion was cooking, and shells."

It fit with the little she knew about CiCi.

"So who are your suspects?" Guin asked, nonchalantly, hoping the detective might answer this time.

"Come now, Ms. Jones," said the detective. "You know I can't tell you."

"Can't blame a girl for trying," said Guin, getting up. "Well, I should get going."

The detective looked up at her.

"I'll follow up with you next week about the autopsy and the horse conch," said Guin. "And I still need to officially interview you."

The detective grunted.

Guin was standing by the door.

"You got plans for the weekend?" she asked him.

"Assuming I don't have to work? Fishing. You?"

"Ris is flying back tomorrow. I'm going to pick him up at the airport."

The detective made a face.

"Well, I should go," Guin said, turning to leave.

"Aren't you forgetting something?" called the detective.

Guin turned back to face him.

"I don't think so."

The detective held up the box containing the two pastries.

"They're for you," she said.

The detective continued to hold up the box.

"If you don't want them, I'm sure there's someone around here who will choke them down," she said, smiling.

She turned once more, then made her way out of his office and back down the hall.

CHAPTER 14

Guin drove back to the condo. She was scheduled to go over to Sam's place at five, which left her time to do some investigating.

She went onto Instagram, found Scott Murray's page (@HotScot), and sent him a message. Then she did a search for CiCi's mother, Kimberly, and found out where she worked. She started to enter the number into her phone, then stopped. Mrs. Rawlins was probably not even there. And if she was, she probably wouldn't want to speak with a reporter.

"Well, nothing ventured, nothing gained," said Guin, calling the insurance office.

A cheerful-sounding woman answered the phone, and Guin asked to speak with Kimberly Rawlins. She was surprised when she was put through.

"Mrs. Rawlins?" said Guin.

"Yes?"

"My name is Guinivere Jones. I'm a reporter with the *San-Cap Sun-Times*."

She waited to see if Mrs. Rawlins would hang up or yell at her, but there was no reply.

"I'm calling about your daughter, CiCi. I'm very sorry for your loss," she quickly added. "She was a lovely young woman."

"Did you know her?" asked Mrs. Rawlins.

"I met her at Samantha Hutchins's," said Guin.

There was silence on the other end of the line for several seconds.

"CiCi was so honored to have been picked. Lots of folks wanted to work on that sculpture, but Ms. Hutchins chose my CiCi."

Guin detected some kind of Southern accent.

"Ms. Hutchins and the other ladies thought very highly of CiCi," said Guin. "And I understand she was an excellent cook."

"She did love to feed people," said Mrs. Rawlins. "Took after her grandmother. They used to bake cookies and pies and cakes together when CiCi was little."

"I hate to intrude on your time of grief, Mrs. Rawlins, but would it be possible to speak with you about CiCi?"

"Aren't we speaking now?" she asked Guin.

"Sorry," said Guin. "I meant, would it be okay for me to meet with you in person? Some of the questions are a bit sensitive."

"Sensitive?" said Mrs. Rawlins.

"I heard there was some issue having to do with some girls at school," said Guin.

"Don't you dare write about that!" said Mrs. Rawlins. "I know what some folks were saying about CiCi, but those were all lies."

Guin was taken aback.

"I'm sorry," said Guin. "I didn't mean to upset you. I'm just trying to find out who did this terrible thing. I don't know if the police mentioned it, but I was the one who found CiCi's body."

Again, there was silence on the other end of the line. Then Guin heard what sounded like sniffling.

"My poor baby."

Guin could tell Mrs. Rawlins was upset.

"I hate to bother you," said Guin, feeling guilty but forcing herself to continue, "but do you know of anyone, anyone at all, who may have wanted to hurt CiCi?"

"As I told the police," said Mrs. Rawlins, still sniffling a bit, "I don't know why anyone would want to harm CiCi. She was a good girl."

"I'm sure," said Guin. "If you don't mind me asking, why had she moved back home? I understood she only had one semester left at FGCU, and I can't imagine anyone choosing to commute during the season if they had a place to live on campus."

Once again, there was silence on the other end of the line. Then Mrs. Rawlins finally spoke.

"There had been talk."

"Talk?" asked Guin.

"About CiCi and this professor she was helping."

"What kind of talk?" asked Guin.

"Oh you know," said Mrs. Rawlins. "That they were carrying on. But I know my CiCi, and she would never do something like that. She was a good girl."

"Do you happen to know the name of the professor?" asked Guin.

"Oh yes," said Mrs. Rawlins. "He was that one all the girls are crazy about. I think that's why they started those rumors. They were just jealous of my CiCi."

"His name, Mrs. Rawlins," Guin asked. She could feel her heart hammering against her chest.

"Dr. Hartwick," she replied. "But the girls all called him Dr. Heartthrob. Silly name, if you ask me."

Guin felt physically ill. She had heard rumors about Ris when she first started dating him, but he swore that they were all untrue. And knowing him as she did, she couldn't believe he would carry on with a student. But why had CiCi suddenly left campus at the end of last year and Ris gone away? Could the two have been related? She tried not to let her imagination run away with her, but it was hard.

"Do you know him?" Mrs. Rawlins asked.

"Hmm?" said Guin.

"Dr. Hartwick. Do you know him? Such a nice man. Always had a kind word to say. And so knowledgeable. Jack and I attended a couple of his lectures. I could see why CiCi liked him. I wonder if he knows. I'm sure he'll be devastated."

Guin wondered if Ris did, in fact, know. If so, he had not mentioned it to her.

"Yes, I'm familiar with Dr. Hartwick," Guin replied, using her professional voice. "I understand he's away this semester."

"Oh?" said Mrs. Rawlins. "CiCi hadn't mentioned anything."

That's odd, thought Guin.

"So why did CiCi move back home? Was she still enrolled at FGCU?"

"She wanted to drop out after those nasty rumors began circulating. But Jack and I convinced her to finish up. She agreed, but only if she could move back home."

Guin heard a beeping on the line.

"Can you hold a minute, Ms. Jones? I need to take this."

"Of course," said Guin.

As she waited, her mind started picturing CiCi with Ris.

"Stop that!" she told herself.

A few seconds later, Mrs. Rawlins came back on the line.

"I need to go, Ms. Jones."

"Would it be okay if I called you again or arranged a time for us to meet?" asked Guin. "I have a few more questions."

"That's fine," said Mrs. Rawlins. "As long as you don't

go printing anything bad about my CiCi."

"I promise, Mrs. Rawlins." Guin just hoped it was a promise she could keep.

Mrs. Rawlins gave her her email address, then they ended the call.

A little after 4:30, Guin left the condo and headed over to Sam's place. She had a lot on her mind and had to force herself to focus on the road. You never knew when or where a cop could be hanging out, waiting to ticket anyone going over 35 mph, the island speed limit.

She arrived a few minutes early and parked in front of the house. She quickly checked her phone, then got out and walked to the front door and rang the doorbell.

"Hi," said Guin. "I hope this is still an okay time to talk."

Rita ushered her inside, then closed the door behind them.

"Is there ever a good time to talk about murder?" she asked.

"No, not really," said Guin. "But sometimes it helps to talk about it."

"I don't know if it'll help, but come on in. Sam and Marta are in back."

Guin followed Rita to the master bedroom. The windows and sliders were open, and Sam and Marta were spraying something on the fountain.

"They're applying the polyurethane coating," Rita explained.

"Ah," said Guin.

Sam and Marta finished spraying, then pulled down their masks.

"Just putting the finishing touches on the fountain," Sam explained. "How does she look, Rita?"

Rita walked around the fountain, which was sitting in several pieces.

"Looks good. I just hope we can put Humpty Dumpty together again."

She stood looking at the fountain for several seconds more.

Guin cleared her throat.

"If you all are done here, I'd like to ask you a few questions... about CiCi."

"Go ahead," said Sam.

"Actually, if you don't mind, I'd like to interview you one at a time."

"No problem," said Sam. "Who do you want to start with?"

"Let's start with you, if that's okay with the rest of you," said Guin.

"Any objections?" Sam asked her crew.

"I need to go to rehearsal," Marta said.

That's right, Guin remembered. Marta sang in the BIG ARTS Chorus, whose spring concert was just around the corner.

"Well, then, why don't I start with you?" said Guin.

"Is that okay, Marta?" Sam asked her.

Marta shrugged.

"Why don't you two go into the kitchen?" Rita suggested.

"Shall we?" said Guin.

The two of them headed down the hall. Guin hadn't realized how tall Marta was. She had to be close to six feet.

When they reached the kitchen, Guin indicated for Marta to take a seat. Then she sat opposite her and took out her notepad, pen, and microcassette recorder.

"Do you mind if I record the conversation?" she asked her.

"If you wish," said Marta.

"Thanks," said Guin.

She hit 'record,' then looked up at Marta.

"So, Marta, how well did you know CiCi?" Guin asked her.

Marta glanced down at the microcassette recorder, then back up at Guin.

"Not well."

"Did you know her before the two of you came to work on the sculpture?" Guin asked.

"No," said Marta.

"Do you know if she was seeing someone, if she had a boyfriend?"

Marta frowned.

Guin waited.

"I don't know if she had a boyfriend," she finally said.

"So she never mentioned anyone while she was working?"

"She may have," said Marta. "I was focused on our work."

"Do you know of anyone who might have wanted to harm her?"

"Harm her?" asked Marta.

"Had she gotten into an argument with anyone? Maybe she mentioned something?" asked Guin.

Marta cast a glance down the hall, back toward the bedroom. She made a face, as though she had eaten something that disagreed with her. Guin waited.

She turned back to face Guin.

"The boyfriend."

"The boyfriend?" Guin said. "I thought you said CiCi didn't have a boyfriend."

"Not her boyfriend, Samantha's," Marta replied.

Guin was confused.

"Did CiCi get in a fight with Denny?"

This was the first she'd heard of it.

"I don't know. But something was going on," said Marta, primly.

"Going on, as in…?"

Marta looked at Guin, as if expecting her to read her mind.

"You think Denny and CiCi were sleeping together?" Guin asked, a bit incredulously.

"I'm sure there was no sleeping involved," said Marta.

Guin was shocked. Granted, she barely knew the girl, but she couldn't imagine CiCi going and having sex with her employer's boyfriend, even if he was a drop-dead sexy guitar player for a rock band. Then again….

"Speaking of Denny," said Guin, "is he around?"

"No," replied Marta.

Guin was running out of questions.

"So I understand CiCi told all of you she was planning on going to Silver Key yesterday morning. Do you know if she told anyone else?"

"I have no idea," said Marta. "Her parents, I suppose."

"Anyone else?" Guin asked.

"I don't know," said Marta. "CiCi wasn't in the habit of confiding in me."

"Did she confide in Sam or Rita?" Guin asked.

"You would have to ask them," said Marta.

"Is there anything else you can tell me about CiCi? Did she happen to mention anything about school or why she was living at home?"

"She may have mentioned something," said Marta. "I don't recall."

She looked down at her watch.

"I need to go. I don't want to be late for rehearsal."

"Of course," said Guin, stopping the microcassette recorder. "Thank you for your time. If you think of anything, anything at all, just shoot me an email."

She handed a card to Marta. Marta glanced at it, got up, then tucked the card into her bag.

Guin watched as Marta made her way to the door and left. Then she got up and went to get Sam.

CHAPTER 15

"So why did you pick CiCi?" Guin asked Sam, after they had sat down in the kitchen.

"There was something about her application."

She paused, and Guin waited for her to continue.

"She explained that she had been going through a hard time at school and that beachcombing, looking for shells, made her forget about the bad stuff. Something I could relate to. I also liked the fact that she was a marine biology major—and that she wrote that if we picked her, she would cook for us," Sam added with a smile.

"Was CiCi a good cook?" Guin asked.

"Oh yeah," said Sam. "She could totally go pro."

"Did she happen to mention any boy trouble?"

"Boy trouble?" asked Sam.

"I understand something happened at school last semester, that caused her to want to move back home," Guin replied. "I was wondering if she had mentioned anything."

"She did mention something, a misunderstanding having to do with a professor. But she said everyone had it all wrong."

"Did she happen to mention the name of this professor?" Guin asked her, trying to sound nonchalant.

"No," Sam replied. "Sorry."

"That's okay," said Guin, slightly relieved. "Did CiCi ever mention a boyfriend, maybe someone she broke up with recently, or somebody named Scott?"

"Scott?" said Sam. "I don't think so. CiCi mostly talked about food, and shells. Though maybe she mentioned something to Rita."

"What about Denny?" asked Guin.

"Denny?" asked Sam, looking puzzled.

As if being psychically summoned, Denny walked through the front door.

"Hey," said Sam. "Were your ears burning?"

He looked confused.

"Guin here was just asking about you."

Denny grinned.

"And what is it you wanted to know?" he said, looking down at Guin.

Denny's hair was tousled, and his shirt was unbuttoned, revealing a lean physique. Guin had to stop herself from staring.

"Were you out on the beach?" Guin asked him.

"How could you tell?" he said, continuing to smile. "The beach here is amazing." He turned to Sam. "We should go catch the sunset."

"If I can," she replied.

"So what were you two chatting about?" asked Denny.

"I was about to ask Sam if maybe CiCi had confided something in you, maybe mentioned a boyfriend," said Guin.

"She mentioned someone named Scott, but I think he was just a friend. Said he was a fan of the band and would be totally jealous."

He grinned.

"Did she happen to mention anything else, any problems she'd been having?" Guin asked.

Denny looked thoughtful.

"She didn't really say too much about her personal life. Just that she was majoring in marine biology over at FGCU and loved to cook."

"Did she mention she was planning on going to Silver Key?"

"Yeah, she mentioned it. Why?"

"She told all of us," Sam interjected.

"Do you know if she mentioned it to anyone else?" Guin asked.

"It's possible," said Sam. "She'd been talking about the storm and going there to see if she could find a Scotch bonnet for days."

"What about people who had applied to be helpers?"

"What about them?" asked Sam.

"Could one of them have held a grudge against her, maybe wanted to get her out of the way?"

"I guess that's possible," said Sam. "Though it seems a bit extreme."

"You don't know the shellers around here," said Guin.

"You should ask Rita," said Sam. "She was in charge of the applications."

"I'll do that," said Guin. "Can you send her out?"

"Sure," said Sam, getting up. "So you're done with me?"

"For now," said Guin, smiling. "If I think of something else, I'll text you."

"That's fine," said Sam.

She turned to see Denny poking his head in the refrigerator.

"What are you doing?" she called over to him.

"Looking for food."

"Come on, let's go get Rita."

He shut the refrigerator door.

"Then can we get something to eat? I'm starving."

Sam smiled.

"After Rita chats with Guin. Come."

Denny followed her down the hall. A couple of minutes later, Rita appeared.

"Please, have a seat," said Guin, gesturing to the empty chair.

Like Marta, Rita towered over Guin. Guin looked for a resemblance between Rita and her brother. They were both tall, with brown hair and long, straight noses, but the resemblance pretty much ended there.

"So, what did you think of CiCi?" Guin asked her, after she had taken a seat.

"CiCi?" said Rita. "She was a hard worker, eager to please. Knew what to look for."

"Did she talk about any friends or mention anyone special?" Guin asked.

"Not that I recall," said Rita. "She didn't talk a whole lot about her personal life."

"So no mention of a boyfriend?"

"I don't think so. Why?"

"No particular reason. Did she happen to mention why she had moved back to Sanibel?"

Rita shook her head.

"I knew she had family on Sanibel and lived here. I didn't pry into her personal life."

"So nothing about a professor?"

Rita looked at her.

"Is there something in particular you want to know?"

"I'm trying to find out if she had been mixed up with someone, someone who might have had a beef with her."

"With CiCi?" said Rita. "I can't imagine that. CiCi was too much of a people pleaser."

"What about someone jealous of her position with Sam? I understand a lot of people applied to help out, but only a couple were chosen. Maybe someone found out about CiCi being picked and wanted to get her out of the way."

Rita stared at Guin.

"Seriously?"

"I know it seems crazy, but I've seen and heard about people doing some pretty crazy things when it comes to shells since I moved down here," said Guin.

"Huh," said Rita, shaking her head. "Still, no one was supposed to know who was helping us. And even if someone found out, we were almost done with the sculpture. Though..."

"Yes?" said Guin, leaning forward slightly.

"There was that crazy real estate agent," said Rita.

"Crazy real estate agent?" said Guin.

"Yeah, the one who rented us the house. Susan Hastings."

"Suzy Seashell?" asked Guin.

Rita grimaced.

"Yeah, that's the one. I caught her snooping around here, and CiCi said she ran into her over at Bailey's. Said she asked her a bunch of stuff."

"Do you think CiCi may have told her she was planning on going over to Silver Key?" asked Guin. (That could explain why she had been there that morning. Though Guin had a hard time imagining Susan killing the young woman.)

"It's possible," said Rita. She paused. "Do you think she could have killed CiCi?"

"I don't know," said Guin. "Susan's done some pretty crazy things, but I just can't picture her braining someone with a shell."

Though as she said it, her brain flashed on a photo she had seen on Susan's blog of her proudly wielding a giant horse conch.

"I should get back to work. You have any other questions for me?" asked Rita.

Guin thought for a minute.

"Where were all of you at the time of the murder?"

Guin knew the detective had already asked them that, but she often found that asking the same question days later could yield a different result.

"I was here, making coffee," said Rita.

"And Sam?"

"Asleep," said Rita. "She didn't stumble into the kitchen until nearly eight-thirty."

"What about your brother?"

"Denny?" asked Rita.

"Unless you have another one staying here who I don't know about," said Guin, smiling at her.

"I assume he was in bed with Sam," she replied.

Guin looked at Rita. Something about the way she had said it, her expression, made Guin pause.

"What about Marta?" she asked, a few seconds later.

"She was baking muffins."

"Here?" asked Guin.

"No, at her place. She got here a little after eight-thirty and brought a plate of them with her."

Guin hit 'stop' on her microcassette recorder.

"Okay," she said. "I think that's it for now."

"Good," said Rita, getting up.

Guin looked up at her. Rita was quite an imposing figure. She would probably have had no problem wielding a large horse conch.

"I hope the police nail whoever did it," Rita said to Guin as Guin gathered her things.

"I hope so, too," said Guin. Though as she headed to her car, she wondered if the killer could have been right there, inside the house.

CHAPTER 16

Guin woke up early the following morning. She had a lot on her mind—Ris was arriving that afternoon, and she needed to type up her notes, among other things—and she was yearning to go to the beach. Some days it felt as though the beach was calling to her in her sleep, and if she didn't obey its siren call, she would be restless the rest of the day.

She glanced down and saw the two cats curled up on either side of her. Why couldn't she be more like them and be content to sleep all day? But that was not her style.

She threw back the sheets, disturbing the felines, and headed to the bathroom. Less than fifteen minutes later, she was dressed and out the door.

Guin could see the moon as she walked down to the water. After running into Susan and the detective by Silver Key the other day, she had decided to go to the beach along West Gulf Drive instead.

As she made her way slowly west, she glanced over at the large houses that were perched just beyond the dunes. One day, she said to herself, when I win the lottery.

She continued to make her way down the beach, staring intently at the wrack line, where the water met the shore. In fact, she was so focused on the sand beneath her that she nearly collided with another shell seeker.

"Hey, watch where you're going!" said the man.

Guin looked up, then smiled.

"Lenny!" she beamed.

But he did not look equally pleased to see her.

"I see you're back from Australia," he said. "How long have you been back?"

Guin felt suddenly guilty. She had been back a week now and hadn't texted him.

"I'm sorry, Lenny. I've just been so busy…"

Lenny, full name Leonard Isaacs, was one of the handful of people Guin had become close friends with since moving to Sanibel a year and a half before. She had met him on the beach, when they both had been looking for shells, and he had picked up a king's crown conch that Guin had had her eye on. They had got to talking and had found out they were both from New York and were both Mets fans.

Lenny, a former science teacher and widower, had retired and moved to Sanibel several years before Guin. He was now a Shell Ambassador, who loved to help children and their parents identify shells. Indeed, Lenny liked nothing better than to pontificate on Sanibel's marine and beach life and preservation. He also had an impressive shell collection, and a couple of times a year opened up his home to members of the Sanibel-Captiva Shell Club.

"Yeah, yeah, yeah," said Lenny.

"I know I should have called or texted you," said Guin. "It's just with work and everything…"

She trailed off again.

"So what's got you so busy you don't have time to text your old friend Lenny to go shelling with you?"

Guin thought about telling Lenny about CiCi.

"I can tell by your expression you're thinking," he said, looking at her.

"You know me so well," said Guin.

"So, what's the story? You got some big piece you're working on?"

"Sort of," said Guin. "You know that sculpture the City commissioned, the one that's going to be unveiled over at the museum at the start of the Shell Show?"

"The one no one's supposed to know anything about?" said Lenny. "Though Suzy keeps talking about it."

"You read Suzy Seashell?" asked Guin, surprised.

"You don't?" said Lenny.

He had a point. Shellapalooza was considered must reading by pretty much everyone on or visiting Sanibel and Captiva who was into shells and shell-related gossip.

"So what's Suzy been saying?"

"Not that much, really. Mostly guesses. Though I don't think she likes the people working on the sculpture so much."

"Oh?" said Guin. "What gives you that idea?"

"She seems a bit PO'd that they wouldn't give her a sneak peek or an interview."

"Do you blame them?" said Guin.

Lenny chuckled.

"So, have *you* seen it?" he asked her.

Guin bit her lip.

"You have!" said Lenny. "I knew it!"

"Keep your voice down," Guin admonished him. She quickly scanned the beach, making sure no one was within earshot. "Ginny arranged for me to interview the artist," she said, keeping her voice low. "I went over there and saw the fou—it. It's pretty amazing."

She had almost said *fountain*, but she had caught herself just in time.

"So what is it?" Lenny asked her. "You can tell me. I promise not to say a peep."

"Sorry, Len, no can do. I signed an NDA."

"NDA, shmendiyay," he said.

"You'll see it at the preview," said Guin. "That is, if you're planning on going."

"I wouldn't miss it," said Lenny. "I've got an exhibit in the Scientific Division."

"Oh?" said Guin, though she was not surprised. "You want to tell me about it?"

"It's top secret," said Lenny. "You'll just have to wait until the preview."

Guin smiled at him. She could tell he was sore about her not revealing anything about the fountain, but she had given her word to Sam and Rita: no squealing.

"Well, good luck to you, Len."

She could tell he was disappointed she hadn't pressed him for details.

"So, what else you know?" he asked her.

Again, Guin thought about telling Lenny about CiCi.

"Ris is flying home this afternoon," she said instead.

"So soon? Someone die?"

Guin was about to say no, but someone had, in fact, died. Though that wasn't why Ris was flying home.

"He's interviewing to be the new chair of the Department of Marine & Ecological Sciences at FGCU," Guin replied.

"Why does he have to interview? They should just hire him."

Guin smiled.

"Well, he's not the only candidate, and he doesn't want special treatment."

Lenny made a shooing motion with his hand.

"I bet you're happy to have him back," he said.

"I guess," said Guin.

"You guess? What's wrong, kid? Something happen?"

"No, it's just…" She hesitated. Then she decided to tell Lenny about CiCi. "So this young woman was found murdered on the beach the other day."

"Murdered? On Sanibel?" said Lenny.

"Yeah," said Guin.

She left out the part about her finding the body.

"Turns out she was a TA of his."

Lenny whistled.

"Yeah," said Guin.

"But he couldn't have had anything to do with it," said Lenny. "He was in Australia. Or do you think he snuck back here without telling you?"

"No, he was definitely in Australia. But there were rumors."

"Rumors?" said Lenny, confused.

"About Ris and this girl," said Guin.

"What kind of rumors?" asked Lenny.

"The usual kind involving a handsome professor and a pretty undergraduate," said Guin.

Lenny made a face.

"Don't believe the rumors."

"I'm trying not to," said Guin.

"Seriously, don't let some silly gossip come between you and the professor. You know he's crazy about you."

"I'm trying, Len," Guin repeated. "But it's hard."

He placed an arm around Guin and gave her a squeeze.

"Come," he said. "Enough talking. Let's go look for some shells."

Guin nodded her head, and they made their way down the beach.

Guin got back to the condo around nine. Lenny had invited her out for breakfast, but Guin had declined. She had a lot of work to do before she headed off to the airport. And she had a feeling she wouldn't be getting much work done after Ris had arrived.

She made a beeline for the kitchen to fix herself some coffee. No sooner had she opened the cabinet than the cats appeared.

"Meow," said Fauna, looking up at her, as Flora gently pawed Guin's shin.

"What?" said Guin. "I already gave you guys food."

Fauna meowed again.

"Fine," said Guin, with a sigh.

She opened the refrigerator and took out the container of milk. Then she got a small bowl from the cabinet.

"There," she said, placing the bowl of milk in front of Fauna.

Fauna immediately lunged for it, while Flora pawed again at Guin's shin.

"Do you need some loving, Flora?" Guin asked the older cat.

Flora looked up at Guin with her big green eyes. Guin knelt and stroked the pretty feline for a minute, then stood up again.

"Sorry, Flora, but I need coffee."

Guin was leaning against the counter, sipping her coffee, when her phone started buzzing. It was a text message from Craig.

"Give me a call when you have a sec," it read.

Guin took another sip of her coffee, then called Craig's number.

"What's up?" she asked him, after he had picked up.

"Heard some interesting gossip at poker last night."

"Oh?" said Guin.

"Seems our little friend wasn't that innocent."

"Little friend?" Guin asked, confused.

"One of the guys saw Caroline Rawlins and that rocker making out by the beach the other day."

"CiCi was making out with Denny Sumner? Are you sure?"

"He swears it's the truth," said Craig.

Guin was at a loss for words.

"When was this?" she asked him. "And how did he know who they were?"

"It was Wednesday evening, and he recognized Denny. Or rather his daughter did. She was with him and is apparently a big fan of that band of his."

"But how did he know it was CiCi in the car with him? It could have been Sam, or someone else."

"He described her. Definitely sounded like the victim."

This was not good, thought Guin. What was CiCi doing fooling around with Sam's boyfriend?

She shook her head.

"Sorry to be the bearer of bad news," said Craig.

"No, it's okay," said Guin. "Do the police know?"

Craig paused.

Ah. No doubt the person who had shared this bit of news either worked at the Sanibel Police Department or there was someone from the police department who had been sitting at the poker table.

"Got it," said Guin. "Anything else?"

"I'm speaking with Jack Rawlins tomorrow."

"Okay," said Guin. "Let me know what he says."

"Will do," Craig replied. He paused. "We know where this Denny guy was early Thursday morning?"

"Supposedly in bed with his girlfriend," said Guin.

"Supposedly?" said Craig.

"Yeah. That's what his sister claimed, but I'm not buying it."

"You think she's lying?"

"I do, especially in light of what you just told me."

"You think he and the girl snuck off together?"

Guin tried to picture CiCi and Denny together, but she was having problems doing that.

"I don't know."

Her phone started beeping.

"Hey, Craig, I've got a call coming in."

"No worries. We can catch up Monday."

"Thanks," said Guin. "I'll text or call you."

She went to get the other call.

"About time you picked up, Guinivere."

Oh no. It was her mother. Why had she picked up?

"Hi mom."

"Hi yourself. When were you planning on letting me know you were back from Australia?"

"I sent you my itinerary."

"It could have changed."

"You could have called me, if you were concerned," said Guin.

There was a huff on the other end of the line.

"I assume you've spoken with Lance," said Guin.

Lance was Guin's brother, full name Lancelot. Her mother had been going through an Arthurian legends phase at the time of her pregnancies, and she thought it would be romantic to name her two children Lancelot and Guinivere, not thinking about the implication.

"Of course. He always makes time to call me."

Guin rolled her eyes. Her brother Lance owned a boutique advertising agency in New York City and was happily married to his long-time partner, Owen, who ran a gallery in Chelsea. The two of them were always doing interesting things, or so it seemed, and shared a love of city life and gossip with Guin's mother. Unlike Guin.

"So what did Lance tell you?" asked Guin.

"Not much. Just that you had returned from Australia."

"Listen, Mom, I'd love to chat, but I'm kind of busy right now. I've got a pile of work, and I have to pick up Ris at the airport in a little while."

"They make you work on the *weekend?* I hope they pay you overtime."

Guin didn't want to tell her mother how much she made as a reporter as she would no doubt be horrified.

"And what's this about Dr. Hartwick flying back? I thought he was on sabbatical this semester."

"He was, *is*," said Guin. "He's flying back to interview for a job at FGCU."

"What kind of job? Doesn't he already work there?"

"He does. It's to be the chair of the Marine & Ecological Sciences department."

"Does it pay well?" asked her mother.

Guin stared out the window.

"I don't know. I assume so. Why does it even matter?"

"Well, if you're going to marry him, one of you should have a decent job."

"Who said anything about marriage?" Guin said, looking down at the phone.

"You're not getting any younger, darling. And if you and he want to have kids…"

Guin wondered if there was steam coming out of her ears. It felt that way.

"Ris already has two kids," Guin replied. She glanced at the clock on her monitor. "Mom, I need to go."

"Not before we arrange a time to have a proper chat."

"Fine. How about tomorrow?" Guin asked.

"We're going out with the Van Burens tomorrow. Give me a call Monday, say around five. I should be home then."

"Fine. I'll call you Monday. Gotta go!"

She ended the call before her mother could reply. Then she turned the ringer off. If she was going to get any work done before she left for the airport, she would need to ignore her phone.

CHAPTER 17

"Ris!"

Guin waved as she saw him coming down the escalator.

He smiled and raised a hand.

"You have an okay flight?" she asked him, as he made his way over to her.

He leaned down and gave her a kiss.

"It was fine," he replied. "Thanks for meeting me."

"Of course!" she said.

Guin glanced down. Ris had only a small carry-on bag with him.

"Did you check a suitcase or is that it?"

"That's it," he said. "Now, let's get out of here."

As they drove from the airport to Fort Myers Beach, Guin asked him how the last week had been. He gave her a quick rundown, but Guin could tell he was tired.

"You want to stop and get something to eat?" Guin asked. "Or we could go to my place. I'd be happy to cook something for you."

"Thank you, but I just want to go home," he replied. "I can run out and get some stuff later or tomorrow."

Guin glanced over at Ris, who was staring out the window. She wanted to ask about CiCi, but she decided now was not the time.

"How was your week?" he asked her, a few minutes later. "Ginny been keeping you busy?"

She wondered if he knew about the murder.

"I found another dead body," she blurted.

"What?" he said. "Are you okay? Where?"

Clearly, he hadn't heard. Or maybe there was some other dead body she didn't know about?

"On the beach, by Silver Key," said Guin. "It was a young woman, one of the people helping Sam Hutchins with that sculpture."

Guin waited to see if Ris would say something, but he remained quiet, waiting for her to go on.

"I believe you know—knew—her," said Guin, a bit nervously. "I heard she TA'd for you last semester."

"CiCi? CiCi is the young woman you found on the beach?"

He seemed to be in shock.

Guin quickly glanced over at him, nodding her head.

Ris ran a hand through his hair.

"But why? That makes no sense."

"I know."

"What do the police say?" Ris asked.

"Not much," said Guin. "Just that they're investigating."

Ris was looking out the window. Several seconds later, he turned back to Guin.

"When did it happen?"

"I found her body Thursday morning."

"On Sanibel?"

"Yes, by Silver Key," Guin repeated

"What was she doing there?" he asked her.

"Looking for a Scotch bonnet."

"But that makes no sense," said Ris. "Why wasn't she at school?"

Guin again glanced over at him. Was it possible he hadn't heard?

"She's been living at home."

"Did she drop out?"

Did he really not know? Guin wondered.

"She didn't drop out. She just moved back home."

"Why?" asked Ris.

"There were rumors," she said, looking over at him.

Ris sighed.

"Were they true?" Guin asked him.

"No!" said Ris. "How could you even think that?"

He seemed genuinely angry.

"I liked CiCi. She was one of the best TAs I've ever had. Always prepared. Never missed a class or a deadline. Very eager to please."

Guin wondered how eager.

"But I would never, Guin. You've got to believe me."

"So how did the rumors start?" Guin asked.

"You know universities. People talk."

"I'm not following," said Guin.

Ris sighed again.

"One of CiCi's sorority sisters saw us."

Guin gripped the steering wheel.

"It was nothing. I was taking her out to dinner as a reward for all her hard work. CiCi wanted to be a chef. So I took her to the Beach House, to meet Chef Tony. I thought maybe she could get a job there, working in the kitchen, after graduation. Or at least he could give her some advice."

The Beach House was one of her and Ris's favorite places, where they often had dinner when she was staying at his place in Fort Myers Beach. They knew the owners, friends of Shelly and Steve's, as well as the chef and most of the front-of-house staff. It made sense that Ris would take CiCi there, but Guin couldn't help feeling a twinge of jealousy.

"And?" said Guin, unable to look at him.

"One of her sorority sisters and her boyfriend were having dinner there and saw us."

"So?" Guin said again.

"It's possible they got the wrong idea," he replied.

"Possible?" said Guin.

"They got the wrong idea," Ris amended. "You know how girls can be."

Guin did know, but she thought that sorority girls didn't make up stories about their sisters. Unless…

They pulled into Ris's driveway a minute later.

"Here we are," she said, forcing herself to smile.

They got out of the car and walked to the front door. Ris found the hide-a-key and opened the door.

"Place looks the same," he said, glancing around.

"Why wouldn't it?" Guin asked.

Ris's place looked like it belonged in the pages of *Coastal Living* magazine. He had hired a decorator to help him, a friend of his ex-wife's, who Ris had briefly dated. And the place had "sophisticated bachelor beach house" written all over it.

"I don't know," said Ris. "I think part of me worried Hank would be holding wild orgies here while I was gone."

"With Hildy right next door? Hardly," said Guin.

Hank and Hilda Ross were Ris's next-door neighbors. Guin had only met them a couple of times. Hank was a pilot and traveled quite a bit, though he must be nearing retirement, Guin thought. Hilda, or Hildy as she preferred to be called, managed a boutique.

"True," said Ris, chuckling. He stretched, then yawned.

"I should let you get some sleep," said Guin, even though it was still early.

"I'm fine," said Ris, yawning again.

Guin smiled up at him.

"Uh-huh."

"Really," he said, coming over and putting his arms around her. "But if you want to go to bed…"

He leaned down to kiss her and the next thing Guin knew, she was being carried to the bedroom.

"What about your things?" she asked him.

"I have everything I need right here," he said, closing the door to the bedroom with his foot.

"I should have picked up food," Guin said, looking around the kitchen later.

"Don't worry about it," Ris replied. "We can run over to Publix in the morning."

Guin's stomach let out a loud gurgle.

"Why don't I take you out for dinner?"

"But you just got home. Do you really want to go out again? Besides, I should get back to Sanibel."

"Nonsense," Ris said. "Let me take you out. We can get something quick."

"Aren't you exhausted from your trip?"

"Do I seem exhausted to you?" he said, his mouth forming a wicked grin.

Guin felt herself blushing.

"Um…"

He went over and put his arms around her.

"Come, let's get you some food," he said, smiling.

"Okay," said Guin, relenting.

They had gone to a little Italian place nearby, then driven back to Ris's. He had asked Guin to stay over, but when he nodded off while they were watching NatGeo, Guin had given him a kiss and told him she was leaving. He had protested, but Guin held firm. She would see him tomorrow. She gave him a kiss on the forehead and let herself out.

The following morning, she made sure she was up by seven, so she could get to the Sanibel Farmers Market when it opened. She made her way around the market, picking up coffee, cheese, a baguette, and a couple of pastries, as well as fish and fresh vegetables. She had forgotten to ask Ris what he was eating these days (he periodically abstained from sugar and dairy), but she figured fish and vegetables were safe.

Her purchases made, she headed back to her car.

It was still early when she got back home, not even nine o'clock, and she thought for a minute about going for a beach walk. But she didn't want to deal with the crowds. Instead, she opted to walk down to the bayou.

Guin passed a number of people out walking their dogs as she made her way down to the bayou. She and Art, her ex, had thought about getting a dog, but they decided against it as they were both rarely at home. Maybe if she got a house she would get one. Though the cats would probably not be happy about it.

She passed by the golf course and looked up. There was a foursome just teeing off. She watched for a minute, then resumed her walk.

As she strolled, she couldn't help thinking about Ris and CiCi. Was it really as innocent as Ris had made out? But then why would CiCi's sorority sister have started such an ugly rumor?

Guin made a mental note to go visit the sorority the next day—and to ask Ris who the gossip was.

She reached the end of the road and looked out across Dinkins Bayou. The water was calm, and several boats were making their way toward Pine Island Sound. No doubt to go fishing. As she was gazing out, a movement caught her eye. She glanced to her right in time to see a pair of dolphins surfacing. She watched for several seconds, as they came up for air and then submerged, until they disappeared from view. Then she turned and headed back toward the condo.

CHAPTER 18

Ris came over for dinner that evening. Guin had avoided the topic of CiCi, as she didn't want to sound insecure or jealous, but her reporter's instincts had gotten the better of her by dessert.

"So did CiCi have a boyfriend?" Guin asked him, over decaf.

"Not that I was aware of," Ris replied.

"And who was it who spotted you two at dinner?"

"One of her sorority sisters, Tanya Harvey."

"Did you know this Tanya?" asked Guin.

"Why all the questions?" Ris asked.

"I'm covering the story for the paper."

"So what does Tanya have to do with it?"

"I'm trying to find out if anyone bore a grudge against CiCi."

Ris frowned.

"What?" asked Guin.

"Tanya had applied to be my TA, same time as CiCi. I think she took it a bit hard when CiCi got the position instead."

"So why did you choose CiCi over Tanya?" Guin asked.

"Tanya's on the tennis team and has a very active social life. I didn't think she'd have enough time. Also…"

"Also?" asked Guin.

"She may have had a bit of a crush on me," Ris reluctantly replied.

"Ah," said Guin, knowing Tanya wouldn't be the first student to have flirted with Ris.

"But I can't imagine Tanya killing her," said Ris. "Gossiping about her, yes; murdering her, no."

They finished their coffees and Ris got up.

"You're going?" said Guin.

"I would love to stay," he said, "but I have a million things to do tomorrow. And if I'm going to get a run in, I need to get up early."

"I understand," Guin said. "When are your interviews?"

"The first round is Wednesday."

"Good luck," Guin said. "Will you be able to make it to the preview Wednesday evening?"

"I was planning on it. And I told Peggy and Lainie I'd help with setup on Tuesday."

"That must have made them happy," Guin said.

Peggy Sifton and Lainie Bianchi co-chaired the Sanibel Shell Festival and were huge fans of Ris, who had served as a judge the previous year.

Ris smiled. "They did seem pleased."

"I'm surprised they didn't ask you to serve as a judge again."

"They said if they had known I'd be back, they would have."

Guin laughed.

"Frankly, I'm relieved," Ris said. "Judging the Shell Show is a tricky business. People can be very sensitive. I've encountered more than one entrant who didn't understand why her exhibit didn't win a ribbon and had burst into tears."

Guin could well imagine it. People on Sanibel took their shells and the Shell Show very seriously. She didn't know how Shelly and the others did it.

"So, I guess I'll see you there Wednesday," said Guin.

"You covering the show again for the paper?"

"You betcha," said Guin, in a faux North Dakota/Minnesota accent.

Ris laughed.

"That bad, eh?"

"Stick to you," said Ris, leaning down and giving her a kiss on her nose.

He yawned.

"Go," said Guin. "Get some sleep."

"Shall we grab a bite to eat after the preview Wednesday?"

"Sounds good," said Guin. "And I may see you over at the Community House Tuesday."

She walked him to the door. Before she could open it, however, Ris took her in his arms and gave her a kiss.

"Maybe I should stay," he said, looking down at Guin.

"Go," said Guin. "We could both use some sleep. I'll see you Wednesday."

"Okay, I'm going," he said, somewhat reluctantly.

Guin opened the door and Ris stepped outside.

"You sure?" he asked.

"We'll have plenty of time to spend together next weekend, once your interviews and the Shell Show and, hopefully, this case are wrapped up."

"You think the police are going to find the guy who did it by next weekend?" he asked her.

"Well," said Guin, hesitating. "Maybe not by next weekend. But hopefully by then we'll have a better idea of what happened."

"We?" said Ris.

"You know what I mean," said Guin.

"I know you want to be involved, Guin, but please let the police handle this. There's a murderer out there, who killed someone on the beach you like to go to. You need to be careful."

"I know," said Guin. "I promise not to do anything stupid. But I need to find out what happened to her."

"I understand," he said. "I just don't want you to get hurt."

He leaned down and gave her a kiss on her forehead.

"Good night, Guin."

"Good night, Ris."

She watched as Ris made his way down the stairs. Then she closed the door.

A little after 8:30 the next morning, Guin headed off to FGCU. She wanted to speak with some of CiCi's professors, as well as her sorority sisters and Scott Murray, aka HotScot.

She parked the Mini close to the building that housed the Marine & Ecological Sciences department and made her way to the office. She had been there a number of times, having visited Ris at work, and knew the department secretary, a woman by the name of Georgia Gleason.

"Hi, Georgia," Guin said, upon entering the office.

"Hi, Guin," Georgia replied. "What can I do for you? If you're looking for Ris, he's not in yet."

"Actually, I was hoping maybe you could help me," said Guin.

"Shoot," said Georgia.

"What do you know about Caroline Rawlins?"

"CiCi?"

Guin nodded.

"I'm sure you heard what happened."

"I did," said Georgia. "I still can't believe it. Just awful. Who would do that?"

"That's what I'm trying to find out," said Guin.

"You covering the story for that paper of yours?" asked Georgia.

"I am," said Guin. She paused. "Have you spoken with the police?"

"There's a Detective O'Loughlin meeting with Dr. Espinosa right now," said Georgia.

Why was Guin not surprised?

"Ah," said Guin. "I was hoping to speak with Dr. Espinosa myself."

"They should be done soon," said Georgia.

"So did the detective ask you anything?"

"Just if Dr. Espinosa was available. Poor CiCi. As if that girl didn't have enough trouble."

"Why do you say that?" asked Guin.

"You didn't know about the rumors?"

"Rumors?" said Guin, playing dumb.

"Someone started a nasty rumor about Dr. Hartwick and her," she replied.

She was about to say more when she was interrupted by the chairman's door opening.

"Sorry I couldn't be of more help," said Dr. Espinosa, standing in the doorway.

"Just let me know if you recall anything else," said Detective O'Loughlin.

He noticed Guin and stopped.

"Ms. Jones, why am I not surprised to find you here?"

"Detective," said Guin.

They stared at each other for several seconds.

"If you're done speaking with Dr. Espinosa, may I have a word with him?" asked Guin.

"Be my guest," said the detective, gesturing with his hand.

Guin walked towards the open door, then stopped.

"You go to the sorority?"

"On my way there now," said the detective.

"Would you wait for me?" Guin asked.

The detective looked like he was thinking about it.

"Please?" said Guin. "Just give me fifteen minutes here."

"I'll give you ten, but if you're not out by then, I'm leaving without you," said the detective.

"It's a deal," said Guin, smiling.

She knocked on Dr. Espinosa's office door, then poked her head in.

"Dr. Espinosa?"

"Guin! How nice to see you!"

He beamed at her from his desk.

"What brings you here?"

"I'm covering the murder of Caroline Rawlins for the paper."

"Awful business," said Dr. Espinosa, shaking his head.

"I know you were just speaking with the detective, but would it be okay if I asked you a few questions?"

"Of course," he said. "Pull up a chair."

Guin grabbed one of the chairs facing his desk and sat down.

"Do you mind if I record our conversation?" she asked.

"Not at all," he said. "I have nothing to hide."

She pulled out her microcassette recorder and began recording.

"Do you know why CiCi didn't return to campus this semester?"

Dr. Espinosa frowned.

"Did it have to do with the rumors?"

He sighed.

"I take it you heard."

"Yes," said Guin.

"Of course, no one here believed it."

"Of course," said Guin, sounding surer than she felt.

"But you can see how something like that could affect a sensitive young woman."

"Was CiCi sensitive?"

"Perhaps sensitive was the wrong word. CiCi wanted people to think well of her and was always going out of her way to try to be helpful. It crushed her when she made a mistake."

Guin understood. She was a bit like that.

"I think Ris had a soft spot for her."

Guin raised her eyebrows.

"No, not like that," Dr. Espinosa hastily added.

"CiCi was having second doubts about marine biology at the end of her junior year. Wasn't sure if she wanted to pursue it. Dr. Hartwick had thought she would be making a big mistake abandoning marine biology. She only needed a few more credits to graduate. So he offered to mentor her her senior year and invited her to be his teaching assistant."

"That was very kind of him," Guin said.

"Indeed," said Dr. Espinosa. "Though some of the other students did not feel the same way. Several had applied to be his TA and were disappointed when they were passed over."

"Anyone in particular who was, shall we say, more disappointed than some of the others?"

"I dislike casting aspersions on any of our students, but..."

Guin waited.

"I told the detective he should speak with Tanya Harvey."

"Tanya Harvey?" said Guin. Why did that name sound familiar?

"She and CiCi were in the same sorority. Both were Marine Biology majors. I think there was a bit of a competition between the two, though I believe it was mostly on Tanya's part."

Guin continued to patiently listen to Dr. Espinosa.

"Tanya thought she deserved to be Dr. Hartwick's TA. She even lodged a protest with the department after he chose CiCi instead of her, claiming favoritism."

"Did the department do anything?"

"We investigated, but it's really up to each professor who he or she chooses to assist them."

"And the rumor?" asked Guin. "Could Tanya have started it?"

"I don't know for sure," said Dr. Espinosa. "But I wouldn't be surprised."

"And do you happen to know a student by the name of Scott Murray?"

"Scott Murray?" said Dr. Espinosa. "I don't think he's one of ours."

"Well, thank you for your time, Dr. Espinosa," Guin said, stopping the tape and standing up.

"My pleasure, Guin. I'm only sorry I couldn't be more helpful."

"And I'm sorry to hear you'll be leaving FGCU," Guin said.

"It's time," he replied. "I'm sure Ris has told you he's interviewing for the position."

"He has," said Guin.

"I think he would make an excellent chairman."

"I do, too," said Guin.

Guin looked around for the detective.

"He left," said Georgia, "about five minutes ago."

Guin made a face.

"He couldn't have waited?"

"You know how men are," said Georgia.

"Maybe I can catch him," said Guin. She paused. "Hey, Georgia, what do you know about Tanya Harvey?"

"Tanya?"

"Yeah. I understand she was upset when Ris asked CiCi to be his TA."

"Oh that," said Georgia. "Yeah, she was pretty pissed."

"How pissed? Pissed enough to kill her?"

"Tanya? Doubtful. She'd be too worried about getting blood stains on her clothes."

Guin snorted.

"What about boys?

"Boys?" said Georgia.

"You ever see CiCi with a boy?"

Georgia thought for several seconds.

"Just that tennis player."

"You wouldn't happen to know his name, would you?"

"I think it's Scott. Cute kid."

"Thanks," said Guin. "I'll check him out."

"Good luck," said Georgia.

Guin said goodbye, then hurried to catch up with the detective.

CHAPTER 19

Guin arrived at the Kappa Delta sorority house, slipping in behind a young woman who had just swiped her key card, but did not see the detective.

"Can I help you?" asked a young woman.

"Yes, I'm looking for a Detective O'Loughlin. I was supposed to meet him here," said Guin.

"I haven't seen a detective," said the young woman. She gave Guin the once-over. "Are you a cop?"

"No, I'm a reporter."

"Like, for the evening news?" asked the young woman. "I'd love to be a reporter. I'm a journalism major. Which station do you work for?"

Guin smiled.

"I work for the *Sanibel-Captiva Sun-Times*."

"Oh," said the young woman, clearly disappointed.

"It's a great job," said Guin. "You get to cover lots of different things, and Sanibel and Captiva are great."

"If you like being stuck in Nowheresville," said the young woman. "Do people even read newspapers anymore?" she asked Guin.

"Lots of people do," said Guin. (She made a mental note to ask Ginny what the circulation of the paper was these days, though she knew many people read it online.)

"So what are you doing here? FGCU isn't exactly close

to Sanibel. And isn't everyone there, like, sixty-five or above?"

Guin told herself to keep smiling and not be defensive. Many people, especially younger ones, thought of Sanibel as a kind of retirement community, even though there were plenty of young families on the island.

"Actually," said Guin. "I'm here doing a little investigative reporting. Maybe you can help me."

The young woman perked up.

"What are you investigating?"

"I'm looking for information about one of your sorority sisters, Caroline Rawlins."

"CiCi?"

"Yes, do you know her?" Guin asked.

"Sure. It's not like Kappa Delta is that big. What do you want to know about CiCi? Is she in some kind of trouble?"

"She was murdered," said Guin, deciding not to beat around the bush.

"Murdered?" said the young woman, clearly shocked.

"I'm afraid so," said Guin.

"Do they know who did it?" the young woman asked.

"Not yet," said Guin.

"Murdered," repeated the young woman. "Wow."

"I didn't catch your name," said Guin.

"I'm Madeline. Madeline Finlay," said the young woman. "Though everyone calls me Maddie."

"Nice to meet you, Maddie. I'm Guin Jones."

She reached into her bag and pulled out her card case.

"Here's my card," she said, handing one to Maddie.

Maddie stared at it.

"So, about CiCi," Guin resumed. "Do you know why she didn't come back to campus this semester?"

Maddie looked like she was mulling something over.

"Did it have to do with the rumor?"

"You know about that?" asked Maddie.

"I've been informed," said Guin.

"Of course, I can't blame CiCi for sleeping with him. Dr. Hartwick is totally hot, even if he is, like, old enough to be my dad."

Guin cringed.

"Do you know where I can find Tanya Harvey?"

"Her room's upstairs, second floor. You want me to show you?"

Guin was about to say "yes" when she heard her name.

"Ms. Jones."

Guin turned to see the detective walking towards her.

"Detective."

Maddie looked from the detective to Guin.

"This is Detective O'Loughlin of the Sanibel Police Department," Guin said by way of introduction. "Detective, this is Madeline Finlay, one of Ms. Rawlins's sorority sisters."

Maddie looked nervously at the detective.

"I was just asking Maddie here about CiCi and Tanya Harvey," said Guin.

The detective glanced at Guin.

"Maddie was going to show me where I could find Tanya Harvey's room."

Maddie nodded her head.

Suddenly Guin had another thought.

"Do you happen to know a Scott Murray?"

"Scott?"

"Yes," said Guin. "I believe he's on the tennis team."

"That's right," said Maddie. "Yeah, I know him. Why?"

"Do you know if Scott and CiCi ever dated?"

Maddie began to fidget.

"Scott's with Tanya."

Guin had the feeling Maddie was hiding something.

"Do you know if Scott had gone out with CiCi in the past?" Guin asked.

The detective was watching Maddie.

"Ms. Finlay, if there's something you're not telling us…"

Maddie quickly glanced around the room. There were girls milling about, a few of them stopping to look in their direction.

"Come with me," said Maddie, leading them into a small room near the entrance to the sorority. It was empty.

"Scott had kind of a crush on CiCi, but CiCi wasn't interested in him that way. They grew up together, and CiCi thought of him like a brother. And she said she'd never date her brother."

"Ouch," said Guin.

"Right?" said Maddie.

"Were the two of them friends?" asked the detective.

"Oh yeah," said Maddie. "CiCi and Scott were real tight, or they were until Scott started dating Tanya."

"So Scott was from Sanibel?" asked Guin.

"Yeah. And they both went to high school in Fort Myers."

Guin glanced over at the detective. He was writing in his little notebook. He finished and looked up at Maddie.

"Do you happen to know where we can find Ms. Harvey and Mr. Murray?" asked the detective.

"Tanya's room is upstairs. She's probably out, but we can check."

"Shall we?" Guin said to the detective.

"After you," he replied.

They followed Maddie up the stairs.

"Tanya?" said Maddie, knocking on the door.

There was no response.

"She must be out," said Maddie.

"Any idea when she'll be back?" asked the detective.

Maddie shrugged.

The detective withdrew one of his cards.

"Please give this to her and ask her to get in touch with me."

Maddie looked at the card.

"You want to just leave her a note? I don't know when I'll actually see her."

The detective made a face.

"Do you happen to have a piece of paper?" he asked Maddie.

She pulled off her backpack and ripped out a piece of paper from a notebook.

"Here," she said, handing it to him.

"Thanks."

He scrawled something on the piece of paper, then folded it up, enclosing a card.

"Just slip it under her door," said Maddie.

He did.

"Maddie, any idea where we could find Scott Murray?" asked Guin.

"Try the tennis center," she suggested.

"Thanks," said Guin.

"No problem," said Maddie. "You two done? I need to get to class."

Guin glanced at the detective.

"You can go," he said. "Thanks for your help."

"Any time," said Maddie.

Then she raced down the stairs.

CHAPTER 20

"Shall we?" said Guin.

"We?" said the detective.

"I'm coming with you, to speak with Scott Murray. I have to meet this HotScot."

"Hot Scott?" asked the detective, confused.

"HotScot is his Instagram handle. That's how I found him."

They arrived at the tennis center a few minutes later. They spied a man in his forties, around the detective's height, dressed in tennis whites, speaking to a group of students.

"That must be the coach," said Guin.

They headed over.

Guin and the detective waited while the man finished speaking. Then the detective signaled to him.

"May I help you?" asked the man.

"Are you the tennis coach?" asked the detective.

"Yes, I'm Coach Cassidy. How may I help you?"

The detective showed him his ID.

"We're looking for a member of your team, a young man by the name of Scott Murray. Any idea where we could find him?"

"Scott? Has he done something wrong?" asked the coach.

"We just need to ask him a few questions," said the detective. "Can you help us locate him?"

"He's practicing for tomorrow's match."

"So he's here?" Guin asked.

"Yeah, over on Court 6."

"Great," said Guin. "Which way?"

The coach gave them directions.

"Thanks," said Guin.

They followed Coach Cassidy's directions to Court 6.

"What happened to you not saying anything?" asked the detective.

Guin rolled her eyes.

"There he is, over there," Guin said, pointing.

The detective followed Guin over to Court 6, where Scott was hitting balls with another student. He and Guin watched as the two young men hit the ball back and forth, each return harder than the last.

"He's good," Guin whispered to the detective. "And cute."

The detective grunted.

When the point was over, the detective cleared his throat and indicated for Scott to come over.

"Yes?" said Scott, walking over to the detective. "Can I help you with something?"

The detective took out his identification.

"I'm Detective O'Loughlin with the Sanibel Police Department. I'd like to speak with you about Caroline Rawlins."

He looked over at Scott's playing partner, who was standing a few feet away.

"Is CiCi okay?" asked Scott.

"Let's talk someplace a little more private," said the detective.

"I'll be back in a few, Tom!" Scott called. "We can go over to the snack shack," he said to the detective.

"Snack shack?" asked Guin.

"That's just what we call it," said Scott, smiling. "It's just over there," he said, pointing. "Coach stocks it with snacks and water and drinks, so we don't get dehydrated and keep our stamina up. Someone back in the day started calling it the 'snack shack,' and the name kind of stuck."

"Cute," said Guin. "I'm Guin Jones, by the way."

"You also a cop?" Scott asked.

"No, I'm a reporter with the *Sanibel-Captiva Sun-Times*."

"My mom loves your paper," Scott said, smiling.

"Thank you. So, your mom and dad live on the island?"

"Yup, I was raised there. Went to the Sanibel School."

"And that's how you know CiCi?" Guin asked him.

"Yup. We rode the bus together. Is she okay?" he asked, looking over at the detective. "I've been trying to reach her, but she hasn't been returning my texts."

Guin glanced over at the detective, who had been listening to their exchange.

"When was the last time you saw or spoke with Ms. Rawlins?" asked the detective.

"Wednesday night. She was pretty upset."

"Upset?" asked Guin. "What about?"

"She said this famous guy was hitting on her, and she didn't know what to do. Said it was a sensitive situation, that she could lose her job if she said something."

"Her job meaning her work for Sam Hutchins, the shell artist?" asked Guin, before the detective could speak.

"Yeah," said Scott.

"Did she say what happened?" Guin asked.

Scott hesitated.

"I'm not sure I should say anything. CiCi could get into trouble."

"I regret to inform you that Ms. Rawlins is dead, Mr. Murray," said the detective. "So if she said something to you that could help us find her killer, we would appreciate you telling us."

"CiCi's dead?" said Scott. He looked from the detective to Guin, then back at the detective. "That's not possible!" He looked distraught. "When? How?"

"Her body was found Thursday morning," replied the detective.

Scott had gone pale.

"No," he said quietly. "It can't be."

Guin thought he was about to cry.

"Who would do such a thing? Is this a joke? Did someone put you up to this?"

"This is no joke, Mr. Murray."

"How? Where?" he asked the detective. "Was it that guitar player?"

"Guitar player?" asked the detective, playing dumb.

Guin bit her tongue to stop herself from saying anything.

"His name's Denny Sumner," said Scott, suddenly looking quite angry. "He plays guitar for that band, No Signal. CiCi said he was hitting on her, that he kissed her and tried to rape her. She pushed him off, but she was afraid he would say something to Sam and get her fired."

Guin glanced over at the detective, but all of his attention was focused on Scott.

"When was this?" Guin asked the young man.

"Wednesday," said Scott, turning to look at her. "She called me right after she got home. She told me she had taken him to Captiva, to show him around. Then they watched the sunset over on Sanibel. Then when they got back to her car, he got all handsy."

"Did she tell you he tried to rape her?" asked the detective.

"Not in so many words," said Scott.

"Is it possible she was mistaken?" asked the detective. "Could she have encouraged him?"

Guin frowned at the detective.

"No way!" said Scott.

"Did she say he harmed her?" asked the detective.

"No," said Scott, in a more subdued tone. "But I could tell she was freaked out."

"Did she say anything else?" asked Guin. "About Denny, or Sam?"

"Yeah," said Scott. "She said she had told Sumner that she would take him shelling with her the next morning, if he wanted to. But that was before he kissed her. And now she didn't know what to do."

"So she was still thinking of taking him with her?" Guin asked.

"Yeah," said Scott. "Like I said, she was worried Sumner would say something to Sam if she didn't play along."

"So what?" said Guin. "They couldn't possibly take his word over hers?"

"Are you kidding me? He's a rock star. Women probably throw themselves at him every day."

"But CiCi wasn't like that, was she?" asked Guin.

"No, but…"

Scott looked uncomfortable.

"But what?" said the detective.

"There was an incident, on campus, last semester," Scott said, not looking at the detective.

The detective and Guin waited for him to continue.

"Rumor had it CiCi was having an affair with a professor."

"Did you believe this rumor?" asked the detective.

Scott continued to avert his gaze.

"I didn't want to."

"But…" said Guin.

"But what was I supposed to think?" said Scott, looking up at her, his expression fierce. "I saw her, having dinner with him. She was all dressed up, and the two of them looked very chummy. And we're not talking Five Guys. This was one of those places you bring a date."

Guin felt ill.

"Did you have a crush on Ms. Rawlins?" asked the detective.

Scott's face reddened.

"Answer the question," said the detective.

"Okay, maybe I did," said Scott, angrily. "Maybe I was a little jealous of her and Dr. Heartthrob. That's what all the girls call him. He's old enough to be their father, for Pete's sake! But they're all crazy about him."

"So you believed the rumor that CiCi was having an affair with him?" Guin asked, trying to keep her voice neutral.

Scott ran a hand through his hair.

"I don't know," he said. "CiCi swore they were just friends, that he was just being kind to her. But you should have seen the two of them together at the Beach House. It's not a place you take your 'friend' to," he said, using air quotes.

"So you think she might have been lying about Mr. Sumner?" asked the detective.

"No," said Scott. "I mean, I don't know. I don't want to believe it. But if she could sleep with Dr. Hartwick…"

Guin looked at the young man. He looked torn.

"Where were you last Thursday morning?" asked the detective.

"On a bus, headed to Miami," said Scott. "We had a big tournament there over the weekend."

"When did you get back?" asked the detective.

"Yesterday."

"And that call Wednesday was the last time you heard from Ms. Rawlins?" asked the detective.

Scott hesitated.

"She sent me a text later that evening, but I didn't read it until Thursday."

"How come?" asked Guin.

"I turned off my phone after we had hung up. Had to get some shut eye. Bus was leaving early the next morning."

"And what did the text say?" asked Guin.

"She thanked me for listening and said she had gotten a text from Sumner. That he had apologized. And that he asked her to forgive him."

"Did she say anything else?" asked Guin.

"No. That was the last I heard from her. I texted her back later Thursday, but she didn't respond."

"And you weren't concerned when you didn't hear back from her?" Guin asked.

"I just figured she was busy. And there was the tournament. I sure as heck didn't think she had been murdered."

"Do you know of anyone who might have wanted to harm Ms. Rawlins?" asked the detective.

"Other than the guitar player? No. CiCi wouldn't harm a fly, except maybe to cook it," Scott said, chuckling at his little joke.

The detective was looking at him, clearly not amused.

"CiCi loved to cook," Scott quickly explained. "She was always trying out these crazy recipes."

"And what was your relationship with Ms. Rawlins at the time of her death?" asked the detective.

"We were just friends," Scott replied.

"I understand the two of you went to school together, on Sanibel," said Guin.

"That's right," said Scott.

"And you attended the same high school."

"So?" said Scott.

"Did the two of you ever date?" Guin asked him.

"No, not seriously."

From his tone and body language, Guin had a feeling he had wanted to, though.

"We went to prom together. But we were just friends."

Even the detective now looked skeptical.

"I'm dating Tanya Harvey. She's on the women's tennis team."

"And how did Tanya feel about you and CiCi?" asked Guin.

"She understood," Scott replied.

Guin doubted that.

"And do you happen to know where Ms. Harvey was Thursday morning?" asked the detective.

"Yeah, on the bus with me."

Scratch two suspects.

"Is there anyone else on campus you know of who might have had a grudge against CiCi? Maybe one of her sorority sisters?" Guin asked.

Scott thought for several seconds.

"Not that I know of, no. Besides, she had been living off campus since winter break. She was barely here. Only came over a couple times a week. I'd barely seen or talked to her the last few weeks. That's why I was kind of surprised when she called me last Wednesday."

"Did she mention anything about anyone on Sanibel, other than Denny Sumner?" Guin asked.

Again, Scott looked thoughtful.

"She did mention being approached by this woman at Bailey's, something to do with CiCi cooking for her. Said it was kind of weird."

"Did she mention the woman's name?" Guin asked him.

"Susan Hastings. Though most people know her as Suzy Seashell. My mom loves her. Reads her blog all the time."

"And what did CiCi say about her?"

"Just that she asked CiCi a bunch of questions about the project and then asked if she'd like to cook for her and her husband."

"And when was this?" asked the detective.

"Last week," Scott replied.

"And did she happen to mention what she said to Suzy?"

"Nothing. She'd signed one of those non-disclosure agreements. Or that's what she told me."

"Speaking of work, did she ever talk about Sam and Rita, the women in charge of the project she was working on?"

"Just that she thought Sam and Rita were cool. She was really grateful to have been chosen, which is why she was so freaked out about Sumner hitting on her."

"What about Marta, the other volunteer?" Guin asked.

"She said Marta was kind of a cold fish."

"Cold?" asked Guin. "In what way?"

"Nothing in particular," Scott replied. "Just that she wasn't particularly friendly. Didn't joke around like the others."

Guin glanced over at the detective. He was scribbling something in his notebook.

As if sensing Guin was looking at him, he looked up.

"Anything else you recall Ms. Rawlins saying to you?"

Scott thought for a minute.

"No, that's pretty much everything."

He paused.

"You're going to find out who did this to CiCi, right?"

"We are," said Guin, before the detective could reply.

"Thank you for your help, Mr. Murray," said the detective. He withdrew a card from his pocket and handed it to the young man. "If you think of anything, give me a call or send me an email or text. My information's on the card."

Scott looked at the card, then pocketed it.

"I need to go," he said.

"That's fine," said the detective. "Thanks for your help."

"I just hope you catch whoever did it," said Scott.

Guin watched as he walked away.

"Well?" said Guin, turning back to the detective.

"Well what?" asked the detective.

"Do you believe young Mr. Murray?"

"No reason not to," replied the detective.

Guin wasn't so sure.

"I'll check out his story, though," said the detective. "Should be easy to find out if he was on that bus Thursday morning."

"You ask me, he was in love with the girl," said Guin.

"What makes you say that?" asked the detective.

"The way he looked when he talked about her. There's a certain way a guy looks when he's talking about someone he really cares about," Guin explained.

"Oh?" said the detective, looking at Guin.

Guin felt her cheeks getting warm.

"I should get going," she said.

"Don't let me keep you," said the detective.

They stood there, looking at each other for several seconds.

"You'll let me know if you find out anything?" Guin asked.

The detective didn't reply.

"You promised to forward me the autopsy results."

"I did?"

"You did," said Guin.

"Fine. I'll send you a copy. Anything else?"

"I'm good, for now. But let me know if you crack the case."

The detective looked amused.

"Well, lovely seeing you, detective. I'll be in touch to arrange that interview."

She turned and headed back towards her car, resisting the temptation to glance back at the detective.

CHAPTER 21

Guin had meant to get into the Mini and drive back to Sanibel. Instead she found herself back at the sorority.

"Excuse me," she asked two young women who were chatting by the door. "Do either of you happen to know if Tanya's around?"

"I just saw her go in," replied one of the girls.

"Thanks," Guin said. She paused. "Would one of you mind swiping me in?"

"Why do you want to speak with Tanya?" asked the other girl.

"I'm interviewing her for a story."

"You a reporter?" the first girl asked.

"I am," said Guin.

"Cool," said the second girl. "Here, I'll swipe you."

She took out her key card and swiped.

"Thanks," Guin said.

She went inside and glanced around.

"Can I help you?" asked a young woman.

"Yes, I'm looking for Tanya."

"Hey, Tanya!" the young woman shouted up the stairs. "You have a visitor!"

A few seconds later an attractive brunette, who Guin thought could have been Kendall Jenner's twin, appeared.

"Yeah?" she said to her friend.

The young woman who had shouted to her pointed at Guin.

"Who are you?" asked Tanya.

"My name is Guin Jones. I'm a reporter."

"You doing a story on the team?"

"No, I'm doing a story on Caroline Rawlins," Guin replied.

Tanya frowned.

"Why are you doing a story on her?"

"Her body was found over on Sanibel early Thursday morning."

Tanya sat down on the staircase.

"What happened?" asked the other young woman, who had been standing close by.

Guin ignored her.

"Is there someplace we can speak privately?" Guin asked Tanya.

Tanya nodded, then got up.

"Let's go to my room."

Guin followed her up the stairs.

"What's this about?" asked Tanya, after closing the door. "Did CiCi kill herself?"

"No, she was murdered," Guin replied.

"Murdered?" said Tanya, looking confused.

"Yes," said Guin, looking right at the young woman.

"Well, don't look at me," said Tanya, regaining her composure. "I was on a bus to Miami first thing Thursday. Ask anyone on the team. They'll tell you."

"What about the rumor?" asked Guin.

"What rumor?"

Guin had to hand it to the young woman, she was a pretty good actress.

"The one about CiCi and a certain professor," said Guin.

"Oh *that*," said Tanya, flopping down on her bed. "That was no rumor."

"Oh?" said Guin, who remained standing.

"They were totally doing it," said Tanya.

"And you know that how?" asked Guin.

"I saw them," Tanya replied.

"At the Beach House Restaurant, you mean," said Guin.

"Not just there," said Tanya.

Guin waited.

"I saw them, in his office."

"In his office?" said Guin.

"The door was unlocked, and there they were, you know."

"I'm afraid I don't know," said Guin, feeling her heart beating faster.

Tanya rolled her eyes.

"Of course, they acted like nothing was going on as soon as they saw me. But I know what I saw."

"And what did you see?" asked Guin.

"Why do you care?" asked Tanya.

Guin wanted to say, because I'm dating that professor, and the thought of him fooling around with a student makes me want to throw up. But she didn't.

"Like I said, I'm trying to find out who might have had a grudge against CiCi, might have wanted her out of the way."

She was looking directly at Tanya.

"Don't look at me, lady. Like I said, I wasn't here. Besides, while I might not have liked CiCi, I would have never killed her in cold blood."

"What time did the bus leave?" asked Guin.

"Seven-thirty," said Tanya.

No way could Tanya have gone to Sanibel and gotten back in time. But she would still check to make sure that Tanya had actually been on the bus.

"So why didn't you like CiCi? Did it have something to do with her getting the teaching assistant position with

Professor Hartwick?" asked Guin.

"She was always acting so innocent and sweet, but I knew better," said Tanya. "Everyone knew the only reason she got the TA gig was because she was sleeping with Dr. Hartwick. It should have been mine, but she stole it. Just like she tried to steal Scott."

"Scott?" Guin asked, innocently.

"My boyfriend. He's on the men's tennis team. He and CiCi grew up together. She was always chasing him, trying to get him to go out with her. But he wasn't interested."

Guin regarded Tanya. This was the opposite of what she had heard from Maddie. Maybe she needed to have another chat with Scott. Though if both of them had been on that bus Thursday, they couldn't possibly have killed CiCi.

"Was there anyone else at the sorority or on campus who didn't like CiCi, who might have had a grudge against her?"

"Probably. But I wouldn't want to name names and get someone in trouble."

Guin nearly laughed out loud. Was this chick for real? Girls like Tanya were the reason why Guin had never pledged a sorority when she was in school.

"Well, thank you for your time," Guin said, opening the door. "If you think of something, shoot me an email or a text." She handed Tanya her card. "And good luck with the rest of your season."

"Thanks," said Tanya, glancing at it. "You sure you don't want to do a piece on the team? We're undefeated this season."

"Thanks for the offer," said Guin. "Another time."

"Suit yourself," said Tanya, who had clearly grown bored and was checking her phone.

"I'll just let myself out," said Guin. But Tanya wasn't paying attention.

Guin shook her head as she left the sorority. No wonder CiCi left.

She made her way to the parking lot and unlocked the Mini. She got in, then remembered she hadn't checked her messages in a while. She pulled out her phone and saw that her message light was blinking. She had several messages, including one from Shelly, checking to make sure Guin would be at the award ceremony that Wednesday.

In all the excitement around CiCi's murder, she had nearly forgotten about the Shell Show.

"I'll be there!" Guin typed back. "Wouldn't miss it."

She quickly scrolled through the rest of her messages. Nothing urgent. Which was good because her stomach was grumbling. She looked back down at her phone. How had it gotten to be noon already? She looked around. There were probably places to grab a bite on campus, but she didn't want to stick around.

She did a quick search and found a poke place not too far away.

"Perfect!" she said.

She wondered if the detective was still on campus and thought about texting him and seeing if he wanted to join her for lunch, then stopped herself. Instead, she got in her car and headed to the restaurant.

After having eaten a large bowl of raw tuna, salmon, avocado, cucumber, and mango, she felt much better.

She pulled out her phone.

"What are you doing?" she texted Ris.

"Preparing for my interviews."

"OK if I stop by?" she wrote him back.

"Do you need to ask?" he typed, adding a smiley face. "Come on by."

"OK, see you soon. Should be there in 30."

Guin then took a last sip of her water, pocketed her phone, and left.

Guin rang the doorbell at Ris's place and waited.

"You know you can just let yourself in," he said, as he let her in. "You still have the key?"

"I do, but it feels weird. What if you were in the middle of something?"

Her mind immediately conjured an image of Ris and CiCi. She winced.

"You okay?" he asked her.

"Probably just a gas pain," Guin lied. "I'm fine."

"So, to what do I owe this unexpected visit? I thought you'd be busy covering the show."

"I need to ask you something," she said.

She looked up into his sea-green eyes and steeled herself.

"I just met with Tanya Harvey."

"Let me guess," Ris said. "She told you I was having an affair with Caroline."

Guin was taken aback.

"She did. She said she saw the two of you together, in your office."

Ris ran a hand through his hair.

"And you wonder how rumors get started."

He sighed.

"Do you really believe I'd have an affair with a student?"

He was looking right at her and Guin felt her heart racing.

"I don't want to, but Tanya seemed pretty convinced something was going on between the two of you. And she said she saw the two of you making out in your office."

He shook his head. Was that disappointment she saw?

"We were not 'making out,'" he said, a few seconds later.

"I was trying to console her. CiCi had just told her folks she wasn't that interested in marine biology or going into the family business, that she wanted to be a chef. Her father took it pretty hard. They had gotten into a big fight, and CiCi had come to my office in tears, asking me if she had made the wrong decision.

"You should have seen her, Guin. She was really broken up, second-guessing her decision. She so reminded me of Fiona. I just instinctively gave her a hug and told her everything would be all right. I was just trying to calm her down. That's when Tanya burst in."

Guin took in everything Ris said. It was so like him. She could just picture him comforting the young woman, imagining it was his daughter. CiCi was only a couple of years older than Fiona, and there was even a slight resemblance.

"Do you believe me?" he asked.

"I do," Guin said. "But why would Tanya spread such an ugly rumor?"

"Tanya," said Ris, making a face, "was clearly jealous. Though I never thought she'd stoop so low. Clearly not getting the teaching assistant position annoyed her far more than she let on."

"She seemed to be under the impression that the only reason CiCi got the position was because she was sleeping with you," said Guin.

Ris had a pained look on his face.

"I promise you, Guin, I have never, not for a minute, thought of CiCi that way. And if anyone was flirting with me, it was Tanya."

That Guin could believe.

"I told her I wasn't interested, that it was against university rules to have relationships with students, but that didn't seem to matter to her."

He shook his head and continued.

"I know we men get a bad rap, much of it deserved. But the things some of these girls do to try to get attention…"

Guin went over to him and gave him a hug.

"Thank you," he said. "I'm just sorry Tanya caused you any pain."

"I'll get over it," said Guin.

They stood there, holding each other, for several minutes.

"I should get going," Guin finally said. "I need to get back to work."

"Any way I could convince you to stay a little longer?" Ris asked her. He had that grin that showed his dimples, the one that made him irresistible to women.

"Very tempting, but I'm going to have to give you a raincheck. You still helping with setup over at the Community House tomorrow?"

"I am," he replied. "I promised Peggy and Lainie I'd be there."

"Then I'll probably see you then."

She got on her tiptoes and gave him a kiss on the cheek. "Gotta run!"

"Guin…" he called after her.

Guin stopped at the door and blew him a kiss.

"I love you," he called. But she had already left.

Guin thought about what Ris had said as she drove back to Sanibel. She could just picture Tanya flinging herself at him. Then her mind began conjuring an image of Ris kissing Tanya.

"Stop it, Guin!" she admonished herself.

She turned on the radio and put it on the '80s station she liked. She cranked the volume, hoping it would drown out the negative thoughts.

CHAPTER 22

Guin made a last-minute right turn into the parking lot of the *San-Cap Sun-Times*. She hadn't planned on stopping by, but she figured she was already there, so why not?

Everyone in the office looked busy. No surprise, as they needed to get copy to the printer by the next day if they wanted to have the print edition on the island first thing Friday.

"Hey, Jasmine," Guin called to the head designer, who was intently looking at her monitor.

"Hey, Guin," she replied, only briefly glancing over.

"Ginny in back?"

"Should be," said Jasmine.

"Peanut here?" asked Guin, looking around.

Peanut was Jasmine's labradoodle, who often hung out with her at the office.

"Not today. Too busy."

"I'll just head back," Guin said.

Jasmine didn't reply. All of her attention was focused on her screen.

Guin made her way to Ginny's office. The door was ajar, and she could hear Ginny on the phone. She knocked, but there was no response. She poked her head in. Ginny indicated she would just be a minute and gestured for Guin to take a seat.

"Yeah, yeah, yeah," Ginny said. "I hear you, Bill. But it's Kingfisher's turn to get top billing this week. You got the top spot last week. Next week it'll be VIP's turn."

Ginny rolled her eyes.

"I don't care if your people sold $100 million worth of houses. You know how this works."

Ginny put her hand over the mouthpiece and looked over at Guin.

"These real estate agents will be the death of me."

She turned back to her caller.

"Look, Bill, I have to go. There's someone in my office. You want to take out an ad, call me back. Bye."

She hung up the phone and shook her head.

"Sometimes I feel like I'm running a daycare center."

"That bad, eh?" said Guin.

"Some of these real estate agents act like children. 'How come Johnny got a better placement than I did?' It's enough to make me take up day drinking."

Guin smiled.

"Come on, Ginny. We both know you've got a bottle of bourbon stashed in your drawer."

"It was a gift," Ginny retorted. "And, for your information, I still haven't opened it."

"Uh-huh," said Guin.

"So, what brings you here on a Monday? You need more work?"

"Hardly," said Guin. "Between the Shell Show, CiCi's murder, and the jewelry show, my plate's full."

"So why are you here? You wanna tell Aunt Ginny what's bugging you?"

"Who says something's bothering me?" Guin replied.

"Please, Guinivere. I may not have known you that long, but I know that look. Give."

Guin sighed.

"So, I found out something disturbing while I was doing some research on Caroline Rawlins, the young woman whose body I found on the beach."

"Go on," said Ginny.

"Turns out, she TA'd for Ris last semester. I didn't even know. And there's a rumor around campus that she and Ris were…"

Guin searched for the right word.

"Indulging in some extracurricular activities?" suggested Ginny.

"Yes," said Guin.

"Did you speak with Dr. Heartthrob?"

Guin made a face.

"You know he hates that nickname."

Ginny grinned.

"He said there was no truth to the rumor," said Guin. "That he would never fool around with a student."

"You believe him?" asked Ginny.

"I do," said Guin.

"You don't sound convinced."

Guin sighed.

"I do believe him. Really. It's just…"

"So, what do you want me to say to you?" asked Ginny.

"I don't know," said Guin. "I'm just confused."

"About?"

"I thought I was over the whole cheating husband thing. [Guin's ex-husband, Art, had had an affair with their hairdresser.] But this rumor has stirred up old feelings. And I don't know if I can have a relationship with a man who I'm going to be constantly worrying will cheat on me."

"I see," said Ginny.

Guin waited for her to say more, but she didn't.

"That's it?" said Guin.

"Is there something you wanted to hear?"

"I, uh…" said Guin.

"Look, Guin. I can't tell you what you should do. Well, I could, but it's not my life we're talking about. And right now, I have a paper I need to get out. My suggestion? Follow your heart. You love this guy, stick with him. You don't, don't drag things out. Life's too short to be wasting time with the wrong man. And now, if you will excuse me," Ginny said, picking up the phone.

"Of course," said Guin, getting up. "Thanks."

She got up and left Ginny's office. She had meant to discuss CiCi's murder with Ginny, but instead she had brought up Ris. She made her way to the front door, waving goodbye to Jasmine on her way out. She went over to the Mini and unlocked it. Then she quickly checked her phone for messages. There was a text from Craig, asking her to call him.

Craig picked up after a few rings.

"What's up?" Guin asked him.

"I talked to Jack Rawlins. And I also had a chat with the guy who runs that culinary club on campus."

"And?" said Guin.

"Jack said he had no idea who would want to harm CiCi, and he didn't know about any boyfriend. And the gentleman who ran the culinary club said Ms. Rawlins was a great cook and would be missed, but he knew nothing about her personal life or who she hung out with."

Guin sighed. More dead ends.

"Well, I guess we have to keep on looking."

"You find out anything?" Craig asked.

Guin debated whether to mention the rumor, then chided herself.

"Apparently there was a rumor going around campus that CiCi was having an affair with Ris. She was his TA last semester, and they supposedly spent a lot of time together."

"You okay?" asked Craig.

"Yeah, I guess. I spoke to Ris. He denied it, and I want to believe him."

"But…?" said Craig.

"No but," said Guin. "I believe him. But it upsets me that people would think such a thing."

"You find out who started the rumor?"

"Yeah, a sorority sister of CiCi's who was also up for the TA position. CiCi beat her out. Also, the girl's boyfriend may have had a crush on CiCi."

Craig whistled.

"Sounds like motive to me."

"Yeah, except they were both supposedly on a bus headed to Miami at the time of the murder."

"They could have hired someone," said Craig.

"They're kids, Craig."

"Rich kids," said Craig. "You wouldn't believe some of the stuff I saw back in Chicago. Kids these days…"

"I'll check out their alibi—or maybe you could? I want to speak with Sam Hutchins's boyfriend, Denny Sumner, again. Seems he may not have told us everything. And I need to speak with Susan Hastings. She may have been following the girl, trying to obtain information about Sam's sculpture."

Craig shook his head.

"What is it about this island and shells that makes people crazy?"

Guin smiled.

"You going to tell me there are no crazy fish people?"

"Not the same," said Craig.

Guin wasn't buying it.

"Oh, by the way, I heard the autopsy report was ready."

"How'd you hear that?" Guin asked him. "Never mind. So, can you get a copy?"

"I'll ask."

"Thanks," said Guin.

"Sorry I don't have better news."

"That's okay," said Guin. "At least we've narrowed down the list. Most likely it was someone who lives on Sanibel or is staying here. What I want to know is whether it was a random killing, which seems unlikely, or if someone was targeting CiCi."

"Well, let me know what I can do to help," said Craig. "I'll be out fishing tomorrow, but if you need me, just send me a text."

"Will do," said Guin.

They said goodbye and ended the call.

Guin looked down at her phone. Her message light was flashing. There was an urgent text from Shelly, asking Guin to call her.

Guin entered her number.

"Can you come over here?" Shelly asked her.

"Is everything okay?" said Guin.

"No," said Shelly. "I have to drop off my entry tomorrow, and I'm worried I'm missing something. Can you come over and take a look? I need someone with an objective eye."

Guin wanted to get back to the condo to type up her notes, but she could hear the anxiety in Shelly's voice.

"Sure," she said. "I'll be right over."

"You sure everything looks okay?" Shelly asked for a third time.

"Everything is gorgeous, Shell. Guaranteed to earn a ribbon, if not first place."

"Really, you think so?" she said, eyeing her mermaid jewelry.

Shelly had found a bust and had made it look like a

mermaid's torso and head, then adorned it with an exquisite necklace made up of over a dozen different kinds of shells, along with matching earrings and a shell crown.

"I wouldn't say so if I didn't mean it," said Guin.

"Thanks. Your opinion means a lot. So, are you going to stop by the Community House tomorrow?"

Tuesday was the day that exhibitors dropped off their entries.

"I'm not sure. Probably. Do you need some help?"

"I should be okay," said Shelly. "Just wondering if you would be there."

"I'll definitely be at the award ceremony and preview Wednesday. You going?"

"Wouldn't miss it," said Shelly. "Though I'll be devastated if I don't win a ribbon."

"Well, that's not going to happen," said Guin.

"You really think I have a chance?" asked Shelly.

"This from the woman who got into the big downtown Naples art show? People love your jewelry, Shelly!"

"My jewelry, yes. But this is the Sanibel Shell Show, the most prestigious shell show of them all. Have you seen some of these Artistic exhibits? People spend years putting together a single sailor's valentine."

"But you're not entering a sailor's valentine. And I bet no one else is entering a mermaid complete with jewelry."

"I hope not," said Shelly.

"I've gotta go," said Guin, wanting to get back to work. "I'll see you tomorrow or else Wednesday."

"Okay," said Shelly.

They exchanged kisses, then Shelly walked Guin out.

CHAPTER 23

When she got back to the condo, Guin spent a few minutes petting the cats, who acted as though they had been left alone for a week instead of less than seven hours. Then she texted Sam, asking her to give her a call when she had a minute.

She debated whether to call the detective, but her fingers had already made the decision for her. As soon as the operator had answered, Guin asked to be put through to Detective O'Loughlin.

"The detective's in a meeting," the operator replied. "Would you like to leave a message?"

"Just put me through to his voicemail."

Guin left a message, then sent him a text for good measure, asking him if he had received the results from the autopsy and letting him know she planned to talk to Denny.

She put down her phone and looked out the window. It was a beautiful afternoon, and there was a foursome on the fairway below. She watched as they took turns hitting their shots.

"What do you think, Flora, should I take up golf?" she asked the multicolored cat, who was lounging on Guin's bed.

Flora gazed at Guin and yawned.

"Yeah, I think I might find it a bit boring, too."

She stared out the window again. A minute later, her phone started buzzing. She went to grab it, hoping it was the detective. But it was Sam.

"Thanks for giving me a call," said Guin.

"No problem," said Sam. "What's up?"

"Is Denny still there?" Guin asked.

"Yeah, why? You want to get his autograph?"

Guin wasn't sure if Sam was teasing her.

"No, I need to speak with him, about CiCi."

"About CiCi?"

"Yes."

There was a pause.

"You still there?" Guin asked.

"Sorry. Why do you need to speak to Denny about CiCi? He barely knew her."

"I know, but I received some new information, and I need to ask him a couple of questions. Would it be okay if I came over there?"

"We're kind of busy…"

"I promise, it should only take a few minutes," said Guin. "I really need to speak with him, Sam."

Sam sighed.

"Fine. But I don't know what Denny could possibly tell you."

"Thanks," said Guin. "I'll be there at…" She glanced down at her clock. "Does five work?"

"Fine, we'll see you then."

It was nearly three. If she concentrated, Guin could get her notes typed up before she headed to Sam's to meet with Denny.

Before she knew it, it was 4:30. Guin had not heard back from the detective and thought about texting him again. She ultimately decided not to. After all, there was a fine line between being persistent and being a pest. If she hadn't heard back from him the following morning, though, she would follow up.

She parked the Mini in Sam's driveway and rang the doorbell. A minute later, Rita opened the door.

"Thanks for letting me stop by," said Guin.

"Did we have a choice?" said Rita, clearly not in a good mood.

"Is your brother around?" asked Guin.

"He's on the lanai," Rita replied.

"Okay if I go speak with him?"

"Be my guest," said Rita, gesturing out back.

Guin made her way to the lanai. Denny was seated on a lounge chair, playing his guitar, his eyes closed. Guin stood there and listened for several minutes.

"That was amazing," Guin said, when he had stopped.

"Practice makes perfect," he said, smiling up at her.

Guin had to admit, the man had charisma in spades. She could see how a young woman like CiCi could have been seduced.

"Okay if I ask you a few questions?"

"Ask away," said Denny.

"Where were you Thursday morning?" asked Guin.

"Here," said Denny.

"All morning?" said Guin.

"I—" Denny began, then stopped.

"Don't let me interrupt."

Guin turned to see the detective walking towards them.

"Detective," said Guin.

The detective was looking over at Denny.

"You were saying, Mr. Sumner?"

"Fine," he said, his smile gone. "I couldn't sleep. So I got up and went for a walk."

"Where?" asked Guin.

"I don't know. Down to the beach."

"Which beach?" asked the detective.

"Whatever the one is that's closest to here."

The detective was giving Denny that look of his.

"And what time did you go for this walk?"

"I don't know," Denny replied. "Maybe six-thirty?"

"And what time'd you get back?" asked the detective.

"I don't know. Around seven-thirty?"

"If it was dark, how did you see?" asked Guin.

"Flashlight on my phone," he replied.

"But you didn't check the time?" Guin asked.

"Should I have?" he replied.

"Were you alone or did someone meet you there?" asked Guin.

Denny turned his attention to her.

"I was alone," said Denny.

"So CiCi didn't pick you up and take you with her to Silver Key?" Guin asked.

"No," said Denny, not looking at Guin.

"Tell me what happened between you and Ms. Rawlins Wednesday evening," said the detective.

"Nothing," said Denny. "She took me sightseeing, we watched the sun set, then she brought me back here, like I told you the last time you asked."

"Aren't you leaving out something?" asked Guin.

"Like what?" asked Denny.

"Like the part about you trying to rape her," said Guin.

Denny laughed.

"Rape her?"

He looked from Guin to the detective.

"You're kidding, right?"

The detective didn't look like he was kidding.

"Since when is kissing considered rape?"

"So you don't deny it?" Guin asked.

"I don't deny kissing her. And, for the record, she kissed me back. She was practically begging for more, but I'm not that kind of guy."

He was looking up at Guin and the detective now.

"Despite what the tabloids may say about me, I've never forced a woman. In fact, I'm usually trying to pry them off me."

"So what happened after Ms. Rawlins asked you to stop?" asked the detective.

"I stopped," Denny replied. "Then we drove back here."

"And did you text CiCi later?" Guin asked him.

"I did. I could tell she was upset. I told her I was sorry and hoped we could still go shelling together the next morning."

"And what did she reply?" asked the detective.

"She said she'd have to think about it."

"And did she write to you again?" asked Guin.

"Yeah," he replied.

This was like pulling teeth, Guin thought.

"What did she say?" asked the detective.

"She said she was heading to Silver Key around six-thirty and, if I was up, I was welcome to join her."

"So, did you?" asked Guin.

"Did I what?" asked Denny.

"Join her," said Guin.

"No, but it wasn't for lack of trying. When I got up and couldn't fall back to sleep, I figured I'd walk over to Silver Key and meet up with CiCi."

"That's a pretty long walk," said the detective.

"Tell me about it," said Denny.

"It must be at least four miles from here to there," said Guin.

"So I found out," said Denny.

"So did you meet up with her?" asked Guin.

"No," Denny replied. "I made it to the beach, but I got kind of confused. So I asked these two ladies how far it was to Silver Key. When they told me, I turned around and headed back here."

Guin glanced at the detective. He was writing in his little notebook again.

"So you never made it to Silver Key," said the detective.

"Nope," said Denny. "Got back here and went right back to sleep."

"And you didn't hear from Ms. Rawlins again?"

"Nope," he said, picking up his guitar and strumming it.

"What about the ladies you ran into?" asked Guin. "Can they verify your story?"

Denny looked up at her and smiled.

"I like you," he said. "You're feisty."

Guin tried to keep her face in check.

"Answer the lady's question," said the detective, staring at Denny.

"I suppose," he replied.

Of course, finding these ladies would be like finding a needle in a haystack, or a wentletrap on Lighthouse Beach: difficult, but not impossible.

"You wouldn't have happened to catch their names…" said the detective.

"I think one of them was named Nancy," said Denny. "And I'm pretty sure the other one was named Bar or Barb."

He continued to strum on his guitar.

"What did they look like?" asked Guin.

He looked up at her.

"Medium height, short hair. Probably in their sixties or seventies. One of them was wearing a visor with a shell on it. The other one had on a shirt with shell on it. They said they were from the Midwest."

Guin sighed. That could describe hundreds of shellers on Sanibel.

The detective continued to look at Denny, who had closed his eyes and was playing something on his guitar.

"If you could indulge us another minute," said the detective, acidly.

Denny stopped playing and looked up at the detective.

"Shoot," he said.

"Can someone here verify when you returned?" asked the detective.

"Ask Sam or Rita," he replied.

"Okay," said the detective, putting away his notebook.

"We done?" asked Denny.

"For now," said the detective.

"Let me know if you have any more questions," said Denny.

He began playing his guitar, singing a few lines of a No Signal song about a guy who got dumped by the girl he adored.

The detective shook his head and headed back inside the house. Guin followed.

CHAPTER 24

"Well?" asked Guin, after she had shut the slider to the lanai behind them.

The detective gave her a look.

"Do you believe him?" Guin asked.

Before the detective could reply, Rita appeared.

"You done?" she asked.

"For now," said the detective. "Though I'd like to ask you and Ms. Hutchins and Ms. Harvey a few questions while I'm here."

"Marta left already," said Rita. "But you can talk to me and Sam."

Guin made to follow the detective.

"Alone," said the detective.

"But," Guin protested.

The detective gave her a quelling look.

"Fine," Guin replied.

"You can let her tag along, detective," said Rita, clearly amused. "We've got nothing to hide."

Guin gave the detective a triumphant look.

"Fine," said the detective. "But not a word out of you, Ms. Jones."

Guin raised her right hand to her mouth and made a zipping motion with her fingers.

Rita escorted them to the back bedroom.

"Wow," said Guin, looking at the fountain. "Is it done?"

The fountain shimmered in the late afternoon light.

Rita smiled.

"I sure hope so," she said. "We've got to get it to the museum tomorrow."

Guin looked around.

"Where's Sam?"

Just then she heard a toilet flush. Sam emerged from the bathroom a few seconds later.

"Greetings," she said. "To what do we owe the honor?"

"The detective here wants to ask us a few more questions," Rita explained.

"Ask away, detective," said Sam.

"I understand your boyfriend had gone sightseeing with the murder victim the night before," said the detective.

"That's correct," said Sam. "But you knew that already."

"Did he go out again with her the following morning?"

"No, he was here with me," said Sam.

The detective gave her one of his looks, the one that made you feel like he could find the piece of information he was looking for with his mind.

"All night and morning?" the detective asked her.

"He was next to me when I went to bed and when I got up to pee later," Sam responded.

The detective continued to look at her.

Sam sighed.

"Fine, he wasn't in bed when I got up. But I saw him in the kitchen."

"Did you happen to see your brother early Thursday?" the detective asked Rita.

"How early are we talking about?"

"Before eight-thirty," said the detective.

"Yeah, I saw him."

"Where?" asked the detective.

"In the kitchen," said Rita.

"Did you speak with him?" asked the detective.

"No, it was early, and I hadn't had my coffee yet."

"And where were you early Thursday morning, Ms. Sumner?"

"As I told you before, here."

"Can anyone vouch for that?" asked the detective.

"Other than Denny?" asked Rita. "No. Sam was asleep when I got up and Marta didn't arrive until a little after eight-thirty."

The detective had taken out his little notebook and was jotting down notes.

"You don't think I had anything to do with CiCi's death, do you?" asked Rita, staring at the detective.

"Just verifying everyone's whereabouts that morning," replied the detective. "You say Ms. Harvey arrived a little after eight-thirty?"

"Yeah, I remember glancing over at the clock. She brought muffins, baked them herself."

The detective was writing again. Guin tried to sneak a peek but was unable to get a close enough look.

"What do you know about Susan Hastings?" asked the detective.

"The real estate agent?" asked Rita.

The detective nodded.

"What about her?" asked Sam.

"I understand she approached CiCi at Bailey's last week," said the detective. "Asked her about the project and offered to hire her as a private chef."

"Oh she did, did she?" said Rita.

"Maybe we should have just let her volunteer, Rita," said Sam. "She was clearly determined to find out what we were working on."

"And have her blab it all over the island?" said Rita. "No way."

"Do you happen to know if CiCi said anything to her about the project?" Sam asked the detective.

"As far as we know, no."

"She was a good kid," said Rita, wistfully. "Now that real estate agent, on the other hand…"

"Did you ask her about CiCi?" Sam asked the detective.

"We did," said the detective.

"And?" asked Rita.

"We're investigating."

That seemed to be the detective's pat line. But Guin had also been wondering about Susan. Could she have killed CiCi? Guin couldn't picture it, but maybe it had been an accident. What if they had gotten into an argument and Susan, in a moment of insanity or rage, had grabbed the horse conch and hit CiCi over the back of the head with it, then panicked and ran away? She could almost picture it.

"Ms. Jones?" said the detective.

"Hmm…?" said Guin, startled out of her reverie.

"I asked if you had any questions," said the detective.

Guin had to work hard to keep her jaw from falling open.

"Questions?" she said, looking at the detective.

"Yes," said the detective, "questions. You know, those things you are so fond of asking."

Guin had had a dozen questions she had wanted to ask. But they had all suddenly evaporated under the detective's gaze.

"I… uh…" she said.

Rita and Sam waited patiently.

"I know I asked you this before," said Guin, trying to focus, "but did CiCi ever mention anyone here on Sanibel who she was friends with or had an issue with? Maybe an ex-boyfriend or another sheller?"

"No, not that I can recall," said Sam.

"Though there was that boy," said Rita. "I think he was a friend of hers. She mentioned him a few times."

"Do you recall his name?" asked Guin.

"Was it Scott?" said Rita, looking over at Sam.

"Sounds familiar," said Sam.

"Did you ever meet him?" Guin asked.

"No," said Rita. "CiCi knew better than to bring anyone around here."

"Did she happen to mention anyone else?" asked Guin.

"Not really," said Rita. "Mostly, she talked about school and food." Rita smiled. "Mostly food."

"She was always asking us what we liked to eat," said Sam, smiling back at Rita.

"I do miss her cooking," said Rita. "She would have made a great chef."

The detective finished writing, then put away his notebook.

"Thank you for your time, ladies."

"That's it?" said Guin.

"For now," said the detective.

He started to leave. Guin followed him.

"Yes, Ms. Jones?"

"I understand you received the autopsy report. Would you send me a copy?"

"It's as we thought: blunt force trauma to the back of the head."

"Anything else?" asked Guin.

"Like what?" replied the detective.

"Had she been raped?"

The detective regarded her for several seconds.

"No."

Thank God for that, thought Guin.

"Anything else you'd like to know?" asked the detective.

There were a lot of things Guin wanted to know, but now was not the time or place.

"Will you be at the preview Wednesday?"

"I will."

"Making sure nothing gets stolen?" Guin asked.

The detective made a face.

"If there's nothing else, Ms. Jones…"

"I'm good," said Guin.

"Then I wish you a pleasant evening."

He turned and Guin watched as he made his way down the hall. She thought about following him out but returned to the bedroom instead.

"You're back," said Rita.

"Just for a minute," Guin replied. "So you're good to move the sculpture over to the museum tomorrow?"

"Yup," said Rita.

"Good luck," said Guin, gazing at the shell fountain.

"Thanks," said Rita.

"Still okay for me to stop by when you're setting it up?"

"As long as you stay out of the way," said Rita.

"I'll do my best," said Guin, smiling.

CHAPTER 25

The next morning Guin went for a run. She hadn't gone for a run in ages, not since Ris had gone off to Southeast Asia. But this morning she felt she had to. She had woken up feeling anxious and hadn't been able to shake the feeling. So she had dug out a pair of running shorts and a sports bra, laced up a pair of sneakers, and headed out.

By the time she got back, she felt much better, and much sweatier. She glanced at the clock on the microwave. She had been gone nearly an hour.

"Not bad," she said, smiling.

She poured herself a glass of water and drank it down in a few gulps. She thought about making some coffee but decided she needed a shower first.

A little while later, freshly showered and dressed, she fixed herself some coffee and eggs and stood at the counter, staring out past the lanai.

"Another beautiful day in paradise," she said with a smile.

She reached for her phone and realized she hadn't brought it into the kitchen.

She padded back to the bedroom and found it on her night table, off. She turned it on and entered her password, then walked back to the kitchen as it started up. No sooner had it booted than it began to buzz and flash.

"I should have waited until I finished breakfast," Guin sighed. "Well, too late now."

She took another sip of coffee, then she opened her messages. There were texts from Shelly, Ris, and Lance. She opened Lance's first.

"Call me when you get this," he had written late the night before. "I have big news!"

Guin ignored the rest of her messages and called him.

"Hello?" came a sleepy voice.

"Am I waking you up?" she asked.

"I had to get up sometime," he replied.

"You said to call when I got your message. What's up? What's the big news?"

"Remember that Paris agency I told you about, the one that wanted to work with us?"

"Vaguely," said Guin.

"Well, it's happening. Owen and I are headed to Paris next month! And we want you to come with us!"

"What?" said Guin.

"Owen and I are going to Paris in April, and we want you to join us there," Lance repeated.

"I just got back from Australia. No way is Ginny going to let me fly off to Paris for a week."

"It's a once-in-a-lifetime opportunity!" said Lance. "How can you say no? The Paris agency is renting us an apartment in the Sixth, two bedrooms, two baths. There's even a kitchen. Though I doubt we'll be doing much cooking. And I'll pay your airfare."

"That's very generous of you, Lance, but I can't accept."

"Why not?"

"You know why not."

Lance rolled his eyes.

"I can see you rolling your eyes," said Guin.

"I always knew you were a witch," he retorted.

"Seriously, Guinivere, come. It's April in Paris! How can you resist?"

Guin had to admit, she was finding it hard to.

"At least think about it," said Lance. "I have loads of frequent flyer miles. Think how much fun we would have!"

"Okay, I'll think about it," said Guin. "How long are you and Owen going to be gone for?"

"At least a month."

"Does mom know?"

"Not yet. I'm worried that when I tell her she's going to insist on visiting. That's why I need you there."

"Aha!" said Guin. "I knew you had an ulterior motive!"

"Pshaw," said Lance. "Okay, maybe having you bunk in the second bedroom would ensure that mother stays in a hotel, but Owen and I really do want you to stay with us. Just think of it, Guin! The food, the sights, the clothes, the food…"

"All right, all right," said Guin, laughing. "You have me craving a croissant and a café au lait."

"So you'll do it?" asked Lance.

"I said I'd think about it," said Guin.

"Just don't take too long."

"Hey, I need to go," said Guin. "It's Shell Show week."

"Ooh! Shell Show week! I wouldn't want to keep the shells waiting."

"Very funny," said Guin, making a face.

It was hard to explain to non-shell people how important the Sanibel Shell Festival was to the thousands of avid shell collectors who came from around the country—the world—to attend the three-day show.

"I love you anyway," she added.

"And I love you, which is why I want you to come to Paris," said Lance.

"I said I'll think about it," said Guin.

"Fine. Gotta run. Talk to you this weekend."

"Bye," said Guin.

She ended the call and scrolled through the rest of her messages.

Shelly wanted to know if Guin would be stopping by the Community House to check out the exhibits and let it be known that she planned on dropping off her bejeweled mermaid around 9:30. And Ris had written to wish her a good morning and sent her the blowing-a-kiss emoji. She texted him back the same emoji and wrote to Shelly that she had decided not to go to the Community House that day but said she would see her the following day at the preview.

She then checked her email. No news about CiCi. Not that she was really expecting any. Though there was an email from Ginny. She wanted to know if Guin could attend the reception for the new art exhibit opening at the Phillips Gallery at BIG ARTS that Saturday. The art reporter had some kind of family emergency and was now unable to attend. Would Guin go in her stead?

"Sure," Guin wrote back. "Happy to. Just send me the details."

She scrolled through the rest of her emails. Then she opened up Instagram, looking at all the new photos that had been posted overnight. She followed a dozen or so shellers. They always seemed to find the most beautiful shells. Looking at their photos made Guin a bit jealous. Still, she couldn't help looking. One day, she said to herself, I'm going to find something exciting, like a junonia or a Scotch bonnet, or a lion's paw. Then I'm going to take a picture and post it on Instagram.

She finished her coffee, which had gone cold, then walked down the hall to her office/bedroom.

By mid-afternoon, Guin was feeling restless.

"What the heck," she said, staring out the window. "May as well head over to the Community House and check out the exhibits."

She glanced over at Flora and Fauna, who were asleep on the bed, then grabbed her notebook and pen and headed out the door.

She entered the Community House, saying hello to the various volunteers who were helping with setup, and made her way to the Scientific area. There were dozens of exhibits, many elaborately displayed. Everything from alphabet cones to zigzag scallops. Guin marveled at the diversity of the local sea life and the good luck and creativity of the exhibitors who had found the shells. She took photos of her favorites and scribbled some notes. When she was done, she made her way to the Artistic division.

There were over a half-dozen sailor's valentines and at least as many floral arrangements, as well as decorative objects and pieces of furniture made out of shells. Guin made her way down each aisle, admiring the exhibits. She paused when she reached the jewelry section.

Shelly had outdone herself. Her mermaid jewelry literally stood head and shoulders above the rest of the jewelry on display. No doubt what Shelly had intended. Her mermaid bust, with its flowing sea-green hair, decked out in jewels from the sea—coquinas and tellins in yellows, pinks, reds, and purples, as well as purple, pink, and orange scallops, and zigzags, and jingles that reflected the light—was dazzling.

"Guin!"

Guin turned to see her friend Bonnie, the treasurer of the Shell Club, coming toward her.

"I was wondering if you'd be here."

"I wasn't planning on stopping by today, but…"

She looked around the room.

"I know! How can you stay away? Aren't the exhibits this year impressive?"

"They are," said Guin. "I don't know how the judges are supposed to choose. They're all amazing."

"I know," said Bonnie. "Did you see my exhibit over in the Scientific room?"

"Which one is yours?" asked Guin.

"Come, let me show you."

She took Guin's arm and walked her back to the other room.

"Come to see my exhibits, have you?"

Guin winced. It was Marty Nesbitt, the head of one of the Facebook shelling groups. Marty was convinced that Guin had a crush on him. Though where he got that idea, Guin didn't know.

"Which one is yours, Marty?" Guin politely asked him.

"Guess!" he said.

Guin looked around.

"Is it in this aisle?" she asked him.

"It is!" he said, grinning.

Guin eyed the various displays.

"I give up," she said, too tired to play Marty's games.

"Ah, come on," he said. "You've barely looked!"

"Fine, give me a hint."

"If you had a cat, she might give it two paws up."

Guin looked around. There was a collection of lion's paws a few feet away.

"That one, over there?" she asked, pointing to the lion's paws.

"That's it!" said Marty, doing a little jig.

Guin had to admit, it was an impressive collection.

"They're gorgeous," said Guin, meaning it. "You find all these yourself?"

"What's that supposed to mean?" asked Marty. "Of course I did!"

"And which is your exhibit?" Guin asked Bonnie, who had patiently been waiting.

"Over there," she said, pointing to a collection of lace murexes.

"They're beautiful, Bonnie!" Guin said. She peered closer. "The detail on them is amazing."

There were a half-dozen lace murexes in a row, ranging from around an inch to three inches.

"I just love lace murexes," she said.

"Me, too," said Guin, admiring them.

"And I have two other exhibits!" said Marty. "You wanna check them out?"

"Thanks, Marty, but I have to be heading out."

"Will you be at the museum for the judging tomorrow? I know my babies are going to win big. Wouldn't want you to miss out!"

"I'll be there," said Guin, suddenly wishing she wouldn't be.

"Okay, see you then," he said.

He continued to admire his handiwork as Bonnie escorted Guin to the exit.

"He means well," said Bonnie.

"I know," said Guin. "And I have no doubt his exhibits will win something. He can just be a bit…"

"Over-enthusiastic?" suggested Bonnie.

"Yeah," said Guin.

They had reached the entrance.

"You hanging around?" Guin asked.

"Yeah, I'm on duty till five-thirty."

Guin glanced up at the clock. It was nearly five.

"I'll see you tomorrow over at the museum," said Guin.

"See you tomorrow," said Bonnie.

CHAPTER 26

Guin turned to go into the Bailey-Matthews National Shell Museum parking lot, but she was stopped at the entrance by a police officer.

"Sorry, ma'am, the museum's closed to visitors."

"I'm with the *Sanibel-Captiva Sun-Times*," said Guin. "They're expecting me."

The police officer hesitated.

"I'm covering the unveiling for the paper. Guin Jones."

The police officer stepped away and spoke into his walkie-talkie. A minute later he returned.

"You can go ahead, Ms. Jones. Parking's over there," he said, pointing to the right.

"Thanks," said Guin.

The police officer removed one of the cones so Guin could enter.

She parked the Mini and walked towards the museum. There was a cluster of people gathered not too far from the entrance. Guin headed over and immediately spied Olive, the director of the museum; Lorna, the assistant director; and George, the head of operations.

"Hey," she said, walking up to them.

"You covering the big unveiling for the paper?" asked Lorna.

"Yup," said Guin. "Got the exclusive."

"Suzy must be furious," said Lorna, a small smile playing across her lips.

"So I hear," said Guin.

She looked around.

"I'm surprised she didn't find a way to sneak in."

"We hired extra security," said Olive.

"I was wondering about the policeman," said Guin. "Probably a good idea. How's it going?"

"See for yourself," said Olive.

Guin watched as a half-dozen men began to assemble the fountain under Rita's supervision.

"How long do you think it will take?" Guin asked.

"I reckon several hours," said George, watching the men work. "Then they have to test it."

"Careful!" said Rita.

Guin turned to see what was going on. Sam and Marta were standing off to the side.

She continued to watch for several minutes. Then she turned to Lorna.

"I'm going to shove off."

"You're not going to stick around, see it all assembled?" Lorna asked her.

"I'll be back for the official unveiling tomorrow, with the photographer. You can let me know if I missed anything."

She said goodbye to the rest of the group, then made her way back to the Mini. The officer moved the cone when he saw her approach and waved goodbye.

Guin got up Wednesday and stared at the ceiling. She thought about going for a run again, then nixed the idea. Maybe a beach walk.

She turned on her phone, then headed to the bathroom. When she got back, her message light was flashing. There were several texts from Shelly (a daily occurrence), who was clearly anxious about today's judging.

"You want to go for a beach walk?" Guin texted her.

"OMG yes!" Shelly typed back. "When?"

"Want to meet me at Bowman's at 7?" Guin wrote.

"See you then!" Shelly replied.

Guin threw on some clothes, then headed into the kitchen. The cats followed her.

"Hold your horses," Guin told Fauna, who was meowing and pawing her.

She grabbed a can of cat food and scooped the contents into the two cat bowls. Fauna and Flora made a beeline for the food.

Guin shook her head, then looked at the clock on the microwave.

"I'll be back in a bit," she called to the cats, who, as usual, ignored her.

She then grabbed her fanny pack and her keys and headed out the door.

"Do you really think I could win for shell jewelry?" Shelly was asking Guin for the second (or was it third?) time.

"I wouldn't have said it if I didn't mean it," Guin replied. "Say, did someone from the paper contact you?"

Guin had told Ginny about Shelly's mermaid jewelry and had suggested Shelly as one of the people the paper was planning to profile for its special Shell Show edition.

"Yeah, a woman named Kathy, with a K, came by the house the other day and took a bunch of pictures of me and the jewelry."

"There you go!" said Guin.

"Yeah, but it's not the same thing as getting a ribbon."

"Well, I'm not a judge, but I don't see how you can lose," said Guin.

Shelly gave Guin's arm a squeeze.

"You're a good friend, Guin. So what's up with you? Are the police any closer to catching that girl's killer?"

Guin had told Shelly about CiCi, and Shelly was understandably upset, her own daughter being not much older than CiCi.

"As far as I know, no. And we're running out of suspects. Though I don't trust Sam's boyfriend—"

"The guitar player?"

"Yeah, and Suzy's definitely hiding something."

"Do you really think she could have killed that girl?" asked Shelly.

"It's possible," said Guin. "Though I just can't imagine Susan clubbing anyone with a giant horse conch. Too messy."

"And the guitar player?" asked Shelly.

"He admitted to being on the beach that morning."

"There you go!" said Shelly.

"But he was on the wrong beach."

"The wrong beach?"

"He thought you could walk to Silver Key from West Gulf. But when he found out how far it was, he turned around. Or so he said."

"Did anyone see him?" asked Shelly.

"Supposedly two shellers, but good luck tracking them down."

"That poor girl," said Shelly, shaking her head. "Here I am worried about winning some silly award when a young woman has been murdered. What's the world coming to?"

They continued to walk along the beach for another half hour, looking for shells. Then they turned around, stopping when they reached the entrance.

"I should get back," Guin said.

"Yeah, me, too," said Shelly. "Thanks for coming out—and for listening."

"No problem," said Guin, smiling at her friend.

They walked together to the parking lot.

"I'll see you at the award ceremony," said Guin.

"Will Ris be there?" asked Shelly. "I didn't see him at the Community House yesterday."

"Oh?" said Guin.

He had told her he would be helping out.

"Maybe he was taking a bathroom break or on a call when you dropped off your piece," said Guin.

"Maybe," said Shelly. "But I was there for a while. Anyway, I'll see you guys later."

They said their goodbyes and Guin headed home.

It was time to go to the museum for the big unveiling. Guin hadn't heard from Ris all day, and he hadn't returned her texts, which was odd. Probably his interviews took longer than expected. Oh well, she'd see him at the museum.

She did a quick check of herself in the mirror—double-checking that her makeup and hair were okay. (She had decided to wear her strawberry-blonde hair, which was quite curly, down.) Then she turned from side to side, admiring how her "mermaid dress," as Shelly referred to it, flowed around her legs.

A quick stop in the kitchen to feed the cats, then she was out the door.

Guin had made sure to get to the museum early, in order to get a parking spot. The photographer, Glen, who was new, would be meeting her there. She had only met Glen once and hadn't really gotten a chance to chat with him. Per Ginny, he was originally from Fort Myers, but he had been living up in New York until recently.

Guin made her way to the museum and spied the fountain, which was surrounded by a metal barricade and covered with a tarp. At least no one had stolen it overnight. As she approached, she saw George.

"Hey," she said, giving him a smile. "All set for the big reveal?"

"As ready as I'll ever be," he replied.

"How late were you here till last night?" she asked him.

"You don't want to know," said George. "Ms. Hutchins and her assistant wanted to make sure everything was perfect for the unveiling."

Guin looked around for them.

"They're inside," he said, following Guin's gaze. "Olive's going to introduce them when we're ready."

"Ah," said Guin.

People started to trickle in and within thirty minutes the area around the sculpture was packed with eager shell lovers who had paid extra to attend the Judges and Awards Reception and Preview. Still no sign of Ris, though.

"Guin!"

At the sound of her name, Guin turned and spied Glen, the photographer, making his way through the crowd.

"Sorry I'm late. I forgot about Sanibel traffic."

"No worries," said Guin. "They haven't unveiled the sculpture yet."

Guin continued to scan the crowd for Ris, but there was no sign of him. Maybe he was inside or at the Community House? She checked her phone for the third (or was it fourth?) time. Nothing. She was about to try calling him when Olive and Lorna appeared at the top of the steps.

"Ladies and gentlemen," said Olive, in a loud, clear voice. "Welcome! This year, as part of the annual Sanibel Shell Festival, we have a very special treat for you. As you may know, the City of Sanibel, together with the Shell Museum, commissioned renowned shell artist Samantha Hutchins to design a commemorative sculpture to be placed outside the museum, to celebrate Sanibel being the seashell capital of the United States. And tonight we will be unveiling it."

A few seconds later, the doors of the museum opened, and Sam and Rita appeared.

"Ladies and gentlemen, I give you shell artist extraordinaire, Samantha Hutchins!"

There was thunderous applause from the audience as Olive introduced Sam.

"Sam, would you do the honors?" said Olive, smiling at her.

"Thank you, Olive," said Sam. "First of all, I would like to thank the museum and the City of Sanibel for bestowing this great honor upon me. Thank you, Mr. Mayor, and thank you, Olive, and the museum board."

She smiled at them, then turned back to face the crowd.

"I would also like to thank my project manager and dear friend, Rita Sumner, without whose help there would be no sculpture."

Rita smiled as the crowd applauded her.

"And I would like to thank the volunteers who helped us gather all the shells for the project."

There was another round of applause.

"And I would especially like to thank Marta Harvey and Caroline Rawlins, who, unfortunately, could not be here with us this evening. This sculpture is dedicated to you, CiCi."

Sam brushed away a tear, then regained her composure.

"Now, gentlemen," she said to several men who had positioned themselves around the fountain. "If you would be so kind."

The men carefully removed the tarp, revealing the fountain.

Gasps were heard all around, then applause. And for good reason. The fountain was amazing. Even more beautiful than Guin remembered it. Though there was no water flowing and no lights.

"Ladies and gentlemen," said Sam. "I give you the Fountain of Life!"

She raised her hand, no doubt a signal to turn on the fountain, but nothing happened.

She turned and looked at Rita, who shook her head.

"Ladies and gentlemen," said Sam, "we seem to be experiencing a technical difficulty. If you will just give us a couple of minutes, I'm sure we can sort this out."

There was murmuring in the crowd as Sam and Rita conversed quietly. Then Rita went over to George. Guin watched as Rita said something to George, who nodded, then disappeared. As they had been talking, Sam had made her way down to the fountain and had stepped inside to inspect something. A few seconds later, water began flowing out of the dolphin's mouth and the fountain lit up, startling Sam.

The crowd oohed and aahed as the fountain burbled to life.

Then Guin heard someone scream. It was Sam.

"Get her out of there!" shrieked Rita, as smoke started rising from the fountain.

One of the men who had removed the tarp reached in and grabbed Sam, pulling her out of the fountain.

She collapsed in his arms.

"Turn off the fountain!" Rita shouted to George, who had reappeared.

A minute later, the water stopped flowing and the lights on the fountain went out.

The man who had grabbed Sam carried her over to a nearby bench. Rita had rushed over to where she was lying, accompanied by Olive and Lorna.

"Is she okay?" several people murmured.

Guin watched the scene open-mouthed as Glen took photos. She made her way over to where he was standing.

"Did you get all of that?" she asked him.

He nodded his head.

"What happened?" Guin asked.

"I'm pretty sure she was electrocuted," Glen replied.

"Electrocuted? But they tested the fountain last night. It was fine."

"I'm no expert, but that's what it looked like to me," Glen said.

Suddenly, the crowd parted.

"Everyone, move away from the fountain."

Guin recognized that voice.

"Police. Step away from the fountain," repeated the commanding voice to the throng of onlookers.

It was Detective O'Loughlin. She had forgotten he was going to be there.

"Everyone!" shouted Olive. "If I could please have your attention. If you could all go inside. The judges should be ready to announce the awards."

The crowd seemed torn.

"Please!" called Olive. "We need to proceed with the Judges and Awards Ceremony. Come inside and let the police do their job."

With the help of Lorna and George and the officers on the scene, people began filing into the museum.

Soon, everyone was inside, except for Detective O'Loughlin and his officers; a man who was seeing to Sam (no doubt a doctor who happened to have been there for the unveiling); Rita; Guin; Glen; George; and the men who had helped pull off the tarp.

Guin went over to where Sam was being administered to, Rita by her side.

"Will she be okay?" Guin asked.

"Yes, fortunately," said the man examining Sam. "She's a very lucky young woman."

"I don't understand," said Rita. "We tested everything last night. Everything was working fine."

Sam opened her eyes.

"Rita?"

"You okay?" Rita asked her.

"I feel like I was being fried," Sam replied. "What happened?"

"That's what we're trying to find out."

Rita turned and looked over at the fountain, where the detective was speaking with the men who had pulled off the tarp.

"I'll be back in a minute," said Rita. "I want to have a little chat with the detective."

She hesitated.

"Go," said Sam. "I'll be fine. Just a little shell-shocked," she added, with a chuckle.

Rita made a face, then headed over to the fountain.

"Thank you for your help," Sam said to the man at her side. "I think I'm okay now."

She slowly sat up, though she looked quite pale.

"You take it easy," said the man. "If you feel dizzy or nauseous, or run a fever, get to the hospital."

"Will do," said Sam. "And thanks again."

He clasped her hands and nodded. Then he got up and joined the others inside the museum.

Sam watched him go, then frowned.

"I forgot to ask him his name."

"I'll find out and let you know," said Guin, who had stood nearby while the man had examined Sam. "I'm going to go chat with Rita, George, and the detective. Will you be okay?"

"Go," said Sam. "I'll be fine."

"I'll keep an eye on her," said Glen, smiling down at Sam.

"Thanks," said Guin.

Then she made her way back over to the fountain.

CHAPTER 27

Rita and Guin watched as the detective and one of his officers circled the fountain in opposite directions.

"Sir," called the officer.

The detective went over to the officer, a woman Guin didn't recognize.

Rita and Guin tried to get closer but were held off by the other officer.

"Sorry ladies," said the officer, a man in his late fifties by the looks of him.

"Please," said Rita. "I'm the project manager in charge of the fountain."

"Sorry, ma'am," said the officer.

Guin looked at the small brass nameplate he wore.

"Please, Officer Mancuso," said Guin. "We just want to speak with the detective for a minute."

She tried to catch the detective's eye. As if sensing her looking at him, the detective turned.

"Detective, a word!" Guin called over to him.

"Let them through," the detective told the officer.

Officer Mancuso allowed them through, and Rita and Guin hurried over to where he was standing.

"You find something, detective?" Guin asked.

"You say you checked the fountain last night?" the detective asked Rita, ignoring Guin.

"Yes, several times. Everything went off without a hitch."

"Did you check it again today?" asked the detective.

"No, there was no need. We had covered the fountain with the tarp and put up the barricade."

"So the fountain is exactly as you remember it?" asked the detective.

Rita glanced at the fountain.

"I can't vouch for it being *exactly* as we left it. It was pretty windy last night. But it looks pretty much like how we left it."

"So there were no exposed wires," said the detective.

"Exposed wires?" said Rita. "Absolutely not. All the wires had waterproof sheathing and were hidden."

"Well, one of the wires somehow became exposed," said the detective. "That's what caused the short circuit."

"That's not possible," said Rita.

"Show her," the detective instructed the female officer.

Rita followed the officer to a spot a couple of feet away.

"There," said the officer, pointing to a spot inside the base of the fountain.

Rita knelt down. Sure enough, a tile had been removed from the interior of the base, and the sheathing covering one of the wires had been cut away, leaving the wire exposed.

Rita continued to stare at the spot.

"I don't understand. I checked every inch of the fountain after we assembled it here. And we ran several tests. If there was a tile missing and a wire exposed, we would have noticed."

"Is it possible some animal could have gotten in and scratched away the tile?" asked Guin.

Rita frowned.

"I guess it's possible, but…"

It seemed pretty far-fetched to Guin, too.

"I think someone deliberately tried to sabotage the fountain," Guin declared.

"But why?" asked Rita.

"Maybe one of the people who had wanted to work on the fountain, who you had turned down, harbored a grudge?" Guin ventured.

Rita thought about that.

"We've had people damage our work before, but it was usually by accident. You know, someone trying to take a selfie," she said. "There was this one guy: Climbed right up on the thing. Broke off a big piece and sprained his ankle when he fell. Then blamed us."

She shook her head at the memory.

"Any cases of vandalism?" asked the detective.

"Well, a couple of people have tried to pluck shells off of a couple of our pieces," said Rita. "But nothing like this."

"Can you think of anyone who might have had a bone to pick with you or Ms. Hutchins?" asked the detective.

"Not off the top of my head."

"But you did turn down a lot of people who wanted to work on the sculpture," said Guin. "Maybe one of those people was so angry that they decided to get back at you, by damaging the fountain."

"That's a little extreme, don't you think?" said Rita.

"You don't know some of these shellers," said Guin.

"So no one tried to sneak a glimpse of the fountain?" asked the detective.

"Just Susan Hastings, our real estate agent," said Rita.

"Hey."

It was Sam. She was leaning on Glen, who didn't look happy.

"What are you doing up?" said Rita.

"I got tired of sitting. And the doctor said I was perfectly fine."

"I tried to tell her she needed to rest," said Glen, but…"

Rita made a face.

"I'm fine," said Sam. "So, what seems to be the problem? Did you figure out why I was nearly electrocuted? I thought we checked this thing last night."

"We did," said Rita. "But apparently someone managed to get under the tarp and remove one of the tiles and the sheathing around one of the wires."

Sam was staring at the fountain.

"Do you know of anyone who may have wanted to sabotage the fountain?" the detective asked her.

"I can't think of anyone, no," said Sam.

"I was just saying to Rita, it could have been one of the people you turned down," said Guin.

"We must have turned down over a dozen people," said Sam.

"More like four dozen," said Rita.

"You really think one of them would try to sabotage the fountain?"

"We don't know," said Guin.

"What about Susan Hastings?" said the detective. "I understand she wanted to work on the sculpture, but you turned her down. And she was caught snooping around the house."

"True," said Sam. "But do you really think she would sabotage the fountain? That seems a little extreme."

Guin glanced at the detective. She wondered if he was thinking what she was thinking.

"Did either of you happen to see Susan here, at the unveiling?" asked Guin.

"I saw her," said George.

Everyone turned to face him. Guin had completely forgotten he was there. But then George had a way of being invisible.

"Did you see her near the fountain?" asked the detective.

"There were lots of people near the fountain," George

replied. "And I think someone would have noticed if someone had bent down and removed a tile."

Good point, Guin thought.

"What about before the preview, like early this morning or last night?" asked Guin.

"It's possible," said George. "Though the fountain was under wraps, and we had put that barricade around it to keep folks away."

"What about the security camera?" asked the detective.

"We can check it, but I don't know if we'll see much," said George. "It's kind of far away. And if it happened at night, it was probably too dark to see anything."

"Send me the footage anyway," said the detective.

"Will do," said George.

"I'd like to see the footage, too," said Guin.

The detective shot her a look, which Guin ignored.

"Shouldn't you be inside, covering the award ceremony?" the detective asked her.

"I can get the list later," she retorted.

She looked over at Glen, who was standing off to the side.

"You should probably get inside, snap a few pics. If I miss you, I'll see you over at the Community House."

"Whatever you say, boss," he said with a smile, then headed into the museum.

"You two going to be okay?" Guin asked Rita and Sam.

"Yeah, we'll be fine," said Rita.

Guin glanced around.

"Where's Denny? Didn't he come with you?"

Rita made a face.

"He's back at the ranch. Said award ceremonies weren't his thing, unless he was the one winning an award."

"Well, I should go see what's going on inside," Guin said. She hesitated.

"Go, we'll be fine," said Sam. "Thanks for your concern." She paused. "Is this going to be in the paper?"

"Probably," Guin said. "Unfortunately, it's news."

Sam sighed.

"At least I hope you got a good picture of the fountain."

"I'm sure Glen did."

Guin then headed inside, in time to catch the end of the award ceremony.

CHAPTER 28

Guin glanced around the room, looking for Ris, but she didn't see him anywhere. She checked her phone. Nothing. It was possible he was over at the Community House, but it was still odd that she hadn't heard from him.

She waited until the last award was announced, then slipped out the door to try to get ahead of the crowd. There was an officer stationed by the fountain, which was once again surrounded by a metal barricade. But there was no sign of the detective. Or Sam or Rita.

Guin walked to her car. As she waited to turn onto Sanibel-Captiva Road, she spied people rushing to their cars. She had left just in time.

Guin was one of the first to arrive at the Community House, where the doors were still locked. She spied Officer Pettit just inside and waved at him. He smiled and waved back at her.

A few minutes later, Peggy, who must have been inside doing some last-minute checking, unlocked the doors and invited people to come in.

"You beat me," said Glen, finding Guin waiting for him in the lobby. "Anything in particular you want me to take photos of?"

"The winners, of course," said Guin, "and anything else that looks interesting to you."

"Got it," said Glen. "I'll shoot whatever I can and then let Ginny and Jasmine decide."

"Sounds like a plan," said Guin.

Glen disappeared inside. Guin followed him.

She debated which half to see first, Scientific or Artistic. As she was already in the Scientific room, she went with Scientific.

As she made her way down each row, reading the descriptions, she couldn't help but be impressed with the entries. Some were quite elaborate. She smiled as she passed by Bonnie's and Marty's entries. Both had won ribbons, as had Lenny's king's crown exhibit.

She ran into a few people she knew and exchanged pleasantries with them. Then she headed to the Artistic area.

She immediately spied Shelly's mermaid, which had been given a prime spot and had already attracted a small crowd.

"Guin!" Shelly called, waving for her to come over. "Can you believe it?"

Guin saw the first-place ribbon proudly displayed.

"Isn't it amazing?" said Shelly, beaming.

"Congratulations!" said Guin. "Totally deserved."

"I didn't see you or Ris at the big announcement," she said, taking Guin aside. "Is everything okay?"

"Everything's fine," Guin lied.

"What about Sam?" Shelly asked. "Is she okay? And how's the fountain?"

"She's okay, fortunately," said Guin. "I'll check on her tomorrow. And there's an officer guarding the fountain."

"They should have been guarding it before," said Shelly. Guin agreed.

"Hey, I need to go," said Shelly, seeing the crowd around her mermaid bust. "Catch you later?"

"Sure," said Guin.

"Over here, Mrs. Silverman."

It was Glen, come to take Shelly's picture.

"See, you're a star!" said Guin, smiling.

Shelly grinned, then shooed her away.

Guin continued down the aisle and stopped in front of a stunning bouquet of shell flowers, a centerpiece designed to adorn a table at a celebration. Next to it was a ribbon. And Marta.

"Congratulations!" said Guin. "It's beautiful."

"Thank you," said Marta.

"I'm amazed you had time to do it, what with the fountain."

Marta didn't reply.

"Were you over at the museum for the award ceremony?" Guin asked her. "I didn't see you there."

"No," Marta replied.

"So you don't know," said Guin.

"Know what?" asked Marta.

"Someone sabotaged the fountain and nearly killed Sam."

"Sabotaged?" said Marta.

"Yes, and nearly killed Sam."

"Is she okay?"

"Yes, she's fine. But it was pretty frightening. She could have been electrocuted."

"How is the fountain?"

"I think it'll be fine," Guin replied.

"Your turn!"

It was Glen.

Marta frowned.

"If you could just stand next to the flower arrangement," Glen directed.

Marta repositioned herself.

"That's great!" said Glen. "Now smile!"

Marta's lips curled slightly upward.

"Great!" said Glen.

He took a quick look at the photo on his camera.

"How about one more?"

Marta stood still and allowed Glen to take another photo.

"That should do it!" he said. "Thanks!"

Guin turned back to Marta.

"Do you know of anyone who might want to sabotage the fountain?" she asked Marta.

"Talk to that boyfriend of hers," Marta replied, curtly.

"You mean Sam's boyfriend, Denny?"

"Him," Marta replied.

"Why would Denny want to sabotage the fountain?" Guin asked, confused.

"He was jealous."

"Of the fountain?" asked Guin.

"Of the fountain, and her."

Interesting, thought Guin. She hadn't gotten that impression. But then again, she hadn't spent that much time around Denny.

"But why sabotage the fountain?"

Marta shrugged.

"To hurt her."

Guin tried to imagine Denny sneaking onto the museum grounds and vandalizing the fountain but was having a hard time. Still, she couldn't discount Marta's theory. Denny's fame had peaked, and Sam was a rising star. Maybe that bothered him. Though, again, she couldn't imagine he would purposely try to electrocute Sam.

"And the way he flirted with Caroline, right in front of Samantha."

Marta looked as though she had eaten something sour.

"Did Sam say anything?" asked Guin.

"Not in front of me," said Marta.

"Maybe she was used to it," said Guin. "After all, Denny is in a band. He must have women flirting with him all the time."

Marta's disapproval was obvious.

"He should not have been flirting. And she should not have encouraged him."

"You mean CiCi? You think she encouraged him?" asked Guin.

"Of course she did," said Marta. "I warned her, but…"

Before Guin could ask Marta another question, she was cut off.

"Your centerpiece is absolutely gorgeous!" said a woman. "How long did it take you to make it?"

"If you will excuse me," Marta said to Guin.

"Of course," said Guin.

Marta turned back to the woman and answered her question, which was followed by several more.

Guin listened, looking at the centerpiece as Marta spoke. She really was quite talented. She could understand why Rita and Sam had hired her.

Guin made her way around the rest of the Artistic exhibits, jotting notes and taking pictures of several of them.

There was still no sign of Ris, and she was starting to get worried.

She spied Peggy and made a beeline towards her.

"Hi Peggy," she said.

"Oh, hi, Guin," Peggy replied. "Great show this year, don't you think?"

"Definitely," said Guin. "Say, have you seen Dr. Hartwick? I thought he was supposed to be here."

"He was, but he left a message earlier, saying he was

unable to make it. He was very apologetic."

"Did he happen to say why?" asked Guin. It was very unlike Ris.

"No, only just that he was very sorry for the last-minute notice."

"Huh," said Guin, at a loss for words. "Well, thanks for letting me know."

That was odd, thought Guin. She checked her phone. Still no word from him. She sent him another text. "You okay?" she wrote. "I'm at the show."

Oof!

She was so busy looking down at her phone, she hadn't been paying attention to where she was walking and had collided into someone. She looked up—and saw the detective.

"Detective."

"Ms. Jones."

"Checking out the exhibits?" asked Guin, with a smile.

"Just making sure everything's okay."

"All good?" Guin asked.

"So far," replied the detective.

He glanced around.

"Dr. Hartwick not here?"

"No," said Guin.

"I would have thought he'd be front and center at an event like this," continued the detective.

"Something came up," said Guin.

She was finding it hard to look at the detective.

"You want to grab something to eat?" he asked her.

"Excuse me?" said Guin.

"You want to get some food? My shift is almost over."

Guin hesitated.

"You need to eat, don't you?"

As if on cue, her stomach let out a low growl.

"Shh!" she hissed at it. "Where were you thinking?" asked Guin.

"You been to the Sandbar?"

"Actually, no," said Guin. "It's over on West Gulf Drive, yes?"

"Yeah. Is that a problem?" asked the detective.

"Isn't that a bit far?"

"You got someplace you need to be?" asked the detective.

Guin hesitated. She should really head home and start typing her notes. But she was rather hungry.

"Fine, the Sandbar it is. I'll meet you over there."

"I can drive."

"What about the Mini?"

"You can pick it up afterwards."

Guin was about to protest but thought better of it.

"Fine. Give me a minute. I need to go find Glen, my photographer. Then we can go."

"I'll meet you outside," said the detective.

CHAPTER 29

"And then what happened?" Guin asked, leaning forward.

The detective took another sip of his beer and smiled.

"You should smile more often," said Guin, taking another sip of her wine and smiling back at him. It was her second glass, and she was feeling a bit lightheaded.

The two of them had shared some boom-boom shrimp and spring rolls to start and Guin was enjoying her black grouper while the detective worked on his ribeye steak. The detective, who was on his second beer, had been regaling her with tales of some of the wackier things he had been called on to investigate since working on Sanibel, a far cry from his prior beat in South Boston.

"The guy says, 'I didn't know she'd be back down during the summer.'"

"Seriously?!" said Guin. "So what did you say to him? Did you arrest him?"

"I said, 'Well, maybe next time someone asks you to house sit, don't invite your friends. And for God's sake, put some clothes on.'"

Guin let out a peal of laughter, her eyes tearing up.

"Did you tell the homeowner?" Guin asked, when she had recovered a bit.

"Had to. It was my civic and professional responsibility," said the detective, adopting a serious expression.

Guin found herself laughing again. The detective smiled at her and Guin felt herself blushing. She immediately chided herself. This was not a date. She had a boyfriend, even if he had gone AWOL. Speaking of Ris... She glanced down at her phone.

"Everything okay?" asked the detective.

"Yeah," said Guin. "Sorry."

They finished their main course and the server took away their plates. A minute later he was back.

"Could I interest the two of you in a little dessert or some coffee?"

"One piece of your key lime pie, two forks," said the detective.

"Would either of you like some coffee?" asked the server.

"I'll have a cup," said the detective.

He looked over at Guin.

"Do you have decaf cappuccino?" she asked.

"We sure do," said the server.

"That's what I'll have. Thanks."

A few minutes later, he brought over a slice of key lime pie.

"I'll be right back with your coffees."

"Have a bite," said the detective, sticking his fork into the pie and moving it toward Guin's mouth.

"I—" Guin began. But as soon as she had opened her mouth, the detective had popped the piece of pie inside.

"Good, isn't it?" he said, as Guin chewed.

She nodded.

"Very," she said, after she had swallowed.

The detective smiled again.

"So, what's the latest on the Rawlins' case?" Guin asked, as soon as he had leaned back in his chair.

The detective frowned.

"You find her killer yet?"

The detective was saved from answering by the server returning with their coffees.

"One coffee," he said, placing the cup in front of the detective. "And one decaf cappuccino," he added, placing the frothy drink in front of Guin.

"Thanks," Guin said.

They each took a sip.

"So?" said Guin.

"I don't like to mix business with pleasure," replied the detective.

Guin rolled her eyes.

"Have another bite of the pie," said the detective, scooping up a forkful and moving it towards Guin.

"Thanks, but I can feed myself."

"Suit yourself," he said, popping the piece of pie into his mouth. "Mmm," he said, smacking his lips. "You don't know what you're missing."

Guin dug her fork into the key lime pie and took a bite.

"Happy now?" she asked, her mouth full of pie.

The detective smiled again.

"So, do you think the incident with the fountain and CiCi's murder could be connected?" Guin asked.

The detective's expression turned serious.

"It seems to me there's a connection," said Guin. "I just need to find the missing piece."

"Why don't you work on your Shell Show story and leave the police work to the police?" said the detective.

Guin made a face.

"Come on, detective. You know I'm just doing my job."

The detective grunted.

"I hope Ginny isn't expecting me to file a story on the fountain tonight," Guin said. "Is it okay if I send her a quick text?"

"Be my guest," said the detective. "But you're missing out on some really good pie."

Guin shot Ginny a message, then took another sip of her cappuccino. Seconds later, her phone started buzzing. It was a text from Ginny.

"Have you seen Shellapalooza?" she had written.

Guin hurriedly typed the address on her phone. There on the Home page was a photo of the fountain, with Sam mid-shriek, and the headline "Fountain Fiasco!"

"Oh no," said Guin, scrolling down.

She handed her phone to the detective. He moved his fingers on the screen, no doubt enlarging the article, or one of the accompanying photos, and continued to frown. Then he handed the phone back to Guin.

"Would you excuse me for a minute?"

Guin nodded.

"I'll be right back."

Guin watched as he made his way to the exit.

She glanced back at her phone and re-read the article. She shook her head. What a poor sport Suzy was. Even with the malfunction, the fountain was amazing and would no doubt be fixed and running very soon.

She looked around. No sign of the detective. Wonder what's up? she mused. She closed her browser and checked her messages again. Still nothing from Ris. She was on the verge of texting him again when the detective reappeared.

"Everything okay?" she asked him.

"I need to go," he replied. All traces of the relaxed, happy dinner companion were now gone. "Check!" he called, catching the eye of the server.

A minute later, the server brought over the check and the detective handed him a credit card.

"May I at least leave the tip?" Guin asked.

The detective always insisted on paying when they went

out together, even if Guin was the one who had invited him.

The detective scowled.

"Fine," said Guin, with a sigh.

The detective signed the check and shoved the receipt into his pocket.

"Let's go," he said, getting up and heading toward the door.

Guin scurried to keep up with him. When they reached his car, he held the passenger-side door open for her and she climbed in.

"You okay?" she asked him, as they drove back to the Community House.

"Fine," he replied.

Guin kept silent after that.

A few minutes later, they had arrived back at the Community House. The detective parked next to the Mini.

"Thanks for dinner," Guin said.

"No problem," he replied.

Guin hesitated, then leaned over and gave him a quick kiss on the cheek. She had turned to go when the detective suddenly pulled her close and placed his lips against hers.

Guin could feel the urgency in his kiss, or maybe she was projecting.

The kiss went on for several seconds. Finally the detective released her.

"You should go," he said.

"Um, okay," said Guin, still a bit stunned. "Thanks for dinner."

The detective grunted and Guin got out of the car.

Guin arrived home a little while later. On the way, she had kept thinking about the detective. What had made him turn so gruff? Did it have something to do with Suzy's blog post?

The cats were there to greet her as she walked in the door.

"You guys behave while I was gone?"

Flora cocked her head and held up a paw while Fauna mewed.

Guin bent down and pet them.

"Sorry, team, I've got work to do."

She straightened up, got her phone from her bag, and headed to her office/bedroom.

She sat down at her desk and checked her phone. Still no word from Ris. Annoyed, she speed-dialed his number. The phone rang and rang, finally going into voicemail.

Could he have been in an accident? Should she start calling the area hospitals?

She made a face, then texted her brother.

"You there?"

"Present. What's up?" he typed back.

"Can you call me?" she replied.

A second later, her phone rang.

"What's up?" asked Lance. "Everything all right?"

"No," said Guin. "Ris is missing. And I kissed the detective."

Rats. She hadn't meant to mention the detective. It had just slipped out.

"You kissed the detective?" asked Lance. "And what do you mean by *missing*? You think he's with another woman?"

That thought had not actually occurred to Guin. But as soon as Lance had said it, Guin's brain went into overdrive. What if the rumors were right and Ris *had* had an affair with CiCi? She only had his word on it. And there was the woman from Australia. What was her name, Ling? And no doubt there were more women, women Guin had no idea about.

"Hello? Anyone there?"

"Sorry. I was spacing," said Guin.

"Uh-huh," said Lance. "So what's up with you and the detective?"

"I don't know," said Guin. "One minute we're having dinner and laughing, the next he's his usually stony, uncommunicative self. I don't get it."

"Which one of those did you kiss?"

"Technically, he kissed me," said Guin.

"Isn't that, like, illegal these days?"

"Only if you didn't want to be kissed," said Guin.

She paced around her bedroom.

"Oho!" said Lance.

"Yeah, yeah, yeah," said Guin.

"And does the professor know about you and the detective?"

"No!" said Guin, a little too loudly. "And there's nothing really to know," she said, though she knew her cheeks were turning pink.

"Please, Guinivere. I can tell when you're lying, even over the phone."

Was it that obvious?

"So what do I do about Ris? I haven't heard from him in over a day, he's not returning my texts, and he didn't show up to the judging tonight. It's very unlike him."

"Did you try calling him?" Lance asked her.

"I did. He didn't answer. And I've left him, like, a dozen text messages. He hasn't responded to a single one."

"Maybe he just lost his phone, or it fell in the toilet. It happens."

Guin hadn't thought of that.

"Huh," she said. "I guess that's possible. But why hasn't he called me? Couldn't he have borrowed a phone? He called the Shell Club to tell them he couldn't make it."

That's right, he had called them. So he was alive. Unless someone faked the call. Oh God, maybe he had been kidnapped or worse! Guin thought.

"You're doing it again," said Lance.

"Sorry. What were you saying?"

"I said, stop worrying and try him again in the morning. Call the university. They probably know where he is."

Guin could've slapped herself. Of course, the university. They would probably know where he was.

"You're a genius, bro."

Guin could tell he was preening.

"So, you coming to Paris with us?"

He started singing "April in Paris."

"I haven't decided. I'll get back to you soon," she promised.

"Just don't wait too long."

"So, how are you doing?" Guin asked.

"Fine. Busy. Have another big client presentation tomorrow."

"Well, don't let me keep you," said Guin.

"Thanks. Good luck with everything," said Lance. "And let me know how things go with the detective."

Guin could feel her cheeks getting warm again.

"Goodnight, Lance."

"Goodnight, Guinivere."

They ended the call and Guin headed back to her computer.

CHAPTER 30

The next morning Guin got up and stretched. She went over to the window and opened the shade. It was still dark, and she thought she heard the sound of raindrops. So much for a beach walk. Though if it wasn't raining too hard….

She headed to the bathroom and splashed some cold water on her face. Then she headed to the kitchen and fixed herself some coffee in her French press. As she waited for the coffee to brew, she walked back to her bedroom and grabbed her phone. As soon as it had booted, the message light began flashing.

She immediately opened her text messages.

"Finally!" she said, seeing a text from Ris.

"Sorry not to have replied," he had written. "Something's come up. Need to talk. Let me know when you get this."

The message had been left late the night before, after Guin had turned off her phone. Was it too early to call? She sent him a text instead.

"I'm up, if you want to talk."

She stared at the phone, waiting to see if he called her, but the phone didn't ring. She opened her news app and began scrolling. When she got to the local news section, she stopped.

"FGCU prof involved in sex scandal," blared the first headline. Next to it was a photo of Ris.

With dread, Guin clicked on the link.

"Noted marine biologist accused of sexual misconduct," read the headline.

Guin quickly skimmed the article, which had posted late the night before and wasn't very long. The author of the piece, someone Guin wasn't familiar with, reported that two students had recently come forward with accusations of sexual misconduct against Ris, who, the author further noted, had been voted one of Southwest Florida's sexiest men and was known as Dr. Heartthrob.

Oh no, thought Guin. This was bad, really bad.

She reread the article. It didn't mention the accusers' names, but Guin had a pretty good idea who at least one of them was. She made to call Ris but as she was about to enter his number, her phone started to buzz. It was Shelly.

"Did you see the news?" asked Shelly, breathlessly.

Had Shelly also seen the article about Ris?

"What news?" Guin asked, playing dumb.

"Suzy Seashell's hit piece on the fountain!"

"Oh, that," said Guin, relieved. "Yes, I saw it."

"Yes, *that*," said Shelly. "It's disgraceful, if you ask me. Totally spiteful. Just because she wasn't picked to be one of Sam's little helpers doesn't mean she should go trashing the thing."

"I agree," said Guin.

"So any idea what happened?" asked Shelly. "To the fountain, I mean."

"It short-circuited," said Guin.

"I thought you said they tested the thing the night before."

"They did," Guin replied.

"And?"

"And, according to Rita, everything worked fine."

Shelly made a face.

"So someone deliberately sabotaged the fountain. My money's on Suzy. She'd do anything for a story. And she was totally pissed at Sam."

"It's possible an animal got into the fountain overnight and managed to scrape away a tile and gnaw through the sheathing covering the wire," said Guin.

"Pretty determined animal, if you ask me," said Shelly, clearly not buying it.

"Yeah," said Guin, who also didn't really buy the animal theory. Maybe in New York City, where there were rats running around in the subway, or in Connecticut, where mice and voles were rampant, could something like that have happened. But on Sanibel? Unlikely. More likely it was a much larger animal, a rat with a file and a pen knife.

"So you going to the show today?" asked Shelly.

"At some point," said Guin. "How about you?"

"I'm going to be selling tickets from eleven to one."

Guin had thought about volunteering, but she had had so much on her plate, she hadn't signed up.

Suddenly her phone started ringing.

"Hey, Shell, I need to get this. Talk to you later."

She hung up on Shelly, which she knew she'd hear about later, and grabbed the call.

"Oh, hi Craig."

"And hello to you, too. I take it you were expecting someone else."

"Yeah," said Guin.

"You have a minute to talk?"

"Shoot," said Guin.

"I just heard that the police are speaking with CiCi's brother, John Jr."

"Oh?" said Guin, her ears pricking up. "How come?"

"Seems like Johnny has a bit of a rap sheet—drugs mainly, and he allegedly roughed up his former girlfriend."

"What's that got to do with CiCi?"

"Hold your horses. I'm getting to that," said Craig. "It seems young Johnny may not have been telling the truth the other day."

"About?" asked Guin.

"About his whereabouts last Thursday morning, among other things."

"And you know this how?"

"You know I cannot reveal my sources."

Guin rolled her eyes.

"But I have it on good authority that Rawlins Jr. and his sister had not been getting along."

"Lots of brothers and sisters don't get along," said Guin.

"Yeah, but they don't threaten to kill each other."

Guin opened her mouth to say something, then shut it. She and Lance had rarely fought growing up, but she had known plenty of other siblings who had fought, some of them viciously.

"That's not all. He has a gun," said Craig.

"But the medical examiner said CiCi had been killed by blunt force trauma to the back of the head. And we found that shell."

"Yeah, but the butt of a gun can also pack a wallop."

Guin paused. She tried to picture CiCi's brother, whom she had only seen in online photos, striking CiCi in a fit of rage.

"Go on," said Guin.

"As I was saying, Johnny and CiCi had not been getting along. No doubt precipitated by Ms. Rawlins's return to the nest. She was a bit of a rules girl, by all accounts, and young Johnny rarely played by the rules.

"The two of them had been going at it more than usual the week before she was killed," continued Craig. "And the neighbors heard the two of them yelling in the backyard the night before you found CiCi. Mrs. Kravitz, she's the neighbor who heard them, said she could have sworn she heard Johnny threaten to kill his sister."

"But wasn't Johnny supposed to have been out on the boat with his father Thursday morning?" asked Guin.

"That's the thing. He showed up late."

"How late?" asked Guin.

"Late enough to have killed his sister and made it to the boat by eight."

"Did anyone see him over by Silver Key?" asked Guin.

She wracked her brain, trying to remember if she might have seen Johnny Rawlins that morning, but her attention had been focused on the wrack line. Indeed, her own mother could have probably walked right by her without her even noticing.

"Not so far," said Craig. "But there's an eyewitness who says she saw him getting into a car and speeding away from the Blind Pass parking lot that morning."

"How did she know it was him?" asked Guin.

"She didn't."

"I don't follow," said Guin.

"Apparently Johnny, in his haste to leave Blind Pass, shoved a woman in the parking lot and didn't stop to apologize. So she wrote down his license plate number and called the Sanibel Police Department to complain. They didn't take the complaint too seriously, at first. Then they got some additional information and took him in for questioning."

"So do they think CiCi's brother did it?" Guin asked.

"They're still investigating," said Craig. "The kid swears he didn't do it."

"So now what?"

"We wait."

"We wait?" said Guin. "For what, the detective to have

us over for tea? You know he won't tell us anything unless we press him."

"Hey, I'm just as interested as you are in finding out who killed that young woman, but it seems as though the police have things under control."

Guin was incredulous. Not that the police had things under control, but that Craig wasn't hot to investigate.

"Are you okay?" Guin asked.

"I'm fine," said Craig.

"Will Betty vouch for that?"

There was silence on the other end of the line.

"Craig? You there?"

He sighed.

"I guess you'll hear it eventually. May as well be the one to tell you."

"Tell me what?" asked Guin. Something about Craig's tone made her nervous.

"The doctor found something."

"Found something?"

"They think it might be cancer."

"Cancer?" said Guin. "Are they sure?"

"No. That's why I'm getting a biopsy."

"When?"

"Next week."

Guin felt her heart start to race. Craig and Betty were like family. She couldn't imagine losing either one of them.

"Do you want me to come with you?" said Guin.

Craig smiled.

"Thanks, but I think Betty and I can manage. I appreciate the offer, though."

"Okay, but you tell me the second you get the results, you hear?"

"I promise," said Craig, with a chuckle.

Just then Guin's phone started to beep.

"I have a call coming in," she said, torn whether or not to take it.

"Take it," said Craig. "I'll let you know if I hear anything else."

"Just take care of yourself," she said. "I'll text you later."

She ended the call and hit 'talk.'

"Hello?"

"Hi."

It was Ris.

"Are you okay?" she asked him. "I saw the piece in the Fort Myers paper."

"I should have warned you," said Ris.

"You knew?" said Guin, taken aback.

"The university alerted me," he replied. "They told me about the allegations. And Georgia told me some reporter had been round, asking questions."

"But the allegations, they're not true," Guin said. "Right?"

"Of course they're not true," Ris replied, sounding slightly irritated. "But the university needs to go through the proper procedures."

"And you're okay with that?"

"Of course I'm okay with that," Ris responded. "I've got nothing to hide."

"Do you need to hire an attorney?" Guin asked.

Ris sighed.

"Probably. I've got some feelers out."

"Good," said Guin. She paused. "Does this mean you're out of the running for the chairmanship?"

Ris sighed again.

"Probably. I spoke with several members of the search committee. They said they believed me, but with the current climate, they can't take any chances. There's a lot of pressure on campuses right now, as you can imagine."

Guin could. #MeToo stories had been everywhere. And

even if Ris was innocent, which Guin fervently believed, having female students come forward and accuse him of sexual malfeasance was not something they could ignore.

"So what are you going to do?" Guin asked.

"Lie low. I have to fly to Japan next week. I was thinking of extending my visit, going back to Australia. I was invited to be a guest lecturer by the Marine Studies Institute at the University of Sydney. I had turned them down, but…"

"You'd move to Sydney?" Guin asked, a bit dumbfounded.

"Only for a semester or two," Ris replied.

"But what about us?"

"Come with me. You had a great time in Sydney, didn't you?"

"Yes, but what about my job, my life here on Sanibel?"

"Didn't you say your unit was about to be sold? And I'm sure you could find some freelance work. It would be an adventure."

Guin felt herself starting to panic. This was not what she had bargained for.

"I… I…" she stammered.

She took a deep breath and tried to pull herself together.

"I need to go. I'll talk to you later."

She ended the call, not waiting for Ris to reply. She stared out past the lanai. What was happening? First Craig, now Ris. It was like her perfect little world was falling apart. And it wasn't even nine o'clock.

She walked over to the sliders. It appeared that the rain had stopped.

"I need to go for a walk," she announced to the cats, who had been following her around.

She hurriedly walked into the bedroom and threw on some clothes.

CHAPTER 31

It was misting outside, but Guin didn't care. She needed the fresh air to help clear her head. As she walked down to the bayou, she took several deep breaths, which she slowly released, closing her eyes intermittently.

She reached the end of the road, where it dead-ended, right at Dinkins Bayou, and stared out at the water. She watched as a couple of boats headed out towards Pine Island Sound. As she stood there watching them, she noticed some bubbles. A few seconds later, a dolphin emerged, followed by two more.

Guin watched, transfixed, as the dolphins made their way across the bayou. She wished she had brought her phone with her, so she could have taken a picture or a video. But she had left it back at the condo in her haste to get out the door.

She continued to stare out across the bayou for several more minutes, watching the birds and enjoying the quiet. She glanced at the nearby docks, some of which had boats attached to them, others set up for sunbathing. If the weather had been sunny, no doubt there would be more people out.

She took a final look around the bayou, then turned and headed home.

As she walked, she was assailed by a variety of thoughts:

Could CiCi's brother have killed her? Was Craig okay? Was Ris telling her the truth about those students? In the case of Tanya Harvey, she could believe that Ris had been the victim of gossip. But according to the story in the paper, more than one student had claimed he had acted inappropriately.

Guin shook her head. Too many questions, and not enough answers.

"I need to speak with you," Guin texted the detective. "It's urgent."

A few seconds later, her phone rang. It was the detective. She immediately picked up.

"You okay?"

"No," Guin replied.

"Please don't tell me you found another dead body."

Guin snorted.

"No," she said. "No dead bodies."

Though that made her think of Craig, and she grew sad again.

"You said it was urgent."

Guin sighed.

"I need your advice."

"You want my advice?"

"Hey, there's a first time for everything," said Guin.

"Mmph," said the detective.

"Could I stop by the station, or take you out for lunch later?"

"I'm a little busy at present, Ms. Jones. Can't you tell me what it is that's bothering you over the phone?"

"I'd rather not," she said.

The detective sighed.

"Meet me over at the Paper Fig Kitchen at noon."

"Thank you," said Guin. "See you then."

She ended the call and looked at the time. It was still early. She thought about going over to the Community House, then nixed the idea. Instead she called Sam.

She picked up after a few rings.

"How are you?" Guin asked.

"Better," Sam replied.

"Good to hear it," said Guin. "How's the fountain?"

"Fine, or it will be. Rita went over to the Shell Museum first thing this morning with Marta to take a look at it. Hopefully the two of them can patch it up."

"I'm sure they'll get it up and running in no time," said Guin. She paused. "So, how long do you and Rita plan on staying on Sanibel?"

"We had planned on leaving this weekend," said Sam. "But with the fountain, and the police wanting us to file a report, and Denny being questioned again…"

"Denny's being questioned, by the detective?" Guin asked.

"Yeah. The detective told him not to leave the island."

"I'm guessing he's not happy about that."

"Actually, he's handling it quite well," said Sam. "He thinks it's funny. And I think he likes it here. He's written several songs. Don't remember the last time he did that."

"What about the tour?"

"I can't imagine the detective will keep him here for that long," Sam replied. "Though, personally, I wouldn't mind if he missed the tour. I know I shouldn't say that, but…"

Guin understood. It must be rough, him touring all the time and her working on sculptures in different cities. They must not get to spend much time together.

"Have the police asked you any more questions about CiCi?" Guin asked her.

"No, just about the fountain. Rita said the detective was going to meet her over at the museum. She said he wanted to take another look before they patched it up."

So that's where the detective was.

"Well, I hope you and the fountain are back in business soon," said Guin.

"Thanks," said Sam.

They ended the call. Guin looked at the clock. If she left now, she would have time to stop at the museum and check on the fountain before she met the detective for lunch. Unless, that is, he was still there.

"Hey," said Guin, walking over to the fountain.

George looked up and smiled.

"How's it going?" asked Guin.

"I think," said Rita, giving the fountain a once over, "we should be good to go. What do you think, George?"

"I think so, too, but let's wait a few hours to test it. Best to let the epoxy set as long as possible."

"Okay. Shall we give it a go after the museum closes tonight? That is if you can stay a little late," Rita said.

"No problem," said George, looking shyly at Rita.

She smiled at him.

Was George blushing?

Guin looked from George to Rita. George was an introvert, and, as far as she knew, very single. Which was a shame, Guin thought, as he was so kind and gentle, and so good at making and fixing things. But whenever a female approached him, he grew shy and tongue-tied. Though that was clearly not the case with Rita.

"George here has been a huge help," said Rita. "Wish I had known about him before. Would have saved me a lot of time and trouble."

George was definitely blushing now.

"Well, I should get going," said Rita. "I'll see you back here at five, George?"

"See you then," said George, who was now grinning.

Rita began packing up her toolbox.

"Um, Rita…"

Rita looked up.

"Yes, George?"

Guin watched and waited.

"Would you, um, like to have lunch with me?"

Rita smiled.

"I made a big salad and a baguette," George quickly added. "There's plenty for two. We could eat over there, at one of the tables, if you have a few minutes."

"You made a baguette? You are a man of many talents, George Matthews."

Yup, he's definitely smitten, Guin said to herself.

"You two enjoy your lunch," said Guin. "Okay if I pop back around five?"

"Sure," said Rita. "Just keep your fingers crossed it works this time."

"It's going to work," said George.

"That's the spirit!" said Rita.

"Did the police post someone to keep watch?" asked Guin, looking around and not seeing a policeman.

"They're sending someone to keep watch after the museum closes," said Rita. "At least that's what the detective said."

"And we have the fencing, though that didn't do much good," added George.

"What about adding another security camera?" asked Guin.

"I thought about that," said George. "We just don't have it in the budget—and it's not like we have an extra one lying around."

"You could always ask your members," suggested Guin. "Maybe someone could donate one."

"I guess," said George. "Though that doesn't help us tonight."

True, thought Guin.

"Well, enjoy your lunch," said Guin.

She turned to go, then turned back.

"Say, where's Marta?"

"She took off," said Rita.

"Will she be back later?" Guin asked.

"I doubt it," said Rita.

"I told her I got it," said George.

"Okay, well, see you two later," said Guin.

She headed to the Mini, then snuck a look back. But she could no longer see Rita and George.

"So, what's so urgent?" asked the detective, when they had sat down at one of the outdoor tables outside the Paper Fig with their sandwiches and drinks.

Guin wasn't sure where to begin.

"It's about Ris."

The detective raised an eyebrow.

"He's been accused of… inappropriate behavior," said Guin.

The detective continued to regard her.

"By some former students. I'm not sure how many. More than one, I gather. Ris says he didn't do it, but…"

She looked at the detective, willing him to say something, but he continued to regard her in his Sphinx-like way.

"I just thought, maybe, you'd have some advice."

"For him or for you?" asked the detective.

Guin thought for a minute.

"For both of us."

The detective took a sip of his LaCroix, then a bite of his sandwich. Then he took another sip of sparkling water.

"You love him?" he asked her.

Guin stared at the detective.

"Love him?" she asked.

"Answer the question," said the detective.

She suddenly felt like she was in an interrogation room, with one of those bright lights shining down on her.

"I…" she began.

She could feel her cheeks growing warm.

"I…" she began again.

She looked down, then up at the detective.

"I don't know."

"He love you?" asked the detective.

"He says he does," Guin replied.

"And you believe him?"

"I…"

Did she believe him? She wanted to. After all, why would he lie to her? Though she had believed Art, her ex, when she had asked him if there was something going on between him and their hairdresser. He had told her that she was being ridiculous. Ridiculously correct, as it had turned out.

"I want to," said Guin.

The detective took another bite of his sandwich and washed it down with more LaCroix. Guin had lost her appetite.

"Do you think they'll arrest him?" Guin asked.

"Only if they can prove abuse," replied the detective. "Most likely they'll just suspend him without pay."

Though that would be devastating for Ris.

"What would you do?" asked Guin. "If you were him."

"If I was innocent? Fight."

But that was not Ris's style. Not that he was a coward. Far from it. She just couldn't picture him dragging those girls through the mud, discrediting them, no matter how much they deserved it.

The thought made Guin think of Ris's daughter, Fiona. She wondered if Ris had told her.

Guin sighed.

"As for you," said the detective.

"Yes?" said Guin.

"I'd dump him."

"Dump him?" said Guin. "Shouldn't I be standing by his side, defending him?"

"These things can get pretty ugly. Are you prepared?"

Guin opened her mouth to speak, then quickly shut it. Was she prepared for all the ugly press, to be contacted by reporters and the police and asked about Ris? Suddenly, she was full of doubt and hated herself. If the situation had been reversed, she knew Ris would stand by her, defending her with his last breath.

And suddenly she knew: She didn't love him. Sure, she cared about him. Felt awful about what was happening. But she wasn't in love with him.

She looked up to see the detective looking at her.

"He says he's going to take a guest lecturer position in Australia, lay low until this thing blows over, assuming they don't arrest him."

"Probably smart," said the detective.

"He asked me to go with him."

The detective had been about to take another bite of his sandwich but stopped.

"What did you tell him?"

"I told him no."

He put the sandwich in his mouth.

"Aren't you going to eat?" asked the detective, when he was done swallowing.

"I'm not hungry," said Guin.

"You should eat," said the detective.

"Fine," she said.

She picked up her sandwich and took a bite.

"Happy now?" she asked him.

They sat in silence for several seconds.

"Can I ask you something, about the case?" Guin asked him.

"You can ask…" replied the detective.

"I heard you had CiCi's brother, John Jr., over at the police department. Is he now the prime suspect?"

"Where'd you hear that?" asked the detective.

"Does it matter?" asked Guin.

"If one of my officers is leaking confidential information it does."

"Was it really that confidential? For all you know, I could have heard it from the father or one of Johnny's friends."

The detective made a face.

"Well?" said Guin.

"Well what?" asked the detective.

"Did you arrest Johnny Rawlins?"

"No," said the detective.

"But you did question him."

"We did."

"And?" said Guin, leaning forward.

"And you know I can't speak to you about police matters," said the detective.

Guin leaned back and huffed.

"What about Denny Sumner?" she asked.

"What about him?" replied the detective.

This was like some bad comedy routine.

"I understand you told him not to leave the island."

"That's right."

"So is he a suspect?"

The detective opened his mouth to speak but Guin put up a hand to stop him.

"I know, you can't discuss police business."

The detective grinned.

He finished his sandwich and balled up the paper it had come in.

"Now I have a question for you."

"Oh?" said Guin.

"What are you doing a week from Saturday?"

"I don't know," said Guin. "Why?"

"I've got two tickets to see the Yankees play the Mets in Port St. Lucie."

"But you hate the Yankees."

"Exactly," said the detective, grinning again.

Guin smiled back at him.

"So, you wanna go?"

Guin thought about it for a second.

"Sure, why not?"

"I need to get back to work," said the detective. "I'll be in touch regarding the game."

"I look forward to it," said Guin. "Thanks for lunch."

The detective nodded, then headed to his car.

CHAPTER 32

Guin watched the detective drive away. Her mind was a jumble. She kept replaying what the detective had said about Ris. Should she break things off with him? It seemed like a crummy thing to do, under the circumstances. But she also didn't think it would be fair to lead him on. She sighed, then took out her phone to call him. She was about to enter his number but stopped. She couldn't do it. Not now.

She looked at the time. It was a little before one. Shelly would be getting off her shift at the Shell Show. If she hurried, she would probably catch her before she left the Community House.

Guin arrived at the Community House a few minutes later and went over to the ticket line.

"Hi there," Guin said to the two women seated at the table. "Do either of you know if Shelly's still here? She was doing the shift before you."

"I think she went to the kitchen," said the brunette.

"Thanks," said Guin.

One perk of volunteering for the Shell Festival was that if you worked at least two shifts, you got free food.

Guin headed to the kitchen and opened the swinging door. Shelly was inside, chatting with a handful of people.

"Hey," said Guin.

"Guin!" said Shelly, her mouth half-full of food. "Wasn't sure if you were coming."

"Neither was I," Guin replied.

"You know Melinda and Tom, I believe."

"Hi," said Guin.

Melinda and Tom were fellow Shell Ambassadors and Shell Club members.

"We were just talking about how busy it's been this morning," said Shelly.

Melinda and Tom nodded.

"We may break a record," said Melinda.

"That's great," said Guin.

"You doing a piece on the show?" asked Tom.

"I am. Actually several," said Guin. "There's going to be a whole section on the show in next week's paper."

"Anyone we know going to be featured?" asked Melinda, looking at Shelly and smiling.

"Maybe," Guin answered, smiling back at her. "There's going to be a spread highlighting a bunch of the winning entries. Mostly photos with captions, which I'll be writing. And I'll be doing a wrap-up piece, talking about attendance and how much money was raised. And I need to do a follow-up on the fountain."

"I look forward to reading them," said Melinda. "Speaking of the fountain, what happened? Is the artist okay? I was there last night, but I couldn't really see what happened. I was too far back. I went to ask Marta, but I couldn't find her."

"Marta was there?" asked Guin. She didn't recall seeing her.

"I'm pretty sure I saw her," said Melinda. "She's pretty hard to miss. She was standing off to the side. But when I went to look for her after, I couldn't find her. So is the artist okay? She had us all pretty scared."

"Sam's fine," said Guin. "Fortunately. And Rita and George were over at the museum this morning, repairing the fountain. Hopefully it will be back in business before the show closes Saturday."

"Good to hear," said Tom.

"Hey, Shell, can I talk to you for a second, alone?" said Guin, pulling her aside.

"Everything okay?" asked Shelly.

"Everything's fine," said Guin. "I just need to ask you something."

Shelly put down her plate.

"I'll be right back," she told Tom and Melinda. "Make sure you save me a cookie."

They made their way out of the kitchen and ran smack into Marty Nesbitt.

"Guinivere! Fancy running into you here!" said Marty, beaming at her.

Not now, thought Guin, but she forced herself to smile. "Marty."

"Here to interview me about my big wins?" he asked her. "Three ribbons! Count 'em."

"That's great, Marty. But I really need to speak with Shelly."

"Girl talk, eh?" he said, waggling his bushy eyebrows.

Guin groaned inwardly.

"Yup," said Guin, eager to make her escape.

"Well, be sure to come back and check out my ribbons!" he called.

Guin smiled through gritted teeth and steered Shelly to the seating area outside the restrooms.

"What's up?" asked Shelly, when Guin finally released her arm.

"I think I need to break up with Ris."

"What?!" said Shelly.

"I spoke with the detective, and he said I should break up with him."

"The detective, eh?" said Shelly, folding her arms across her chest and giving Guin a look.

"What's that look for?"

"You know what that look's for," Shelly replied. "Why were you discussing your love life with the detective?"

Guin could feel herself blushing.

"It just kind of came up, okay? I was asking him for advice."

"Advice? About your love life?"

"No!" said Guin, a little too loudly. "I was asking him for advice about Ris."

"I'm not following," said Shelly.

Guin sighed.

"I wanted his opinion about the sexual harassment charges."

Shelly grabbed Guin's arm.

"What sexual harassment charges? Has Ris been accused of sexually harassing someone?"

"Don't you read the Fort Myers paper?" asked Guin.

"I've been too busy," said Shelly. "It's Shell Show week."

Right.

"Spill."

"Well," said Guin, "apparently a couple of former students accused Ris of inappropriate behavior. He swears he didn't act inappropriately, that it was a misunderstanding, and I want to believe him."

"But," said Shelly.

"But there's a part of me that wonders if there could be some truth to the allegations. Though I'm pretty sure I know one of the girls. And if anything, she was the one who threw herself at Ris, and he rejected her."

"I'm all for #MeToo and all that jazz," said Shelly, "but maybe you should give Ris the benefit of the doubt here. It's not his fault women are crazy about him. Heck, I've seen eighty-year-old women practically throw their panties at him after one of his lectures."

Guin laughed, despite herself.

"When were these alleged trysts supposed to have taken place?" asked Shelly.

"I'm not sure," said Guin. "Before we became serious."

"And what does the university say?"

"They're investigating."

"What about his teaching gig?" asked Shelly. "Has FGCU suspended him?"

"I don't know. But he withdrew his application for the department chair position."

Guin suddenly felt bad for Ris. If he was innocent, and she fervently wanted to believe he was, this was a serious blow to his career.

"So is he going to fight it?" asked Shelly.

"He's conflicted. He wants to prove he's innocent, but he hates all the mud that will no doubt be dredged up. And he's worried about his accusers."

"Seriously?" asked Shelly.

"I know," said Guin. "But that's Ris."

Shelly shook her head.

"So what will he do if they fire him?"

"He says he was offered a guest lecturer position in Australia."

"Australia?!" said Shelly. "Wasn't he just there?"

"Yeah. Apparently, the University in Sydney had asked him to stay on, but he'd said no. Now he's reconsidering."

"What about you?"

"He asked me to come with him," said Guin.

"This is like déjà vu all over again," said Shelly.

"I know, right?"

"So what did you say?"

"I told him I couldn't leave Sanibel."

"Well, there you go," said Shelly.

"So you think I'm doing the right thing?"

"By not flying off to Australia with a guy who you'll be worried about cheating on you every second? Absolutely."

If possible, Guin felt worse than before.

"Thanks," she replied. "So, I need to tell him, right?"

"That you're not going to go to Australia with him?"

"That, and that I'm breaking up with him."

"You could always ghost him," suggested Shelly.

"That doesn't seem right. Besides, I could run into him. I don't want things to be awkward."

"Fine," said Shelly. "But do it on neutral ground, someplace public. Don't let him seduce you into going to Australia with him. I'd miss you too much."

Guin smiled at her friend.

"Now come back to the kitchen and get some food," said Shelly. "I don't know about you, but I need a cookie. Make that a brownie."

"Thanks, but I'm not really hungry," said Guin. "And I need to do a quick walk around, make sure I got everything."

"Suit yourself," said Shelly.

"You volunteering again tomorrow?" asked Guin.

"Yeah, I'll be back here at eleven tomorrow morning, selling tickets again. But I'm off on Saturday."

"I'm sure the Shell Club appreciates it," said Guin.

"You going to be okay?" asked Shelly.

"Yeah, eventually," said Guin. Right now, though, she just wanted to curl up in bed with the cats.

Shelly leaned over and gave her a kiss on the cheek, followed by a hug. It felt good.

"Thanks," said Guin.

"Now go take that walk, and be sure to ooh and aah when you pass by my exhibit," said Shelly, grinning at Guin.

Guin smiled back at her.

"You bet."

Shelly reached over and gave Guin another hug.

"I'll text you later," she called, as she made her way back to the kitchen.

CHAPTER 33

Guin spent the rest of the afternoon working on her Shell Show stories for the paper, stopping a little before five. She was eager to get back to the museum, to see what was up with the fountain. She arrived there just before 5:30 and found Rita and George pretty much right where she had left them. She wondered if they had spent the afternoon together.

"How's it going?" asked Guin.

"We're about to find out," said Rita.

Guin looked around.

"Where's Sam?"

"Back at the house, resting. Denny's looking after her. She wasn't feeling so great."

"Sorry to hear that," said Guin. Sam had told her she was fine when she had spoken with her that morning. Had she just been putting on a brave face?

"You ready, George?" Rita asked him.

"Ready."

George disappeared inside the museum. A few minutes later, the fountain lit up.

Guin stared at it.

"It's beautiful. But I don't see any water."

"We're testing the electrical first," explained Rita.

George came out of the museum a minute later.

"How does it look?" he asked Rita.

"Good! Let's just check one more time that there are no exposed wires before we test the water."

George nodded. Then he and Rita began to slowly examine the fountain.

"What are you looking for?" asked Guin.

"Any smoke or a fizzing sound," replied George.

"Well, I don't see or hear anything," said Guin, leaning over the fountain.

Rita was inside the fountain, sniffing.

"I don't smell or see anything. I think we're good! Of course, I thought that the last time."

They stood staring at the fountain for several minutes.

"What do you say, George? Should we try it with the water?"

He looked a bit unsure.

"I say we give it a go," said Rita. "Nothing ventured, nothing gained."

"Just get out of the fountain. I don't want you to get injured in case something goes wrong."

Rita smiled at him.

"Why George, I didn't know you cared."

George blushed furiously, then turned and went back into the museum.

Guin and Rita stood a foot or two away from the fountain. As they watched, water began flowing from the mouth of the dolphin.

"Success!" shouted Rita.

They continued to watch the fountain. Then George joined them.

"We did it, George!" said Rita. "Well done!"

George looked less sure.

"I need to do one last check."

He headed toward the fountain, rolled up his pants,

removed his shoes, then stepped inside. Guin held her breath.

Slowly, George walked around the inside of the fountain. He made two circuits, then he stepped out.

"You okay?" Guin asked him.

"Fine. Just a bit wet."

Rita went over and gave him a kiss on the cheek, which caused George to blush anew.

Guin smiled.

"Well done, you two. The fountain looks great."

"I only wish Sam could have been here," said Rita. "But I'll drag her over tomorrow."

Guin looked around.

"So, are the police going to send someone to stand guard?"

"That's what they told us," said George.

"Hey, can you two help me with the barricade?" called Rita. She was trying to drag the metal fencing closer to the fountain. "Not that it will do much good."

She had a point, thought Guin. The barricade wasn't very high, and pretty much anyone could climb over it. It was mostly used as a deterrent, to let people know they weren't supposed to go near the fountain.

The three of them repositioned the barricade, so it encircled the fountain.

"There," said Rita, a few minutes later. "That should do it."

Guin walked over to the museum and eyed the security camera.

"Hey, George, did you give the detective the footage from the other night?"

"I did. Why'd you ask?"

"Could I see it?" asked Guin.

"It's kind of late, Guin, and the museum's technically closed."

"It will only take a few minutes," said Guin, giving him a beseeching look.

"I'd like to see that footage, too," said Rita. "That is, if that's okay with you, George?"

Did Rita just bat her eyes at George? Guin had to keep herself from laughing.

George looked like he was clearly struggling.

"Fine," he finally said. "Just don't tell anyone I let you in."

"Mum's the word," said Rita.

Guin made a zipping motion with her fingers across her mouth.

"Okay, follow me," said George.

They followed George inside the museum, then down the stairs. He led them to a room with several computers and a bunch of other equipment.

"Hold on a sec," he said, going over to one of the computers. "I'll cue it up. Though I'm warning you, there's not much to see."

"Understood," said Guin.

"Is there something specific you're looking for?" asked Rita.

"I want to see if anyone showed up at the museum after you left," said Guin.

"It was pretty dark," said Rita.

"I know," said Guin.

"And the camera isn't exactly state of the art," said George. "We should really get a new one, with a telephoto lens and infrared capability."

Guin waited patiently as he continued to fuss.

"Okay, it should be all set," said George, a couple minutes later. "Here, have a seat."

He pulled out the chair in front of the computer. Guin sat and Rita stood over her.

"You want to take a seat?" Guin asked her.

"I'm good," said Rita.

"So what do I do?" Guin asked George.

"Just use the mouse to hit play or fast forward or rewind or pause it."

He gave her a quick demonstration.

"Looks pretty straightforward," said Rita. "You going to hang out with us?" she asked George.

"I need to go upstairs and do some work. Just text me when you're done."

He gave Rita his number.

"I just need to leave by seven."

"Gotta big date?" asked Rita, smiling up at him.

George blushed.

"Just text if you need me."

George left, and Guin and Rita turned their attention to the screen.

Guin began fast forwarding. As George had said, there wasn't much to see. Guin fast forwarded past midnight, then two a.m., then four.

"I don't see anything suspicious," said Rita.

"Neither do I," said Guin.

"Could we have missed something?"

"Maybe. Let me keep going a little more."

Guin continued to fast forward the footage.

"Wait. There! What's that?" asked Rita.

Guin hit the rewind button.

"There!" said Rita. "See that light?"

Guin looked at the time stamp. It was just after five a.m. It was still dark, but it looked as though there was a light, like a flashlight, moving towards the museum.

Guin pressed 'play.' Then they watched as the light

stopped near the fountain.

"Can you make it brighter or zoom in?" asked Rita.

Guin looked at the controls but was at a loss.

"Okay if I take a look-see?" asked Rita.

"Be my guest," said Guin.

She and Rita exchanged places.

Rita fiddled with the computer. She was able to zoom in a bit, but it was still too dark and blurry to see much.

She made a face.

"George did warn us we wouldn't be able to see much," said Guin.

Rita rewound the footage, then played it again.

"That's definitely some kind of light," she said.

"I agree. And it seems to be headed right toward the fountain," said Guin.

Suddenly the light went out. Then a smaller light flicked on.

"I think someone's in the fountain," said Rita.

Guin nodded.

"I wish we could see what they're doing. Maybe we should call George?"

Rita mulled it over.

"Fine."

Guin texted George, and he replied that he'd be right down.

"Any way you can make it brighter and zoom in more?" she asked him, when he arrived.

"I'm afraid not, at least not with the software we have here," George replied.

"But someone with the right software could?" asked Guin.

"Sure, if they had some expensive editing package."

"I know someone who can help us," said Rita.

"I don't know," said George, rubbing the back of his head.

"Come on, George. I promise not to tell anyone," said

Rita. "Remember, whoever vandalized the fountain nearly killed Sam. Don't you want to catch whoever did this?"

George was clearly conflicted.

"But the footage is property of the museum."

"You could make us a copy though, couldn't you?" asked Guin. "That's what you did for the police."

George rubbed the back of his head again.

"We promise not to say a thing," said Guin.

"No one would know," added Rita.

"If it got out that I gave you guys museum footage," said George, "I could lose my job."

"Understood," said Guin.

George was still conflicted.

"Fine," he said, a few seconds later. "Just give me a minute." He looked around.

"What are you looking for?" Rita asked him.

"A thumb drive. I think I have one up in my office. Be right back."

A few minutes later, he returned and inserted the thumb drive into the computer.

"Just make sure you get this back to me," he said, handing her the thumb drive.

"Will do," said Rita.

"Thanks George," said Guin.

She resisted the urge to kiss him.

"And don't tell the detective I gave you that footage."

"I promise," said Guin, though George looked distinctly dubious.

"I need to shut down the computer," he said.

He waited for them to move away. Then he sat down, closed the file, and powered off the computer.

"Let's go," he said.

He led them to the side door, ushering them out. Then he turned off the lights and locked the door behind them.

CHAPTER 34

Guin got up Friday morning determined to take a beach walk, even if it was a short one. She had stayed up late the night before, working on her Shell Show stories for the paper, and then had trouble sleeping, her mind fixated on the fountain and Ris.

She had been too chicken to call or even text Ris, and he had not gotten in touch with her. Maybe she should just avoid him. She debated what to do as she got dressed and fed the cats.

"I should just call him, arrange to meet," she said to the cats, as they inhaled their food.

As usual, they did not reply.

Guin sat in the Mini, deciding which beach to go to. Bowman's was the closest, but she still felt funny about going there, as it was close to Silver Key. So she once again headed to West Gulf Drive.

She parked her car by Beach Access #4, then walked down the path, past Mitchell's Sandcastles, to the beach. The sun was just starting to peek above the horizon, turning the sky shades of pink and purple. Guin closed her eyes and took a deep breath, raising her arms as she did so and inhaling the fresh sea air. Slowly she exhaled, lowering her arms. Then she repeated the exercise two more times.

"You flap a little harder, you might fly away," came a voice.

Guin opened her eyes to find Lenny standing a few feet away from her, smiling.

"I was just clearing my head," she said.

"Well, you looked like you were ready to take flight," said Lenny.

"If only I could," Guin said with a sigh.

"What's ailing you, kid? You seem a bit down."

"Does it show that much?" Guin asked.

"Only to someone who knows you," said Lenny. "So, professional or personal?"

"Personal," said Guin.

"You want to tell me about it?"

"I don't want to bore you."

"Bore me? Please. I guarantee your personal life is way more exciting than mine. Though Annie and I won duplicate bridge the other night. That was pretty exciting," he said with a smile.

Guin smiled back.

"How's Annie doing? I still don't think she's forgiven me for finding that dead body at her listing."

"Water under the bridge," said Lenny. "So, what's troubling you, kid?"

"It's Ris."

"Ah," said Lenny, in that knowing kind of way.

"I assume you saw the story in the Fort Myers paper."

"And it was on the news," said Lenny.

"It was?" said Guin, taken aback.

Guin didn't tend to watch the local news, except during hurricane season.

"Oh yeah."

"I take it it wasn't good."

"Not if you're Professor Hartwick. Though the university didn't throw him under the bus."

"Did they speak to any of the young women?"

"Just some girl named Tanya. She claimed she knew several young women who had been seduced by your Dr. Hartwick, including the dead girl. She was pretty convincing."

Guin made a face.

"She's lying," said Guin. "I met her. I wouldn't trust her as far as I could throw her. She and CiCi were both up for the TA position. But CiCi got it. And Tanya's held a grudge against Ris ever since."

"Ah," said Lenny. "I thought she was overdoing it a bit, with all that 'hashtag me too' stuff. But what do I know? I'm just an old man."

"You are not old!" said Guin.

"Too old to understand young people these days," he replied. "So, is he innocent?"

"That's what he says," said Guin.

"You believe him?" asked Lenny.

"I want to. I do. It doesn't seem like something he would do. But I haven't spoken with his accusers. Though I wouldn't put it past Tanya to have bribed someone."

"Don't you think that's a bit harsh?"

"You haven't met Tanya."

Lenny shrugged.

"Anyway, Ris claims he didn't do anything improper, and I believe him. Unless I hear otherwise."

"He hire a lawyer?"

"He said he would. This whole thing derailed his getting the chairmanship position. He's talking about going back to Australia."

"Australia?" said Lenny. "That seems a bit drastic."

"Yeah, well, he was offered a guest lecturer post there. He says he's going to take it, lay low until this whole thing dies down."

"Sounds like he's running away," said Lenny.

Guin stared at Lenny. He had a point.

"So what are you planning on doing?"

"He asked me to go with him, to Australia."

Lenny raised his eyebrows.

"You going to go?"

"No way," said Guin.

Lenny looked relieved.

"As a matter of fact, I'm breaking up with him."

"Because of the accusations?"

"No," said Guin. "Because I realized I'm not in love with him."

"Ah," said Lenny. "Then you're doing the right thing."

"I hope so," said Guin.

They continued walking down the beach, looking for shells. It was a beautiful morning, and Guin was glad to be outside.

"So, what's going on with you?" Guin asked.

"The usual. Been volunteering at the Shell Museum, playing bridge, Kiwanis stuff. Keeps me busy."

They turned and headed east. As they were walking, Guin saw two French bulldogs dashing across the sand, their owner chasing after them. Guin recognized the dogs, whom she had encountered on the beach before.

As if sensing she was a friend, they ran over to her, sand flying everywhere.

"Hi Napoleon. Hi Josephine," Guin said, bending down and petting the dogs, who were jumping all over her. She laughed as they tried to lick her face.

"Napoleon! Josephine! Down!"

It was their human, a woman who looked to be around Guin's age.

"I'm so sorry," said the woman. "They just love the beach. And people."

Guin laughed as the dogs continued to clamor for her attention.

"Yes, well, they know better than to jump all over strangers," said the woman.

"Well, I'm not a stranger, am I?" she said, talking to the dogs.

"Oh?" said the woman.

"I met them here before," Guin explained. "Your mom was watching them."

"Ah," said the woman. "I'm Lou, by the way."

"Guin," said Guin, getting up. "They're lovely dogs."

"They can be," said Lou, looking down at her charges. "No! Down!"

The dogs had discovered Lenny and were now jumping on him.

"That's okay," said Lenny, chuckling.

He scratched the dogs behind their ears.

Lou looked mortified.

"Clearly, we need another trip to the trainer," she sighed. "Come along, you two."

"Nice meeting you, Lou," said Lenny. "And you, too, Napoleon and Josephine."

"Nice meeting you, too," Lou said. "Gotta go!"

The dogs were pulling her down the beach, anxious to introduce themselves to a snowy egret standing a few feet away.

Guin and Lenny watched as Napoleon and Josephine bounded after the bird.

"Cute dogs," said Guin.

She took out her phone and looked at it.

"And I need to get going, too."

"Gotta lot of work?"

"I do," said Guin. "Shell Show week is always busy. Plus, I'm still trying to figure out who killed CiCi Rawlins and sabotaged the fountain."

"I meant to ask you about that," said Lenny.

"CiCi or the fountain?"

"Both."

"Well, I'm afraid I don't have much to tell you," said Guin.

"No idea who did it?"

"Which?"

"Both," said Lenny.

"There are several suspects for each, but I haven't been able to come up with enough evidence to point my finger at anyone. Frankly, I'm frustrated."

"What about the police?"

"You know the detective," said Guin. "I'm on a need-to-know basis, and he doesn't feel as though there's much I need to know."

"Well, good luck to you. I guess I'll have to wait and read about it in the paper, like everyone else."

"Sorry about that Lenny."

He held up a hand.

"That's okay. I understand. But if you ever need someone to help you do a little detective work, don't be afraid to ask. We former science teachers make pretty good detectives."

Guin smiled.

"I bet you do. Well, gotta run. Let's meet up for lunch."

"I'd like that," said Lenny.

"Good!" said Guin. "It's a date!"

She turned and made her way back towards where she had parked the Mini.

As Guin showered, thoughts about both cases kept running through her head. She had a nagging feeling she was missing something. But what?

As she rinsed the conditioner from her hair, she made a note to call the detective and reach out to CiCi's brother. That is, if he wasn't in jail.

She finished up, then got out of the shower and put on some clothes. Then she called over to the police department and was told the detective was busy. Of course he was. She left a message on his voicemail, then sent him a text, asking him to call her as soon as he got her message. Then she looked up CiCi's father's charter boat company and called over there.

"Rawlins Reel Good Fishing Charters."

"Hello," said Guin. "Is John Jr. there?"

"He's out with a group. Would you like to leave a message?" asked the woman.

Guin thought about saying no, that she'd call back later, then decided she might as well leave a message.

"Yes. Could you tell him that Guinivere Jones called and ask him to call me back?"

"Guinivere?" asked the woman. "Would you mind spelling that?"

"Just tell him Guin Jones called. That's G-U-I-N."

"Okay," said the woman. "What's your number?"

Guin gave her her mobile.

"Is there something I can help you with?" asked the woman.

"Thanks, but I need to speak with Johnny."

"He know who you are?" asked the woman.

"I'm a reporter with the *San-Cap Sun-Times*."

"A reporter? You investigating the murder of his sister? 'Cause I'll tell you right now, Johnny had absolutely nothing to do with that."

"And you are?" asked Guin.

"Becky Marlin."

"And how do you know Johnny had nothing to do with his sister's death?"

"'Cause he was staying at my place."

Oh really? thought Guin.

"I heard he was seen at the Blind Pass parking lot shortly after his sister's body was found," said Guin.

"Like I told that policeman, that's because he was staying at my place, and he was late for work."

"If he was staying at your place, what was he doing parking over at Blind Pass?"

"My place is right by there, and between me and my roommate, there's no place to park," said Becky.

Guin wasn't buying it.

"You don't believe me? Ask my roommate."

"And when did you say Johnny left your place?" asked Guin.

"Must have been around 7:45. We'd forgot to set the alarm, and he was real pissed. Said his dad would kill him if he was late again."

Guin made a face. If Becky was telling the truth, there went another suspect.

"Well, thanks for your help," said Guin.

"You still want to speak with Johnny?"

"Please," said Guin.

She wanted to hear directly from him where he was that morning. Though no doubt the two of them had made sure to sync their stories.

She ended the call and sighed.

CHAPTER 35

Guin spent the rest of the morning working on her articles and waiting for the detective to call her back. He still hadn't returned her call by lunchtime, and she hadn't heard from Ris either.

She made herself a peanut butter and jelly sandwich in the kitchen, which she ate standing up, staring out past the lanai. She knew she should call or text Ris, but she still didn't know what to say.

"Hi, Ris. We need to talk."

It sounded so cliché.

She sighed. Well, may as well get it over with.

She retrieved her phone from her desk and sent him a text.

As she stood there, staring at her phone, it started to buzz. It was a call from Rita.

"Hey, Rita, what's up?"

"I thought you'd like to know, I got the edited film back from my buddy."

"That was fast," said Guin.

"I told him we were in a hurry, and a life depended on it."

"You shouldn't have scared the guy."

"It's fine. He owed me."

"So, can you send it to me?"

"I'll send you the link. The file's pretty big."

"That's fine," said Guin. "Have you looked at it yet?"

"No, he just let me know that he edited it and had sent me the link."

"You want to come over?" Guin asked her. "We can look at it together on my monitor."

"Hold on," said Rita. "Let me just check that Sam doesn't need me."

"How's she doing?" asked Guin.

"She says she's fine, but I can tell she's still not a hundred percent. Hold on. I'll just be a sec."

Guin waited for Rita to come back on the line.

"Sam told me to get out of here. Give me your address."

Guin gave it to her.

"Okay, I'll be right over."

"Just text me when you get here, and I'll let you in."

"Sounds good," said Rita.

Rita arrived nearly an hour later.

"I was getting worried," said Guin.

"Sorry," said Rita. "Had an urgent call."

"Everything okay?"

"Yeah. Just had to rearrange a bunch of stuff back up north."

Guin gave her a quizzical look.

"We've decided to stay on Sanibel a little while longer. Work from here."

"That's great!" said Guin.

"Yeah," said Rita. "Frankly, neither Sam or I were jazzed about heading back up north and dealing with winter."

"What about your brother? Doesn't he have a tour coming up?"

"He says he's thinking about bagging it."

"What?!" said Guin. "Can he do that? What about No Signal?"

"No Signal will be fine. Plenty of guitar players out there who would love an opportunity to tour with them."

"But what about Denny?"

"He's been thinking of going solo for a while now. Been writing a bunch of stuff. Some of it's pretty good, too," she said, with a smile.

"And how does Sam feel about that?"

"She's thrilled, though she feels a bit guilty."

"Guilty?" asked Guin.

"Yeah, she thinks he's bagging the tour because of her. But really, she's just an excuse. He's been looking for one for a while now."

"Ah," said Guin. "So will he stay on Sanibel, too?"

"For now," said Rita. "The detective still hasn't given him permission to leave the island."

So clearly the detective must think Denny was involved in CiCi's death, thought Guin.

"Well, now that you're here, let's go check out that video."

Guin led Rita to her bedroom/office. She had grabbed a folding chair and had placed it next to her office chair.

"Sorry about the chair," she said. "I don't get a whole lot of company."

"It's fine," said Rita, taking a seat. "I mailed you the link before I left. Just go to your inbox."

Guin did as she was told and clicked on the link after opening her mail.

"Here goes," she said, hitting 'play.'

"Micah said he took the liberty of just editing the part he thought we'd want to see," explained Rita.

Guin and Rita watched as the screen went from almost pitch black to gray.

"That definitely looks like a flashlight," said Guin.

They watched as the flashlight approached the museum, then stopped by the fountain. The screen got lighter, allowing them to see there was a person, dressed seemingly in black pants and a black hoodie, holding the flashlight. But they couldn't see the person's face.

They continued to watch as the person, who appeared to be on the tall side, climbed into the fountain, then squatted down.

"What's he doing?" asked Guin.

"I'm guessing removing a tile," said Rita.

They continued to watch as the person continued to squat in the fountain. Finally, a few minutes later, the hooded stranger stood up and swiped his arm across his forehead, knocking back the hood of his sweatshirt, showing what appeared to be a thatch of light-colored hair.

Guin willed the person to turn around, but he didn't. Instead, he flipped his hood back up, quickly glanced around, stepped out of the fountain, and headed back toward the parking lot.

"Well, that wasn't very helpful," said Guin. "Though please thank your friend for me."

Rita was still staring at the screen.

"Do you mind?" she said, leaning over and grabbing Guin's mouse.

"Not at all," said Guin.

Rita rewound the video and stopped on the frame showing the back of the man's head.

Guin stared at the screen. Something about the man seemed familiar, as though she had seen him, or that head of hair, someplace before. She looked over at Rita, who was also staring.

"Well, whoever he is, he's tall with light hair," said Guin. "I just wish he had turned around, so we could have seen his face."

Rita was still staring at the screen.

"You okay?" Guin asked her.

"Yeah," said Rita.

But she didn't seem fine.

"I need to go," she said.

"Of course," said Guin. "Thanks for coming over."

"No problem," said Rita.

She had gotten to her feet and was heading toward the door.

"You sure you're okay?" asked Guin.

Rita seemed to be very preoccupied.

"I'm fine. I just need to go speak with someone."

"Okay," said Guin, trailing her. "By the way, if you hear anything from the detective, would you let me know?"

"Sure," said Rita, whose attention was focused straight ahead of her.

They got to the front door and Guin opened it for her.

"Bye," said Guin.

Rita didn't reply.

I wonder what that was about? thought Guin, as she closed the door.

She shrugged and went back into the bedroom. As soon as she had sat back down, Fauna jumped into her lap. Guin petted her as she clicked on the link to the video and watched it again, pausing at the frame where the back of the stranger's head was exposed. Again, Guin felt like she had seen that head before. She just couldn't place it.

She reached for her phone, then realized she must have left it in the kitchen. She got up, much to Fauna's annoyance, and went back into the kitchen. Her phone was on the counter, and her message light was blinking.

She hurriedly unlocked the device and checked her messages.

There was a voicemail from Ris, asking her to give him a

call. There were also several emails.

Why was it that as soon as she was busy doing something, or didn't have her phone, people returned her messages?

She sighed and checked her messages, sending a few quick replies. Then she called Ris back.

"Hey," he said, picking up.

"Hey," said Guin. "How're you doing?"

"I've been better," he replied. "Sorry I've kind of been incommunicado. Guess I've got a lot on my mind."

"We should talk," said Guin, deciding not to beat around the bush. "In person."

"You want to come over?" Ris asked. "I'll make us dinner."

"Thanks, but no," said Guin.

"Where then? You want to go to the Beach House?"

That was the last place Guin wanted to go.

"How about…" she searched for a place in between the two of them where they could meet. "Let's meet over at the Bimini Bait Shack. I've been meaning to try it out."

"You sure?" said Ris. "I don't mind cooking."

"Thanks," said Guin. "I need to check it out for the paper," she lied. Though Ginny would probably welcome a restaurant review.

"Okay, if that's what you'd prefer."

Guin didn't prefer it, but she needed a neutral place, someplace that wasn't special to them, and she could really use a drink.

"What time?"

Guin looked at the clock on her microwave. It was just past 3:30.

"How's five-thirty?"

She wanted to say "now," to get it over with. But she fought the urge, trying to make it sound like no big deal.

"Fine. See you then."

They ended the call, neither of them having said "I love you."

Guin tried to do more work, but it was useless. Her mind was on her meeting with Ris. She practiced what she was going to say:

"Ris, I care deeply for you, but I realized I don't love you. And it would be unfair to both of us to go on like this, especially with you going to Australia."

She sighed. Was she crazy to break things off, to let him fly off to Australia, to possibly never see him again?

She tried to envision life without him. Well, she had been without him for the better part of the last two months, more if she counted the months he was busy training for the Ironman up in Panama City, when she barely saw him. Had he been carrying on with someone else?

She had difficulty imagining it. Then she remembered what Tanya had said. She tried to picture Ris and CiCi together. But again, she just couldn't.

Guin glanced at the clock on her monitor. It was 4:30.

She got up and changed her clothes, putting on a sundress and applying some makeup.

She glanced at herself in the mirror. Her strawberry blonde curls were behaving, for once, so she left her hair down.

"Show time," she said, giving herself one final look.

She headed to the kitchen, to give the cats some food before she left, though she didn't anticipate being gone that long. Then she grabbed her bag and her keys and headed out the door.

CHAPTER 36

Traffic getting off the island was horrible, worse than usual, thanks to the Shell Show. Guin, in her preoccupied state, had totally forgotten and wound up texting Ris that she would be a little late.

Finally, around 5:45, she pulled into the Bimini Bait Shack. She immediately spied Ris's red Alfa Romeo convertible. She'd miss that little red car. It was a classic, Ris's baby. She wondered if Ris's neighbors would be taking care of it while he was back in Australia, along with his house.

She climbed the steps and entered the restaurant. The place was packed. Of course, it was a Friday night, at the peak of the season. What had she been thinking? Clearly, she hadn't been.

She made her way towards the bar, where she spotted Ris. He already had a drink.

"Hey there," she said, tapping his shoulder.

He turned and smiled at her.

"What are you drinking?" she asked him.

"What?" he said, the noise by the bar drowning out conversation.

"I said, what are you drinking?" Guin repeated, pointing at his drink.

"A G and T," he said. "Here, have a seat."

He removed the book he had placed on the seat next to him. It was a tome on Australian marine life.

"Brushing up?" Guin asked, smiling at him.

"Just some light reading," Ris replied, smiling back at her.

He signaled for one of the bartenders. A few seconds later, an attractive brunette came over. She smiled at Ris.

"What can I get you?"

"Guin?" asked Ris.

Guin looked at the female bartender. Was that a flicker of disappointment?

"You have any special cocktails?" Guin asked her.

"Here," said the bartender, handing her a drink menu.

"Thanks," said Guin, taking it.

"Be right back," said the bartender.

Guin glanced down at the menu, smiling at the names of the various drinks. Should she have the Ginger and Mary Ann, the Gilligan's Island, the Beach Bum, or the Shell Stopper? They all sounded good, if a little on the fruity side.

"What'll it be?" asked the bartender, a couple of minutes later.

"Just a Scratch Margarita, no salt," said Guin.

"Coming right up."

"So," said Ris, turning to face Guin. "What's up?"

Guin looked up at him.

"Up?" she said.

"I know that look," Ris replied. "Why did you want to meet me here instead of at the Beach House or dinner at my place?"

Guin wished the bartender would hurry up with her drink.

"I told you, I needed to write up this place for the paper."

"Uh-huh," said Ris, clearly not believing her.

"Here you go," said the bartender, placing Guin's margarita in front of her.

"Thanks," said Guin.

She took a healthy sip. Then another.

"I'm waiting," said Ris.

Guin took another sip of her drink.

"You may want to slow down," he said, knowing that Guin was a bit of a lightweight.

"Ris, I…" she paused. "Ris, you know I care about you."

He was looking right at her, and Guin could feel her heart racing.

"I care about you a lot. But…"

"But…"

"But I can't go to Australia with you."

"I understand," said Ris. "It'll be tough, but we did it before. And, of course, I'll fly you down to visit."

"No," said Guin. "What I mean is…"

She took another sip of her margarita.

"I'm breaking up with you."

There, she said it.

"You're breaking up with me?" said Ris, taken aback. "Why? Is it because of the accusations?"

"No, it's not because of the accusations," said Guin.

"You of all people," he said, shaking his head.

"It's not because of the accusations," Guin repeated.

"Then why?" he asked her. "I thought we had a good thing. I thought you thought so, too."

"We did. We do," said Guin, feeling her heart slamming against her chest.

"Then why?" he repeated, staring at her.

"I don't love you," she blurted out.

"Ouch," he said.

"I'm sorry," Guin said, feeling miserable.

"Well, thanks for letting me know."

Guin reached into her bag and pulled out an envelope.

"Here," she said, placing the envelope in front of Ris.

"What's this?" he asked her.

"Your key."

"You're giving me back my key?"

"I thought you'd want it back," Guin replied.

Ris ran a hand through his wavy brown hair. She would miss running her hands through his chestnut-colored locks, so thick, yet so soft.

"Thanks," he said.

Guin stared down at her drink.

"So when did you have this revelation?" Ris asked her.

"I was speaking with the detective, and…"

"The detective?" said Ris, interrupting her. "You were discussing our love life with Detective O'Loughlin?"

Guin could feel her cheeks reddening. This was not going as planned.

"No, I mean… I…"

"Forget it," said Ris, tossing a twenty-dollar bill on the bar.

"Ris, don't…"

"Don't what, Guin?" he said, turning to look at her again.

She could see the anger and pain on his face.

"I'm sorry," she said, lamely.

"I'm sorry, too. Goodbye, Guin."

She opened her mouth to say something, but nothing came out.

Ris shook his head, then made his way out of the bar.

Guin watched him go, then turned back to her drink.

"If you don't want him, can I have him?" asked the bartender, leering at Guin.

Guin glared at her.

Guin remained at the bar for another half hour, sipping her drink and watching the people around her.

"You want another one?"

It was the other bartender, an older man.

Guin looked down. She hadn't realized she had finished her margarita.

"Sure," she said.

"Coming right up," said the bartender. "You want some food to go with that?"

"I'm not hungry," Guin replied.

"Suit yourself," he said. "But a bitty thing like you, you should have some food. Those margaritas pack quite a wallop."

"Thanks," said Guin, her tone a bit surly. "I'm good."

She turned her attention to one of the TVs. Some sporting event was on.

"This seat taken?" asked a male voice.

Guin didn't bother turning.

"Go ahead," said Guin.

"Thanks," said the stranger.

"Here you go," said the bartender, placing the margarita in front of Guin.

"Thanks," Guin replied, picking it up and taking a sip.

"What can I get you?" asked the bartender to the man seated next to Guin.

"A Fort Myers Brewing," said the man.

"You got it!" said the bartender.

"You come here often?" said the man, addressing Guin.

Guin turned to tell the man she wasn't interested.

"Sorry, but I'm…"

It was the detective.

"What are you doing here?" she asked him. With all of the ambient noise and being so distracted, she hadn't recognized the detective's voice.

"Just grabbing a drink after work," he replied. "Though I'm surprised to see you here. You writing up the place for the paper?"

The bartender brought the detective his beer, placing it in front of him.

"Thanks," said the detective.

Guin let out a sigh.

"Something wrong?" asked the detective, taking a sip of his beer.

"No. Yes," said Guin, feeling her head start to throb.

"Which is it?" asked the detective.

"I just broke up with Ris. He didn't take it very well."

"You were expecting him to be happy about it?"

Guin glared at him.

"Breaking up with him was your idea, remember?"

The detective held up his hands.

"Hold on there. I never told you to break up with the guy."

Guin continued to glare at him.

"You told me that if I didn't love him, I should let him know."

The detective took another sip of his beer.

"Well?" said Guin.

"Well what?" asked the detective.

They sat there, looking at each other for several seconds. Then Guin looked down at her margarita and took another sip.

"You eat anything?" asked the detective.

"Why do people keep asking me that?" Guin snapped. "I'm fine. All right?"

The detective held up his hands again. Guin made a face and took another sip of her drink. Truth be told, she was starting to feel a bit lightheaded, but she wasn't going to tell the detective that.

"Well, I'm going to get some food," said the detective. "Excuse me," he said to the bartender. "Can I get a menu?"

"Coming right up!" said the bartender.

A minute later he deposited a menu in front of the detective.

"Hmm…" said the detective, poring over the menu.

Guin surreptitiously glanced over.

"Yes?" said the bartender.

"I'll have some fried calamari," said the detective.

"And what about you, Miss?" asked the bartender. "I highly recommend our conch fritters. Best on the island."

"Fine," said Guin. "Bring me an order of conch fritters."

"Very good. I'll be back in a few with your orders," said the bartender.

Guin took another sip of her drink.

"Maybe you want to slow down a bit," suggested the detective.

Guin glared at him.

They sat in silence for several minutes, both watching the television.

"Here you go," said the bartender, ten minutes later, placing the fried calamari in front of the detective and the conch fritters in front of Guin. "Enjoy!"

Guin stared down at her conch fritters.

"*Bon appetit!*" said the detective.

Guin stared at him.

"What?" said the detective, swallowing a piece of fried calamari. "My mom used to watch Julia Child."

He shrugged and popped another piece of fried calamari into his mouth.

Guin turned back to her food.

"Go on, eat something," said the detective.

Guin picked up a conch fritter and bit into it. It wasn't bad. She had another bite. In fact, it was pretty good.

She signaled to the bartender.

"What can I get you?" he asked.

"May I have a glass of water?" Guin asked him, sweetly.

"Coming right up!" said the bartender, smiling back at her.

"See, you're feeling better already," said the detective, grinning at her.

Guin didn't know how long they stayed there for. A while. The detective had ordered another beer and some clams and insisted on Guin having a few. She had to admit, it felt better being there with the detective than being home alone.

"You want another margarita?" asked the bartender.

Guin looked down. She hadn't realized she had drunk the second one already.

"No thanks," she said. "Just some more water."

He refilled her glass.

"Well, I should be heading out," said the detective, when he finished his beer.

He signaled for the check.

"You going?" said Guin, suddenly feeling a bit panicky.

"Yeah, I've got some work to do."

"But it's the weekend," said Guin, not wanting him to leave her. "Stay."

"Shouldn't you be going, too?" he asked her.

She sighed.

"I suppose you're right."

She caught the bartender's eye and mouthed "check." He nodded back at her. For once, the detective didn't offer to pay for her. She wasn't sure if that made her glad or upset. Her head was starting to pound, and she felt a bit woozy as she got up.

The detective immediately grabbed her arm.

"You sure you're okay?"

"Just had a little more to drink than I had planned," she responded.

The detective made a face.

"You're coming with me."

"Excuse me?" said Guin.

"You heard me. You're coming with me, at least until you've sobered up."

"I'm perfectly fine," said Guin.

She took a couple steps toward the exit and stumbled.

The detective looked at her. Was that pity? Guin shook her head, but that only made it hurt more.

"Where do you live?" she asked him.

She realized she had no idea. She assumed he lived on Sanibel, or else nearby.

"Close to here. Come on," he said, taking her arm.

She followed him outside, her head pounding as she made her way down the stairs.

"Easy does it," he said, continuing to hold onto her.

He led her over to his car and opened the passenger-side door.

"What about the Mini?" she asked, looking around, trying to spot it.

"You can get it later, when you're feeling better."

Guin opened her mouth to say something but quickly shut it. She got in the detective's car and stared out the window.

"Here," said the detective, reaching around her to put on her seatbelt.

She felt his arm brush her breasts as he reached over and felt her face growing warm.

"Thanks," she said.

He replied with a grunt, then started the car.

CHAPTER 37

A few minutes later, the detective pulled into an apartment complex. It was dark out, so Guin couldn't see much.

"Here," said the detective, opening Guin's door and helping her out.

Guin followed him up a flight of steps. He opened the door and turned on the lights. Guin followed him inside.

"It's nothing fancy, but..."

He hung his keys on a hook by the front door.

Guin took a quick look around. There was a kitchen to the right and the living area was straight ahead.

"Come on in," said the detective. "Would you like the guided tour?"

"Sure, why not?" she replied.

"This is the kitchen," he said, making a sweeping gesture with his hand.

"I kind of figured that," said Guin, trying to quash a smile.

"And over there is the living room," said the detective, gesturing toward the living area.

Guin giggled.

"Over here," he said, turning around and taking a few steps, "is the guest room and bathroom."

He opened a door and turned on the light. Guin could see what looked like a queen-size bed and a dresser, and there were posters of various Boston sports teams on the walls.

"For when Joey comes to visit," said the detective.

Joey was the detective's adult son, who Guin had only recently learned about.

"Does he visit you often?" asked Guin.

"Not so much. But I keep the room ready for him."

"And where do you sleep?" asked Guin.

He led her past the kitchen and living room.

"This," he said, opening the door and turning on the light, "is my room."

Guin peered inside. The room was sparsely furnished. There was a queen-size bed with a night table next to it and a chest of drawers with a poster of Fenway Park above it. But that was about it.

She took a few steps into the room, to get a better look. Then she turned around and nearly crashed into the detective, who she hadn't realized had followed her in and was standing directly behind her. He automatically reached out his hands to steady her, then hurriedly removed them and took a step back.

Guin giggled again.

"Nervous, detective?" she said, taking a step toward him. He didn't move.

Guin took another step, then got up on her tiptoes.

"Ms. Jones... Guin... don't," said the detective.

A second later, Guin was kissing him.

Guin opened her eyes and looked around. Then she panicked. She was in the detective's bed. She looked over to her right, but there was no one else in the bed. She glanced around again. Had she slept with him? She couldn't recall. Everything after the kiss was a blur, and her head hurt.

Never ever have two margaritas on an empty stomach, she told herself. She lifted the sheet and looked down at her body. She was dressed in a Boston Bruins jersey. How the heck had that happened?

She rubbed her head and glanced over at the night table. There was an alarm clock on it, and a glass of water and two aspirin. The clock read 5:34. She swallowed the two aspirin and took a sip of the water. Then she closed her eyes. She prayed she hadn't done anything foolish. Though considering she was in the detective's bed, wearing his Boston Bruins jersey, it didn't look good.

She got up and went in search of the bathroom. When she was done, she climbed back into the detective's bed, but she was too restless to fall back asleep. Where was the detective?

She glanced back down at the table. There was no note. Just the glass of water.

She got out of the bed again and made her way to the kitchen. A light was on, and there was a nearly full pot of coffee in the coffee maker.

"I hope I didn't wake you," said the detective.

Guin jumped, then put a hand over her heart.

"You scared me."

"Sorry."

He was eyeing her.

Guin instinctively moved her hands to cover herself. The jersey was big but barely covered her bottom. At least she still had on her underwear.

"Did you happen to see my clothes?" Guin asked him, her face turning pink.

"Probably still on the floor, where you left them," said the detective, taking a sip from his mug. "Would you like some coffee?"

"Please," said Guin.

The detective opened a nearby cabinet and got out a mug.

"Black?"

Guin nodded.

He poured some coffee into the mug, then handed it to her.

"Thanks," she said, taking it from him. She took a sip. "Not bad."

She smiled up at him.

"You want something to eat?" he asked her. "Not that I have much to offer."

"I'm fine," she replied, taking another sip of coffee. It was strong, just how she liked it.

She peered over her mug at the detective.

"So, um, what exactly happened last night?"

The detective regarded her.

"You had a little too much to drink, so I took you back here."

"I got that part," said Guin. "I meant after. Like, how did I wind up in *this*," she said, sweeping her hand over the jersey.

The detective grinned.

"It looks good on you."

"Yes, but how did it wind up on me?"

"You don't remember?" asked the detective.

"If I remembered, would I be asking you?" asked Guin, a bit snippily.

"Well, first you kissed me…" began the detective.

Guin waited for the detective to continue, dreading what was to come.

"Then I kissed you back…"

Guin could feel her face turning a bright shade of red.

"Then you pushed me onto the bed and nearly ripped off my shirt."

"I did *what*?!" Guin screeched.

"I have the loose button, if you want to see it."

Guin felt mortified.

"Then what?" she asked, dreading the answer.

"Then we kissed some more."

"And?" said Guin.

"And then you fell asleep."

"I what?" said Guin, not sure she heard him correctly.

"You snore, by the way."

"I do not snore," said Guin.

"I hate to break it to you but…"

The detective was grinning. Guin was infuriated.

"But how did I wind up in your jersey?" Guin asked, taking a piece of it between her fingers and pulling it out.

"You insisted."

"I insisted?" said Guin, confused.

"You did. After you fell asleep, I gently woke you back up and suggested you change into something more comfortable. I didn't want you to get that nice dress of yours all wrinkled."

Though no doubt after their tussling, it already was.

"So you, what, undressed me?" asked Guin, her hands now on her hips.

"No," said the detective. "You did that all by yourself. Though you did ask me if I'd like to do the honors."

Yup, Guin was totally mortified.

"And the jersey?"

"I told you to help yourself to whatever was in my closet, and you came out wearing that. And I must say, it looks better on you than it ever did on me."

"Thanks," said Guin. She paused. "So we didn't… you know…"

"No," said the detective. "Though you were more than willing."

Ouch, thought Guin.

The detective continued to sip his coffee.

"So what are you doing up so early—and where did you sleep last night?" she quickly added.

"In the guest room," replied the detective. "And I've been working."

"At five in the morning?"

"I typically get up around five," said the detective.

"What were you working on?" asked Guin.

"The Rawlins case. We got some new evidence."

"Oh?" said Guin. "Care to share?"

The detective gave her a look, the one that said, 'You know I can't, or won't, do that. So why are you asking?'

"Well, I came across some new evidence, too," said Guin.

The detective raised his eyebrows.

"And, unlike you, I'm willing to share. You have a computer?"

"In the living room," said the detective.

"I'll send you the link. Then I'll show you."

Guin went to look for her purse.

"Where's my bag?" she asked him.

"Didn't you see it?" he asked her.

"No. Where is it?"

"By the bed."

Guin went back into the bedroom, turning on the light. There was her bag, on the dresser. She reached in and pulled out her phone, which was still on, and opened her email. She found the one from Rita, with the link to the video, and forwarded it to the detective.

"You should have it any second," she told him, when she emerged from the bedroom.

He was looking at her again.

"Maybe you should change," he said, his face partially

hidden behind his mug of coffee.

"How come?" asked Guin, putting her hands on her hips, which caused the jersey to inch upwards.

"Because I have work to do, and I don't need any distractions."

Guin walked over to him, standing directly in front of him.

"You find me distracting?" she asked him.

He didn't answer.

She took his mug and placed it on the counter, then took a step closer to him.

"You didn't answer me, detective," she said, placing her arms around his neck. "Do you find me distracting?"

Part of Guin felt horrified, but the other part of her was thoroughly enjoying this, no doubt the part that told her drinking two margaritas on an empty stomach was just fine.

"This isn't a good idea, Ms. Jones…" said the detective. Though he made no move to remove her arms from around his neck or push away her body.

"Yes?" said Guin, still clinging to him.

The detective sighed.

"What am I going to do with you?"

"I have a few ideas," said Guin, smiling up at him.

She liked how he looked first thing in the morning, his curly reddish brown hair, tinged with gray, a little wild, his tawny eyes wary but soft. She could make out the freckles across his face, his firm jaw and strong neck. She ran a hand down his muscular arm and wondered if he worked out. He had always reminded her of a boxer.

He looked down at her hand, then gently pushed her away.

"Like I said, I have work to do."

"Fine," said Guin. "I'll go change. Wait for me before opening that link I sent you."

Guin went back into the bedroom.

"I took out a towel and a washcloth for you," called the detective, through the closed door.

"Thanks," Guin called back.

She thought about taking a quick shower but decided to wait until she got home. Instead, she washed her hands and face, then slipped back into her sundress. She glanced in the mirror. Her hair was a mess. She searched for a comb and ran it through her hair.

"What's the point?" she said.

She emerged from the bedroom and headed over to where the detective was seated, a laptop in front of him, several file folders next to it.

"Better?" she asked him, twirling around.

He looked up but didn't answer.

Guin looked down at the laptop. He had the video up.

"I told you to wait," she said.

"Sue me."

Guin sat down next to him. Without looking at her, he started the video from the beginning.

"There!" Guin said. "Pause it there," she commanded, at the place where the fountain vandal's hood fell back.

The detective was staring at the screen.

"That must be who was responsible for causing the fountain to short circuit," said Guin. "If he had only turned around, so the camera could have gotten a look at his face."

"How do you know it's a he?" asked the detective, looking at her.

Guin opened her mouth to say something, then quickly shut it. How did she know it was a he? She had just assumed it was a he because the vandal was tall and had short hair. But it could have been a woman.

"You know who it is, don't you?" asked Guin, looking right at the detective.

Again, the detective didn't speak.

Guin reached for the top file.

"What else aren't you telling me?"

She opened the file and saw several clippings inside, including a photo from the *San-Cap Sun-Times*, taken at the fountain ceremony. Why would the detective have that? She scanned the photo, taking in the crowd of onlookers. Nothing popped out at her. But the detective must have had the photo for a reason. She slowly scanned the photo again. Then stopped. She looked over at the laptop.

"Play the video one more time," she commanded him.

He pressed 'play,' and the video started streaming. Once again, she watched as what looked like a flashlight approached the fountain, then stopped. Then the screen lit up, as Rita's editor friend had no doubt increased the brightness, to allow the viewer to see the person attached to the flashlight.

Again, Guin watched as the vandal squatted down inside the fountain and remained there for several minutes, then stood up and brushed an arm across his—no *her*—face, causing her hood to fall back and reveal her white-blonde hair.

Of course, thought Guin, mentally kicking herself. That's why she looked familiar. But why?

"So, are you going to arrest her?" asked Guin, looking at the detective.

"We'll need to question her first."

"I need to make a phone call," said Guin.

"At six a.m.?" asked the detective.

Good point, thought Guin. But this couldn't wait.

CHAPTER 38

The detective dropped Guin off at the Bimini Bait Shack on his way to Sanibel. On the way there, she had asked him about CiCi, but he had remained tightlipped.

"Would you at least confirm my theory that the two crimes are connected?" she had asked him. But he hadn't replied. Which only served to frustrate Guin further.

"I just know the two are somehow connected," she grumbled, glancing out the window. "I just need to figure out how."

"Take my advice and stay out of it," the detective had told her.

Guin had shot him a look.

"I have a job to do, too," she had retorted. "A job that would be made much easier if the police would just answer a few simple questions."

But the detective had just stared straight ahead.

"Thanks for last night," she said, as she got out of the car.

She slammed the door shut and stared, but the detective ignored her. She then watched as he drove away. Why did he have to be so difficult? She sighed and got into the Mini.

The cats were there to greet her as soon as she walked in the door. Fauna acted as though she hadn't been fed in days, while Flora looked up at Guin with her big green eyes, as if to say, "Why did you abandon us?"

"I'm sorry," said Guin. "Though it really hasn't been that long."

She walked into the kitchen and gave the cats some food, which they began wolfing down. Then she refilled their water bowl.

"Slow down!" she admonished them. "I don't want to be cleaning up cat puke five minutes from now."

But they paid her no mind and continued to scarf their food.

Guin shook her head and leaned against the counter. Her stomach growled.

"Right. Food."

She was still feeling lightheaded.

"Probably should have picked up something on my way home," she chided herself.

She opened the refrigerator and grabbed the carton of eggs. Then she reached into the freezer and pulled out a loaf of bread. A few minutes later, her scrambled eggs and toast were ready. She ate them standing up, leaning against the counter, watching as the sun lit up the golf course.

She reached for her phone and realized she had left it in her bag. She quickly retrieved it and saw that the message light was flashing. There was a message from Ris. She froze, unable to decide what to do. After a few seconds of hesitation, she opened it.

"Can we talk?" read the message.

Guin stared at it. What had they left to talk about? She deleted the message and checked the rest.

Lance had written her, as had Shelly.

She opened Lance's text first, which was from the night before.

"Let me know when you're coming to Paris. Call me!" It was followed by an emoji blowing a kiss and a picture of the

French flag and an airplane.

Guin stared at the text.

"Paris," she said. She could use a trip to Paris. "Screw it," she said.

"I'm in," Guin wrote him back. "Let me know when's a good time to chat."

She hit send and smiled. Then she opened Shelly's message.

"Need to talk to you about the Naples show. Want to do brunch tomorrow?"

It had been ages since Guin had had Sunday brunch with Shelly. When she had first become friends with her, before she had begun dating Ris, the two of them had had brunch nearly every Sunday, usually at the Over Easy Cafe.

"Count me in!" wrote Guin.

Next, she checked her email. There was a message from Ginny with the subject line "New stories." Guin opened it and scanned the body. Ginny wanted her to review Malia's Island Fusion, a new restaurant that had just opened where the Blue Coyote had been. And she wanted Guin to profile a volunteer at Ding Darling, who was celebrating his 40th anniversary volunteering there. Ginny also reminded her about the gallery opening that evening, letting her know that Glen would meet her over there.

Guin sighed. She enjoyed working for a small-town paper, but she was suddenly feeling a bit claustrophobic. Though that wasn't the right word. What she really needed was to get away from Sanibel for a few days, even though she had just been away. Maybe a week in Paris with Lance and Owen would help. Though a small part of her worried that a trip to Paris would only make her restlessness worse.

"What do you think, Fauna? Will Ginny give me another week off?" she asked the black cat, who was rubbing herself against Guin's legs.

"Meow," Fauna replied, clearly wanting to be pet.

Guin bent down and rubbed the side of Fauna's face, then scratched her back. Fauna purred in response.

As she was petting the cat, her phone started buzzing. She straightened up and grabbed her phone. It was Rita.

"Thanks for calling me."

"No problem," she said. "What's up? Your text sounded pretty urgent."

"I need to speak with you and Sam. Can I come over?"

"Sam's still in bed, but sure. Come on over. I'll brew up some coffee."

"I'm good," said Guin. "But thanks. I'll be by around nine."

"Sam should be up by then," said Rita. "See you then."

Guin quickly took a shower and changed. Then she got on her computer. She opened her search engine and typed in "Marta Harvey and Tanya Harvey."

Guin arrived at Sam's place a little after nine.

Rita led her into the kitchen, where Sam and Denny were seated at the kitchen table, nursing mugs of coffee.

"Hi," said Guin.

"Hi," said Sam. "What's up? We got your message. Seemed pretty urgent."

"I know who vandalized the fountain," said Guin.

The three of them looked at her.

"It was Marta," said Guin.

"Marta?" said Sam, confused. "Why would she want to damage the fountain? She spent months working on it."

Rita looked over at Guin.

"I thought it was her, but I wasn't sure."

"You knew?" said Sam, turning to her friend.

"Not for certain. It only came to me when I saw the video Micah sent. The 'guy' with the short blonde hair, it had to be Marta."

"That's why she looked familiar," said Guin.

"But why?" said Sam. "I don't understand."

"I'm not entirely sure," said Guin. "But I'm working on a theory. And I think she may have killed CiCi, too."

"Marta? You can't be serious, Guin," said Sam.

"Marta damaging the fountain is one thing, but murder?" said Rita, staring at her.

"I'm afraid I am," Guin replied.

"I believe it," said Denny.

They all turned to look at him.

"There was something off about that chick."

"You think there's something off with any woman who doesn't fall under your spell," Rita retorted.

Denny made a face, and Rita stuck out her tongue.

"Children, behave," said Sam.

"What made you think there was something 'off' about her, Denny?" Guin asked him.

"She kept giving me these looks."

Rita rolled her eyes.

"And she kept saying God was watching and didn't approve of fornicators."

"Huh," said Sam. "She never said anything to me."

"Nor me," said Rita. "Not that she ever really said much. Marta was the strong, silent type," she explained to Guin.

"I got that impression, too," said Guin. "Did she ever say anything about CiCi to any of you?"

"I don't think the two of them got along," said Rita. "But I don't recall Marta saying anything."

"CiCi told me Marta scared her," said Denny. "That she always felt Marta was judging her."

"What?" said Sam. "She never said anything to me."

"She was probably scared of you, too," he said, smiling at her.

"Me?" said Sam.

"You can be pretty intimidating," said Denny.

Sam hit him.

"See what I mean?"

"I still don't understand why Marta would want to harm the fountain," said Rita. "She of all people would appreciate the hard work we put into it. Have you seen her work?" Rita asked Guin. "I'm surprised the City didn't ask her to design something."

"About that," said Guin. "Did you know she had applied to the committee to create the shell sculpture?"

"No," said Sam. "Did you, Rita?"

"I did not," said Rita, frowning. "How did you find out?"

"I did some digging," said Guin.

"So you think there were some bad feelings there?" asked Sam.

"It's possible," said Guin. "I need to go chat with some of the Shell Crafters. Maybe one of them knows something."

"But if she wanted to sabotage the fountain, why wait until just before the unveiling?" asked Rita.

"To have the biggest impact," said Guin. "Maybe she wanted to make you seem incompetent in front of all those people, unworthy."

Sam and Rita looked thoughtful.

"Wow," said Sam. "I would have never suspected Marta. I still can't believe it. You're sure she's the one?"

"Not a hundred percent," said Guin. "But the saboteur in the video was tall and thin with short, light hair. Even though the video was grainy, I'd lay odds it was Marta. Besides, how many people knew exactly where the wires were? It had to have been her."

"Even if she wasn't awarded the commission, everyone knew she had helped with the fountain," said Sam.

"Only after you unveiled it," Guin pointed out. "And it still wasn't her creation. She was just a helper, not the artist."

"But why kill CiCi?" asked Rita. "What did CiCi ever do to her?"

"I think I may know," said Denny.

Once again, all eyes turned to him.

"I think Marta saw us."

"What do you mean, 'saw us?'" said Sam, looking at him.

Denny sighed.

"I was just horsing around."

Sam and Rita continued to look at him.

"I saw the way CiCi looked at me, and I figured I'd have a little fun."

"What do you mean by 'fun,' Dennis?"

Rita was giving him the hairy eyeball.

"You know, flirt with her a bit."

All three women were eyeing him.

"It was no big deal. But I could tell Marta was not amused."

"I'm not particularly amused either," said Sam. "Go on."

"I think that's why she said what she did, about God not liking fornicators. It was a warning for me to stay away from CiCi."

"But what does that have to do with CiCi?" asked Rita. "It sounds more like she was warning you."

"Oh no," said Guin, the missing piece of the puzzle snapping into place.

"What?" said Sam.

"Of course. Stupid, stupid, stupid."

"What?" said Rita.

"Marta must have known about the rumor," said Guin.

"What rumor?" said Sam.

"About CiCi and Ris."

"Who's Ris?" asked Rita.

"Sorry, Dr. Harrison Hartwick. He's a professor at FGCU. CiCi was his teaching assistant."

"What was the rumor?" asked Rita.

"That they were sleeping together," said Guin.

"I can't imagine CiCi sleeping with a professor," said Sam.

"Me neither," said Rita.

"I can," said Denny. "I mean, if I was her professor, I'd totally sleep with her."

Rita and Sam both glared at him.

"Just being honest."

"Dr. Hartwick said the rumor wasn't true," Guin explained. "But the young woman who started it, Tanya Harvey, was pretty convincing."

"Wait a minute," said Rita. "Did you say the girl's name was Tanya *Harvey*?"

Guin nodded.

"I did some checking. She's Marta's granddaughter."

"But I still don't understand why Marta would kill CiCi," Sam said.

"I suspect it was an accident," said Guin. "Marta probably just wanted to warn her, put the fear of God in her about being a Jezebel, and didn't want to do it in front of all of you."

"She put the fear of God in me," said Denny.

Sam and Rita ignored him.

"I never pictured CiCi as a Jezebel," said Sam.

"Me neither," said Rita.

Guin continued.

"So when CiCi said she would be going to Silver Key early the next morning, Marta figured she would confront her there."

"So what happened?" said Sam.

"They probably got into some kind of argument," said Guin. "Maybe Marta got all righteous on CiCi, and CiCi told her to go to Hell and mind her own business, and Marta lost it."

"What did you say the murder weapon was?" Rita asked her.

"A giant horse conch," said Guin. "Marta must have picked it up somewhere along the beach, then hit CiCi on the back of her head with it when she wasn't looking."

"I must have been on Sanibel too long," said Rita, "but I can actually picture that."

"Me, too," said Denny.

"You can?" said Sam.

"You ever see *Vikings* on the History Channel?" asked Denny. "Marta totally reminds me of one of those Viking chicks."

"Or Cersei Lannister," said Rita.

Denny nodded his head.

"I still don't understand, though," said Sam. "If Marta was so holier-than-thou, how could she stand working for me?"

"She probably didn't know about you and Denny," said Guin. "I certainly didn't."

"You guys do kind of fly under the radar," said Rita.

"Besides," said Guin, "her original goal was just to be a part of the sculpture."

"So do you think it was her intent to destroy the fountain from the beginning?" asked Sam.

"I don't know," said Guin.

"So now what?" asked Rita.

"Now the hard part: proving Marta was responsible for killing CiCi, destroying the fountain, and nearly killing Sam," said Guin.

CHAPTER 39

"How are you going to prove it?" asked Rita.

"Isn't that the police's job?" asked Sam.

Guin was thinking.

"If only someone saw Marta on the beach that morning."

"I'm surprised you didn't see her," said Rita.

"I suffer from shell blindness," said Guin.

"Shell blindness?" asked Denny.

"When I'm on the beach, looking for shells, I'm oblivious to anyone around me. My own mother could walk right by me and I probably wouldn't notice her."

"I understand," said Sam. "I'm like that when I'm working on a new sculpture. I get into the zone."

"Exactly," said Guin.

"Still, you would think someone would have seen her," said Rita. "Not like Marta is hard to spot."

"True," said Guin. "But not a lot of people make it all the way down to Silver Key. It's a bit of a hike to there from Blind Pass. And it was early. The sun had just barely risen. Only crazy shellers like Suzy—"

Guin stopped. Suzy! I bet Suzy saw Marta, she said to herself.

"What is it?" asked Rita. "You've thought of something, haven't you?"

"Susan Hastings was on Silver Key that morning," said

Guin. "At first I thought she might have been responsible, but I just couldn't picture her clubbing CiCi over the back of the head. But she saw Marta. She just didn't realize it."

"I don't understand," said Sam.

Guin smiled.

"As the island's resident Gossip Queen, Suzy mentally records everything suspicious or unusual that she sees, so she can use it later in her blog."

"But wouldn't the police have already arrested Marta if Susan had reported she saw Marta arguing with CiCi?" asked Rita.

"Susan said the person she saw was wearing a hoodie, so she didn't see his face," said Guin. "But what if Marta ditched the hoodie someplace and just walked down the beach dressed normally? Suzy probably wouldn't have paid her any mind. Just another person out looking for shells."

"That actually sounds plausible," said Sam. "So are you going to talk to Susan, find out if she saw Marta on the beach that morning?"

"Actually," said Guin, looking over at Sam, "I was hoping you would talk to her."

"Me?!" said Sam. "But you're the reporter!"

"I know, which is why you should be the one to speak with her. Suzy hates me. She thinks we're in some kind of competition. But if you invited her over here, told her you wanted to give her an exclusive…"

"Then what?" asked Sam.

"Then, after you've buttered her up, you tell her our theory about Marta, and ask her if she happened to see Marta on the beach that morning," said Guin.

"You mean *your* theory," said Sam.

"Does it really matter?" asked Guin. "The point is to find out if she saw Marta by Silver Key."

Sam looked pensive.

"Fine, but how am I supposed to butter her up? And shouldn't we tell the police what we're up to?"

"As soon as we get Suzy's testimony and can put Marta at the scene of the crime, I'll call Detective O'Loughlin."

"Okay, but what do I say to Suzy?"

"Just call her and say you feel bad that you didn't include her, and that you'd like to make it up to her by giving her a scoop on your next big project," said Guin.

Sam looked at Rita, who shrugged.

"And then what?" she asked.

"You arrange to have her come over or have her meet you someplace. You tell her what you're working on next. Then you tell her you heard she was on Silver Key the morning CiCi was killed, and how that must have been so dreadful for her. And, oh, by the way, did she happen to see Marta shelling that morning on the beach?"

"You sure you don't want to be the one doing the talking?" said Sam. "I'm afraid I'm going to screw it up."

"You'll do fine," said Guin.

"You really think it'll work?" Rita asked.

"It's worth a shot," said Guin.

"I still think we should go to the police," said Sam. "Tell them your theory and let them handle it."

"I promise, we'll call the police. Right after you talk to Suzy."

Sam sighed.

"Fine. Let's get this over with. Rita, grab my phone."

Rita went to get Sam's phone, then handed it to her.

"What if she doesn't answer?" said Sam.

"Leave a message," said Guin.

Sam entered Susan's number.

"It's ringing."

The three of them waited.

"Hi, Susan! It's Sam Hutchins."

Rita, Guin, and Denny all watched as Sam spoke.

"I'm good. Hey, I feel really badly about not including you in the fountain project."

There was a momentary silence.

"That's very kind of you to say," said Sam. "But I want to make it up to you by giving you the scoop on my next project."

Again there was silence as Suzy said something to Sam.

"Great. Well, if you're free, you can come over now," said Sam.

Guin waited.

"Okay, I'll see you in around half an hour," Sam said.

She ended the call and looked at Guin.

"How'd I do?"

"Great!" said Guin.

"So now what?" asked Rita.

"Now, I leave," said Guin.

"You're not going to stay and listen?" asked Sam.

"Trust me, it's better if I'm not here. Just text me when Suzy's left."

"Fine," said Sam. "But I'd feel better if you were here."

"I'll be here," said Rita.

"I'll be here, too," said Denny.

"Thanks," said Sam.

"See, you'll be fine," said Guin. "Well, I should get going. Good luck. And call me as soon as she's gone."

"Will do," said Sam.

"I'll see myself out," said Guin.

Guin paced around the condo, waiting for Sam to call her. More than an hour had passed since she had gotten home, and she hadn't heard from Sam or Rita. She was starting to get nervous.

Suddenly, her phone started ringing. She lunged for it.

"Hello? Sam?" she said, not bothering to look at the Caller ID.

"Nope, Polly."

"Oh, hi, Polly. What's up?"

Polly Fahnestock was Guin's real estate agent. And between her jet lag, covering the Shell Show, and CiCi's murder, Guin had been too busy to follow up with Polly regarding the cute cottage Polly had shown her just before she had left to meet Ris in Australia.

"Remember that adorable little cottage we saw off of West Gulf, the one you said you really liked?" asked Polly.

"I remember it. How much did it go for?" asked Guin.

"That's why I'm calling," said Polly. "It's back on the market."

"Really?" said Guin, taken aback.

"Really," said Polly.

"How come? Did it not pass inspection?"

"Nothing like that," said Polly. "The prospective buyers withdrew their offer. They're buying in Naples instead. So the house is available. You still interested?"

"Wow," said Guin.

"Yeah," said Polly. "So, you want to make an offer?"

Guin sat down on the couch.

"Can we go see it again?"

"Of course. Do you want Ris to come with you?" asked Polly.

"We broke up," said Guin.

"Wow," said Polly. She paused. "Did it have something to do with what I've been hearing on the news?"

"Not really," said Guin. "I just realized we weren't a good fit."

"Well, his loss," said Polly. "So, when do you want to see the place?"

"Do you think we could go over there tomorrow?" asked Guin.

She was thinking she'd invite Shelly to go with her.

"Let me call over to the listing agent and get back to you."

"Great," said Guin.

She was about to say something else when she heard another call on the line. It had to be Sam.

"Hey, Poll. I've gotta go. Leave me a message if you get my voicemail, or text me."

"Will do."

Guin quickly ended the call and grabbed the incoming one.

"Sam?"

"You owe me," she replied.

"That good, eh?" said Guin.

"I thought she would never leave," Sam replied.

"Sorry. So, did she recall seeing Marta?"

"At first she was pretty coy. Then I told her your theory. That got her talking."

"What did she say?" asked Guin.

"She said she thought she had seen Marta on the beach that morning, had said hello to her, but that Marta had ignored her. Though she said she wasn't that surprised. Marta wasn't exactly the friendliest person. And Marta seemed to be in a hurry."

"Anything else?" said Guin.

"Nothing important."

"Thank you," said Guin.

"Now what?" asked Sam.

"Now I'm going to go over to the Sanibel Police Department, to have a little chat with Detective O'Loughlin," said Guin.

CHAPTER 40

Guin drove as fast as she dared (the Sanibel speed limit being 35 mph) to the Sanibel Police Department. She parked in the lot, then ran up the stairs. She tapped on the glass to get the woman inside's attention and asked to speak with Detective O'Loughlin.

"I'm sorry, he's unavailable," said the woman.

"Tell him it's urgent," said Guin.

"He's not in right now," said the woman. "But you can use the phone to leave him a voicemail," she said, pointing to the phone to Guin's right. "His extension is..."

"I know his extension," said Guin.

She picked up the phone and dialed it.

"This is Guin. Ms. Jones. I know who killed Caroline Rawlins. Call me."

She hung up the phone and looked down at the woman, whose attention was focused on her computer monitor.

"Thanks," said Guin.

The woman glanced briefly at Guin, then returned to her screen.

Guin left the police department and headed back towards the stairs. Then she stopped. She grabbed her phone and entered the detective's number. It went directly to voicemail. He was probably out fishing.

"It's Guin Jones," said Guin. "I know who killed Caroline Rawlins. Call me."

She quickly sent him a text, put her phone back in her bag, then trotted down the steps. She was heading to her car when she remembered that Ginny wanted her to cover the new exhibit opening that evening at the Phillips Gallery, part of BIG ARTS, Sanibel's center for fine and performing arts.

She turned around and headed towards the gallery, which was just a short walk from the police department. The gallery door was open, so Guin let herself in. There were several women inside, placing or adjusting paintings and sculptures. No doubt preparing them for the opening later.

Guin looked around, admiring the artwork, then stopped dead. There, across the room, adjusting a vase filled with shell flowers, was Marta. There was no mistaking her. Fortunately, she had her back to Guin.

"Hello there," came a pleasant voice. "May I help you? The exhibit doesn't officially open until five-thirty."

Guin turned to face the woman.

"I'm sorry," said Guin, smiling at the woman, who was around Guin's height and looked to be in her sixties. "I'm Guin Jones, with the *Sanibel-Captiva Sun-Times*," she said, extending her hand. "Ginny asked me to cover the opening later as Beth had a family emergency."

"I do hope everything is okay," said the woman.

"Me, too," said Guin.

"I'm Harriet Geller," said the woman. "I'm in charge of the gallery."

"Nice to meet you, Harriet."

"Let me know if I can answer any questions," she said.

Guin quickly scanned the room. She didn't see Marta.

"What do you know about Marta Harvey?"

"Marta?" said Harriet. "Not a whole lot. She's a rather private person. Though what she does with shells is truly amazing."

"I know," said Guin. "I saw another piece of hers over

at the Shell Show. I'm surprised she had time to make more than one, what with her work for Samantha Hutchins."

"I know," said Harriet. "It would take me a year to do a piece like that. But she bangs them out like it was nothing."

She shook her head.

"Frankly, we were all a bit surprised when the City awarded that commission to Samantha Hutchins," said Harriet. "Not that she isn't amazing, too. But we thought it should have gone to a local. And, though Marta would never say anything, I think she took it pretty hard."

"Yet she volunteered to work on Sam's piece," said Guin.

"It did seem strange when I heard. She kept it a secret."

"She had signed a non-disclosure agreement," said Guin. "That's probably why."

"Ah," said Harriet.

"So are you and Marta friends?" Guin asked her.

"I don't know if I would call us friends," said Harriet, "We're both in the Shell Crafters and have had the occasional meal together."

"Did you, by chance, ever happen to hear her mention the name CiCi or Caroline Rawlins?"

Harriet looked thoughtful.

"No, not that I can recall," she said. "Why?"

"Did she seem particularly religious or self-righteous to you?" Guin asked her.

"A little bit," said Harriet. "I know she attended church regularly and could quote the Bible. And I did hear her complain a time or two about young people these days. Mainly young women. She didn't get the whole #MeToo movement. I remember her saying, 'If these young women don't want men pawing at them, they should stop dressing like whores and parading around in front of them.'"

"Wow," said Guin.

"I know," said Harriet. "Mostly, though, she kept her opinions to herself."

"Well, thank you for your time," said Guin. "I'm going to take a look around if that's okay. Then I'll be back later to officially cover the event."

"That's fine," said Harriet. "I'll be around if you have any questions."

"Actually," said Guin, "would you mind walking around with me? I have to confess, I'm not familiar with the local art scene. So some insider knowledge would be appreciated."

Harriet smiled. "I'd be happy to," she said.

Guin reached into her bag and pulled out her little notepad and a pen.

"Lead on," she said.

Harriet proved to be an excellent guide. As Guin discovered, she had been a docent at the Museum of Fine Arts in Boston for many years, before moving to Sanibel. And she had an in-depth knowledge of art history, as well as a familiarity with the local art scene. She made each piece come alive, giving Guin plenty to write about.

Harriet also introduced Guin to two of the artists exhibiting.

They made their way over to Marta's piece, but there was no sign of her.

"I think she left," said the artist Guin had just been chatting with.

"Thanks," said Guin.

She and Harriet stood looking at Marta's shell-flower arrangement.

"It really is lovely," said Guin.

She put away her notepad and pen.

"Well, I think that does it for me," she said. "I'll see you later. Thanks for the tour."

"My pleasure," said Harriet. "I'll see you later."

Guin checked her phone after exiting the gallery. No word from the detective.

"Come on!" she said, looking down at the phone. "Call me or at least text!"

As if by magic, her phone started to buzz. It was the detective.

"Finally!" she said, picking up. "Where have you been?"

"I do have a life, you know."

"Did you get my messages?"

"That's why I'm calling."

Guin waited.

"So, don't you want to know who killed CiCi Rawlins?"

"I have a feeling you're going to tell me, regardless," said the detective, in his usual deadpan tone.

"It was Marta Harvey. She did it. And she was the one who short-circuited the fountain."

"And you know this how?"

"I saw the video from the museum's camera. It had to be her."

"And Ms. Rawlins?"

"Run DNA tests," said Guin. "I'll bet you anything the DNA on the shell and on CiCi will match Marta. Suzy says she saw her there. And it fits."

"Mrs. Hastings is not the most reliable of witnesses," said the detective.

"I know," said Guin. "But I think she's telling the truth. Just do me a favor and get Marta to give you a DNA sample, then compare it with the DNA on the shell we found."

The detective sighed.

"Will you do it?" asked Guin.

"I need to go," said the detective.

"But—" said Guin. But the detective had already hung up.

"Great," said Guin, putting her phone back in her bag.

"Ms. Jones."

Guin looked up to see Marta staring down at her.

"Where did you come from?" asked Guin.

"I forgot something in the gallery."

They stood there, looking at each for several seconds. Guin's heart was pounding. How much of her conversation had Marta heard? Guin instinctively reached into her bag for her phone.

"Well, don't let me keep you!" said Guin, nervously.

Marta continued to look at her.

"I have to be going," said Guin. "Nice seeing you, Marta!"

Marta made a face, then turned and headed into the gallery.

Guin's heart was still racing. She watched as Marta entered the gallery, then hurried to her car.

Guin returned to the Phillips Gallery a little before 5:30. She had arranged to meet Glen, the photographer, there beforehand, so they could discuss strategy.

"We meet again," he said, smiling at Guin.

Guin smiled back at him. She hadn't really looked at him before, but Glen was rather good looking, in that Southern California surfer kind of way. Though she knew he was originally from Florida. With his mane of dark blond hair and smiling brown eyes, he reminded her a bit of Art, her ex. He was probably around Art's age, too, in his mid-forties.

"We do, indeed," she said, smiling back at him. "Busy week for you."

"This is nothing," said Glen. "I've sometimes had to cover a half-dozen events over the course of a weekend. Gotta take the work when you can get it."

"Have you always been a photographer?" Guin asked him.

"As long as I can remember," said Glen. "Though it hasn't always been my profession."

"Oh?" Guin replied, intrigued.

"I actually worked on Wall Street, until I got burnt out."

"Really?" said Guin, eyeing his tanned face and nearly shoulder-length hair.

"I know. Hard to believe," he said, his eyes twinkling. "But it's true."

"So what happened?" asked Guin.

"Life," he said. "Marriage broke up. Then my dad got sick and my folks needed me here." He shrugged.

"Wow," said Guin. "That's rough."

"Hey, I know people who've had it much worse," he said.

Guin had more questions she wanted to ask Glen, but people were starting to file into the gallery.

"We should head in," she said.

"So what's the plan?"

"I was here earlier and took notes," said Guin. "You may want to come back tomorrow and get photos of the actual artwork. But for tonight, you can take photos of whatever interests you. Just be sure to get lots of people shots. Ginny loves those. Though remember to ask for permission first and get people's names."

"Aye, aye, captain. Anything else?"

"Nope. That should do it. We don't have to stay too long. Just check in with me before you leave."

"Will do," he said. "So, shall we?"

He gestured toward the door.

"We shall," said Guin.

Guin watchèd as Glen went around the gallery, taking photos of the exhibits and chatting with the artists and visitors. He was a natural. In a way, he reminded her of Birdy. She smiled at the memory of him. She hadn't heard from Bertram "Birdy" McMurtry, the noted ornithologist, bird photographer, and flirt, since she'd had drinks with him and Ris in Australia. He was probably off photographing some exotic bird somewhere.

She turned back to watch Glen. He was chatting with an older couple. Then he took their picture. She looked forward to seeing his photos, and to learning more about him.

CHAPTER 41

The gallery continued to fill, and Guin had made the rounds again, avoiding Marta.

"I think I'm good," said Glen, his camera slung over his shoulder.

"Me, too," said Guin.

"You want to go grab a drink?" he asked her.

Guin was about to say, "sure, why not?" when there was a rustling in the crowd.

Guin turned to see Detective O'Loughlin, accompanied by two uniformed officers, enter the gallery. Guin watched as they made their way over to where Marta was chatting with some couple, then stopped.

"Excuse us," said the detective to the couple, who looked at each other, then took a step back. "Ms. Harvey, if you would come with me."

It was a statement, not a question.

Marta frowned.

"We can do this the easy way or the hard way, Ms. Harvey. It's up to you."

She glared at the detective.

"I have done nothing wrong, detective," she said, stiffly.

"Great," replied the detective. "Then you shouldn't mind answering a few questions over at the police department."

It looked as though Marta would be doing this the hard

way when one of the officers stepped forward. Then she seemed to have second thoughts.

"Fine, I will accompany you to the police department," she said, her head held high, her tone imperious.

Guin noticed that she was several inches taller than the detective.

She watched as the officers led her out of the gallery. Looking at Marta from behind, with her tall, narrow build and short hair, Guin could understand how she could be mistaken for a man.

She had hoped to catch the detective's eye as he passed. But either he didn't see her or he was ignoring her.

"What was that all about?" asked Glen, after the detective left.

"I'm pretty sure the detective just caught the person responsible for vandalizing the fountain and killing Caroline Rawlins," she replied.

"Really?" said Glen.

But Guin's attention was focused elsewhere.

"I've gotta go," she said, taking a step towards the door.

"No problem," said Glen. "Raincheck on that drink?"

Guin stopped and turned back to him.

"Sure. Let me know when you're back on the island."

Then she turned and hurried out the door.

She had hoped to catch the detective, but it was too late. Fortunately, the police department wasn't very far away.

She debated whether to take the Mini or walk, finally deciding on walking. The walkway between the buildings was lit, but it was still dark in spots, and Guin cursed herself for wearing heels.

She climbed the steps to the police department and went inside. There was no one sitting in the booth. She tapped on the bulletproof glass.

"Hello? Anyone there?" she called.

She waited several seconds, then picked up the phone and called the detective's extension. No answer. She left a message, telling the detective she was in the vestibule. Then she waited a few more minutes, in hopes that someone would show up.

She was about to leave when a young officer walked into the booth.

"May I help you?" he asked her.

"I need to speak with the detective," said Guin.

"He's kinda busy," said the young officer. Yet another policeman Guin didn't know. "Can I help you, Miss?"

"No," said Guin. "I really need to speak with the detective."

"You could always leave him a message," suggested the young officer.

Guin sighed.

"Thanks. I already did."

She stood there, not sure what to do. The young officer waited.

"I'll just go," she announced.

She turned and headed back outside.

Guin paced around her condo, unable to concentrate on anything.

As she made her way back towards the kitchen, her phone started buzzing. She had placed it on the kitchen counter and ran over to grab it.

"Hello?" she said.

"Hello yourself," came the reply.

"Oh, hi, Ginny."

"Well, that's a fine how-do-you-do," Ginny replied.

"Sorry, I was hoping it was Detective O'Loughlin."

"Sorry to disappoint you," said Ginny. "Speaking of the

detective, I heard there was some excitement over at the gallery this evening."

Of course Ginny knew. Ginny knew everything that happened on Sanibel, often before the police did.

"How did you hear?" asked Guin.

"I have my sources," Ginny replied. "So?"

"So what did your sources tell you?" said Guin, a bit peevishly.

"Now, now. No need to get snippy with me," said Ginny. "I want to hear it from you."

"All I know is that the detective showed up with a couple of officers and asked to speak with Marta Harvey."

"And?" said Ginny.

"And they took her with them to the police department."

"And why did Sanibel's finest wish to speak with Ms. Harvey at the police department on a Saturday night? Could it not have waited until Monday?"

"No, it could not have," said Guin. Then she told Ginny about her theory and what she had learned about the fountain and CiCi's killer.

"When can you get the story to me?" asked Ginny.

"I need to speak with the detective," said Guin.

"Well, get on it, girly. We don't want to get scooped."

Guin sighed.

"I'll get it to you as soon as I can, Gin."

"That's my girl."

They ended the call, and Guin resumed her pacing.

"Come on, detective," she said, looking over at her phone. "Call me."

But her phone remained silent.

Guin felt bad about blowing off brunch with Shelly Sunday morning, but she couldn't take the morning off if she was to write up her piece on the gallery opening and the police showing up to arrest Marta. Of course, she couldn't submit her piece on the fountain and CiCi's murder until she had spoken with the detective. But she could prepare a rough draft, to be finalized later.

She thought about canceling her appointment to go see the beach cottage that afternoon with Polly. But she was worried this would be her last chance to bid on the place. So she kept the appointment.

She was busy typing away when her phone started buzzing. She normally kept it in a drawer, with the ringer turned off, when she was writing, but she had kept it on vibrate on her desk in case the detective called or messaged her.

She picked up the phone and saw she had a text. It was from Shelly, checking to see how Guin was doing.

"I'm fine," Guin typed back. "Just super busy. Sorry about brunch. You want to go look at a house with me later?"

A second later, Shelly had written her back.

"You bet! Where and when?"

Guin sent her the details, then she put the phone down and continued typing.

She was still working when her phone started buzzing and an alert popped up on her screen. Right, the house. She had to meet Polly and Shelly over there at 2:30.

She finished the sentence she was working on and saved the document. Then she headed to the bathroom. A few minutes later, she was out the door.

"Hey, sorry I'm late," she said, as she hurried over to Polly and Shelly.

"No problem," said Polly. "Shelly and I were just chatting."

"So I see," said Guin smiling.

"You ready?" Polly asked her.

"As ready as I'll ever be," said Guin.

Guin watched as Polly took out her phone, pressed a few numbers, and got the key out of the lock box. Then she and Shelly followed her inside.

"Nice place," said Shelly, as she glanced around. "You want to give me the tour?"

Guin showed her around. In each room, Shelly stopped to open doors and peer inside of cabinets or drawers. And she checked the water pressure in the bathrooms and kitchen. Guin shook her head and smiled.

Shelly finished her inspection. Then they returned to the main living area, where Polly was waiting for them.

"Well?" asked Polly.

"It needs some work," said Shelly.

"What house on Sanibel doesn't?" said Polly. "But you're never going to find a place this close to the beach for this price, Guin."

"I know," said Guin. "It's just…"

"Go ahead and make an offer," said Polly. "You've got nothing to lose."

Except money, thought Guin. She looked at Shelly, who whispered something in her ear.

"I think it's going to take more than that," Guin said to her.

Aloud, to Polly, Shelly said, "I agree, it's a nice place." Then she turned to Guin. "If you can get it for a good price, go for it."

"So?" said Polly.

"What do you think I should offer?" asked Guin.

Polly threw out a number.

"No way," said Guin.

She gave Polly a lower number.

"I'll go write it up and get back to you."

"You okay if we take another look around?" Guin asked her.

"Be my guest," said Polly.

Guin grabbed Shelly and the two of them went around the place one more time.

"You good or you want to stay a few more minutes?" Polly asked them, after they had returned from the master bedroom.

Guin looked at Shelly, who nodded her head.

"We're good," said Guin. "I just want to take a walk around the outside."

"I'll join you," said Polly. "I just need to lock up."

Polly made sure all the doors and windows were shut and the lights off. Then the three of them left.

"There's room for a pool, if you want to put one in," she informed Guin, as they walked around the back of the house.

"A pool will have to wait," said Guin.

"I know," Polly replied. "Just saying."

"I'll need to have a landscaper in," Guin said, looking around. "I don't know the first thing about native plants, or any plants, for that matter."

"No problem," said Polly. "I can give you names."

"Thanks," said Guin.

They finished their circuit of the grounds. The property wasn't that big, which suited Guin, but it still felt private, with bushes and trees obscuring the nearby homes.

"So, you'll let me know if they accept my offer?" asked Guin.

"As soon as I hear back from the listing agent," said Polly.

"Okay," said Guin. She took a deep breath. "Wish me luck."

"Good luck!" said Shelly.

"You got this," said Polly.

"You want to go grab a drink?" asked Shelly.

Guin hesitated. She could use a drink, but she really needed to get back to work.

"Just a quick one," she replied.

CHAPTER 42

It was Monday morning and Guin hadn't heard from Polly or the detective. Was he avoiding her? She had left him several voicemail messages and texts. Surely he had gotten them.

After pacing around the condo, trying to decide what to do, she decided to go pay the detective a visit. She got her things and was about to head out when she decided to call over to the police department first, to make sure he was in. He was, the operator informed her. Would she like to be transferred? Guin said that wasn't necessary.

Instead she grabbed her keys and headed out the door.

She stopped at Jean-Luc's Bakery to pick up some croissants, *pains au chocolat*, and other goodies, as well as two large cappuccinos. Thus armed, she headed to the police department. When she got there, she asked for the detective and was buzzed back a few minutes later.

She knocked on his door, which was ajar, then entered, placing the box of pastries and the tray with the two cappuccinos on the detective's folder-strewn desk.

"What's this?" he said, looking down at the box.

"Open it," said Guin, taking one of the cappuccinos out of the tray and placing it in front of him.

He glanced at the cappuccino and opened the box.

"You trying to bribe me?"

"Did it work?" she asked.

"No," he said.

"Go ahead and take something anyway," Guin replied. "You can give whatever you don't want to whoever's on desk duty today. I'm sure they'll appreciate it."

The detective continued to examine the contents of the box.

"Go ahead. Take a croissant or something. And drink your cappuccino before it gets cold," Guin admonished him.

She took a seat across from the detective and sipped her cappuccino.

"Fine," said the detective, looking up at her.

He reached into the box and withdrew a *pain aux raisins*.

"Go on," she said.

Guin watched as he took a bite. Then she turned her gaze to his cappuccino.

He picked it up and took a sip.

"Happy now?" he asked her.

"Ecstatic."

He took another sip and then another bite of the pastry.

"So, you book her?" asked Guin.

"Who?" said the detective.

"You know who," said Guin. "Marta."

"We're waiting," said the detective.

"For?" said Guin.

"The DNA results," replied the detective.

"How long will that take?" asked Guin.

"We should have them back later today, tomorrow morning at the latest. I told Mike it was urgent."

For the sake of her article, she hoped the detective found out later that day.

"Will you let me know the results?" asked Guin.

He gave her a look.

"I have to file my story by tomorrow or Ginny will have my head."

"Well, if I charge the wrong person, the state's attorney will have mine."

He had a point, thought Guin. But who else could it be other than Marta?

"So, are you holding her?" asked Guin.

The detective didn't reply.

"Did you get her to confess?"

"She claims she had nothing to do with the girl's death or the fountain."

"You saw the video," said Guin. "Who else could it have been, other than Marta? And Susan saw her."

"The video doesn't conclusively prove anything," said the detective. "And Mrs. Hastings only thinks she saw her."

Guin huffed.

"Fortunately, we have other evidence tying her to the crimes," said the detective.

Was that a hint of a smile Guin saw upon the detective's usually stoic face? She leaned forward.

"You do?"

"I know this may surprise you, Ms. Jones, but the Sanibel Police Department has been investigating this case, both cases, quite thoroughly. And I am proud to say, we are rather good at our jobs."

"I would never suggest otherwise," said Guin. "But I saw you at the gallery opening, speaking with Marta. That must mean you think she did it."

"Like I said, we're waiting for the DNA results."

This was going nowhere, thought Guin.

"Well, I should get going," she said, getting up. "Let me know when you formally charge her. Ginny will want a quote for the paper."

The detective made a face.

"Just doing my job, detective." She paused. "We still going to the game Saturday?"

For a moment the detective looked confused.

"Sorry, I've been so busy, I nearly forgot. Yeah, we're still on. You good?"

"I'm looking forward to it," she said. "Our first Spring Training game of the season! Just let me know when we need to head out."

"Will do," he said. "Now if you will excuse me…"

Guin walked to the door, then stopped.

"And don't forget to let me know the DNA results," she said, smiling at him.

He frowned, and she let herself out.

Guin spent the rest of the day working, or trying to work. It was now six o'clock, and she had given up hope of hearing back from the detective when her phone started buzzing. It was a text. From him.

"Got the DNA results. Officially booking Marta Harvey for criminal mischief and first-degree murder."

"Thank you!" said Guin, resisting the urge to kiss her phone.

She texted him back, asking for a quote, then added, "If you won't give me one, I'll just make something up."

"Go ahead," he wrote back. "Just let me see it first."

She turned back to her computer and opened the rough draft she had prepared. She read it over quickly, then began to type. When she was done, she read it over one more time. She wanted to sleep on it and review it in the morning, but she knew Ginny would want it right away.

She sent the detective the two quotes she had attributed to him and asked him to get back to her ASAP. Then she waited.

A few minutes later, her phone rang. It was the detective.

"I would never say something like that," he said.

"Well, then, tell me what you would say."

They spent several minutes going back and forth, until the detective was satisfied.

"Thank you," said Guin.

She then fixed the article and sent it off to Ginny.

She waited nervously for Ginny to respond. When she didn't immediately hear back from her, she went into the kitchen to fix herself something to eat. She was about to put a forkful of food in her mouth when her phone started ringing. It was Polly calling.

"Did they accept my offer?" Guin asked her.

"They countered."

Guin listened as Polly gave her the number.

"What should I do?" Guin asked.

"Meet them in the middle," Polly advised. "It's still a good deal."

"Yeah, but that means less money for renovating."

They went back and forth. Finally, Guin gave her a number.

"That's the highest I'll go, Polly. If they don't accept it, I'll keep looking."

"Got it," said Polly. "It's late. So I may not get back to you until tomorrow."

"That's fine," said Guin.

They ended the call and Guin took a deep breath. She felt too nervous to eat but didn't like to waste food. So she forced herself to eat several bites.

The cats were already asleep on Guin's bed by the time she got in it, several hours later. She nudged them over, so she could squeeze in. Fauna glanced at her, clearly not appreciating being awakened from her slumber, then closed her eyes again.

Guin gazed down at them, watching as their bodies rose and fell. She yawned and reached over to turn off the light, but she couldn't sleep.

She turned back on the light. It was just after ten. She grabbed her phone and called her brother.

"I thought you had forgotten all about me," said Lance.

"Sorry, I've been busy," said Guin.

"Oh?"

"Been working on a big story."

"On the weekend?"

"Gotta write when the story's hot."

"You want to tell me about it?"

"We found the person who killed that young woman I told you about."

"We?" said Lance.

"You know what I mean," said Guin.

"So, who done it?"

"It was the other volunteer working for Sam, Marta Harvey."

"Is that her real name? It sounds like something in a spy novel."

"I hadn't thought about that," said Guin. "Though now that you mention it…"

"So what are you doing up?" asked Lance. "Isn't it past your bedtime?"

"Got a lot on my mind."

"Oh? You want to tell big bro about it?"

Guin sighed.

"I broke up with Ris."

"No! Really?"

"Really," said Guin.

"How come?" asked Lance.

"I realized I didn't love him."

"What's that got to do with it?"

"Lance!"

"Seriously, Guin, at our age love matters less than finding someone to share your life with."

"But you and Owen love each other."

"Yes, but not everyone can be so lucky."

"Well, I'd like to think it's never too late to fall in love," said Guin.

"Suit yourself. Speaking of *l'amour*, when are you coming to Paris?"

"I still need to speak with Ginny."

"Well, go talk to her. I want you there with us."

"And I'd like to be there with you, but I may have just bought a house, and Ginny may not be so amenable to me taking off again."

"You bought a house?" asked Lance. "You tell Mom?"

"I haven't bought it yet. And no, I didn't tell Mom. And please don't go telling her. I'll let her know after I've closed. If I close."

"That's asking a lot, Guinivere. A breakup and a new house? You sure you're not having a mid-life crisis?"

"I don't know. Maybe."

Guin yawned.

"I should try to get some sleep."

"Nighty-night," said Lance. "Don't let the bed bugs bite."

"Thanks," said Guin. "Love you."

"Love you, too," said Lance.

Guin was in bed till nearly seven the next morning, which was late for her. She had had a restless night and kept getting up. She thought about going for a beach walk, but she still had work to do.

She padded to the kitchen, the cats trotting behind her, and fixed herself some coffee. As the coffee was brewing in her little French press, she gave the cats some food and water.

She looked around for her phone and realized she had left it on her nightstand.

She retrieved it and waited for it to boot. As soon as it had, her message light began blinking. There was a message from Ginny.

"Well done, you!" read the text. "This is front page news. Suzy will be furious."

Guin smiled, then she sent a text to Sam and Rita.

EPILOGUE

It was a beautiful, sunny day. The temperature was in the 70s, and they had excellent seats.

Guin and the detective had stopped for lunch at the Five Guys near First Data Field. Five Guys being one of the detective's favorite fast food joints. Then they had parked in a nearby lot and walked to the ballpark.

"These are great seats!" said Guin, as they sat down. "Thank you for taking me."

"No problem," said the detective.

The game lasted just over two hours. The Mets weren't great, but they managed to edge out the Yankees, who were fielding their B-Team.

"Thanks again," said Guin, as they exited the ballpark.

"Always happy to see the Yankees lose," replied the detective.

"Though it wasn't really the Yankees," said Guin.

"Hey, a win is a win is a win," said the detective.

"True," said Guin.

Guin hadn't heard from the detective since the beginning of the week, except for a text telling her he'd pick her up that morning at eight to go to Port St. Lucie. She wondered if she had done something to annoy him—something more than usual.

"I have an idea," said Guin, as they arrived back at the detective's car.

The detective raised an eyebrow.

"Let's go to Hutchinson Island. It's not that far from here, and I hear Jensen Beach is really nice."

"You want to go to the beach?" asked the detective.

"Come on. It's not far from here, and I haven't been to the Atlantic coast in ages."

The detective looked hesitant.

"Please?" said Guin. "I'll buy you a beer afterward."

"Fine," said the detective. "If it will make you happy."

"Very," said Guin, giving him a radiant smile.

Around 40 minutes later, they arrived at Jensen Beach Park.

"Come on!" said Guin, getting out of the car.

The detective followed her down to the beach.

Guin ran to the shore. She stretched out her arms and closed her eyes, feeling the sea spray on her face as the waves crashed around her. When she opened her eyes a minute later, she found the detective looking at her.

"What?" she said, smiling at him.

"Nothing," he replied.

"Come on," said Guin. "Give."

"I like how you look."

"You do?" said Guin, smiling.

"Yeah, you look happy," he said.

"That's because I am happy," she said.

They stayed there for several minutes, looking out at the waves.

"Let's go for a walk," she said.

The detective hesitated.

"Come on," she said. "Walking's good for you."

He grumbled a bit, then acquiesced.

A little over an hour later, they were nursing beers at the Magic Oyster. The detective hadn't said much on their walk, but that was fine by Guin. She had been busy scanning the beach for shells and hadn't felt much like talking either.

"You want some food?" asked the bartender.

They ordered some peel-and-eat shrimp and fresh fried clam strips. When they were finished, the detective asked the bartender for the check and paid.

"Let's go watch the sunset!" said Guin, after they had stepped outside.

The detective didn't seem enthusiastic.

"Oh, come on, detective!" she said, pulling him toward the crosswalk that led back over to the beach side. "When was the last time you saw the sun set? And it looks to be a beauty!"

He allowed her to lead him back across the road and down to the beach. There were people scattered all along the sand, gazing out as the sun slowly sunk into the sea. The sky had turned a fiery reddish orange, the clouds glowing with the sun's rays.

"Isn't it beautiful?" said Guin, glancing over at the detective.

He was looking at her, not at the sunset.

He gently reached out and placed a stray copper curl behind her ear.

"Very beautiful," said the detective.

He took a step closer and Guin held her breath.

"Look!" someone shouted.

Guin turned to see.

The sun was about to vanish beneath the waves and a flock of birds was flying by.

She turned to look back at the detective. He was still looking at her. She suddenly felt all tingly. A breeze blew by them, causing Guin to shiver.

"You cold?" asked the detective.

He took a step closer to her and rubbed her arms.

"Thanks," said Guin. "I think I'm okay now."

They stood there for another minute, as the sky turned pastel.

"I love this time of day," she said. "It's so beautiful and peaceful. Don't you agree?"

She turned to look at the detective. He was looking at her again.

"Very beautiful," he said. Then he gently pulled her toward him and kissed her.

To be continued…

Look for Book Six in the Sanibel Island Mystery series, *Trouble in Paradise*, in 2020.

Acknowledgments

First, I'd like to thank you for reading this book. If you enjoyed it, please consider reviewing or rating it on Amazon and/or Goodreads.

Next, I'd like to thank my first readers, Amanda Walter, Linda Friedrich, and Robin Muth, who made sure there weren't any plot holes or inconsistencies, made great suggestions, and helped make this a better book. I also have to thank my two terrific copy editors, Lisa Thibos and Sue Lonoff de Cuevas (aka Mom), who made sure *Shell Shocked* wasn't full of shocking grammatical, style, or spelling errors.

I'd also like to thank my very talented cover designer, Kristin Bryant, and Polgarus Studio for making this and all my other books look so good, inside and out.

Lastly, thank you to my husband Kenny, who has supported and nurtured me every step of this journey. Guin should be so lucky.

About the Sanibel Island Mystery series

To learn more about the Sanibel Island Mystery series, visit the website at http://www.SanibelIslandMysteries.com and "like" the Sanibel Island Mysteries Facebook page at https://www.facebook.com/SanibelIslandMysteries/.

CPSIA information can be obtained
at www.ICGtesting.com
Printed in the USA
BVHW030236080421
604472BV00015B/58